THE LAST ELECTION

by Andrew Yang
and Stephen Marche

BROOKLYN, NEW YORK

This is a work of fiction. All names, characters, places, and incidents are the product of the authors' imaginations. Any resemblance to real events or persons, living or dead, is entirely coincidental.

Published by Akashic Books
©2023 Andrew Yang and Stephen Marche

Paperback ISBN: 978-1-63614-150-3
Hardcover ISBN: 978-1-63614-149-7
Library of Congress Control Number: 2023933944

Akashic Books
Brooklyn, New York
Instagram, Twitter, Facebook: AkashicBooks
info@akashicbooks.com
www.akashicbooks.com

To those who are willing to see the future, so they can change it

Table of Contents

November 23

THE LAUNCH

(424 days until)

The message that means the end of the American republic arrives at just the wrong moment. Martha Kass is sitting down to a chopped salad of pickled beets, goat cheese, candied pecans, and radicchio.

By late morning, Martha needs to sit by the light in the kitchen even more than she needs to eat. Martha runs the *New York Times*'s tip line and today she has already looked over a video of Oregon militia members planning to purchase Americium for a dirty bomb, a memo between coaches at a California university's swimming program covering up for a sexually abusive team doctor, and a drone shot of a woman being burned alive in a Bangladeshi refugee camp. These are the morning's highlights. None of them will make it into the paper.

American journalism, when you get right down to it, is a lot of interesting salads at a lot of bright desks, asking the question, *Does this suffering matter?* The view from Martha's kitchen is a quiet stretch of Clinton Hill. Its wide street, with a housing project across from the gentrifying apartments, is calm.

Before she notices the message that means the end of the American republic, before she can take a bite of salad, Martha hears a rustling at the front door, and it's Zayn. She forgot that her husband was coming home for the sex scheduled so meticulously by their fertility doctor. They have been trying for a baby for eight months now. "You there?" she asks.

Zayn is already unbuttoning his shirt. "Want to forget

about the world for a while?" he asks, kissing her forehead and strolling to the bedroom.

She would rather have the salad than the sex. She would rather look out the window. An old lady in a blue and gold babushka is pushing a cart of shopping bags awkwardly across the sidewalk, and Martha is curious how the sequence will play out. The salad won't be as fresh after.

But she can hardly complain. Zayn had to take the A train all the way from Harlem and then transfer to the G at Hoyt-Schermerhorn. He has half an hour. Then he will have to rush back to City College to teach Intro to Communication to a class of two hundred.

So the spark that sets America on fire has to wait. The spark that sets America on fire is a message on the *New York Times*'s SecureDrop server that arrives to Martha Kass with a blank subject heading; the sender is a string of numbers. The message contains an audio clip, three minutes and fourteen seconds long.

Martha doesn't know, at this point, that the way she puts down her fork and pulls the sweatshirt over her head en route to the bedroom is being watched.

11:32 a.m., 820 Fifth Avenue, Manhattan, NY
Michael Ricci, Mikey to everybody, has received sixty-four new messages in the past hour but hasn't read them. Only one message matters anyway. It is a three-figure text from his director of digital: *F2F*. To the message requesting a face-to-face meeting, Mikey replies with a single number: *1*.

He cannot write more because he is watching American politics in its advanced state of decadence up close, in action. He needs to study his candidate, Cooper Sherman, independent leader of the Maverick Party, working the selfie line.

American politics, when you get right down to it, is a lot of selfies in a lot of fancy apartments.

Cooper is not a professional politician, and it shows. He talks to people.

There are only four supporters left who want selfies: an elder WASP banker complete in bow tie and suspenders, some trust-fund kid all in gray with a nine-hundred-dollar, orange Hermès scarf, and two teenage girls from Trinity who came with their bubbe. Mikey can't quite tell if they're there to see Cooper because of his politics or his celebrity.

Cooper Sherman is the founder of a multibillion-dollar tax-compliance software company, but he has a shot at the presidency because he starred in *Build It and They Will Come*. For seven seasons, he helped the owners of failing small businesses, and his catchphrase was, "Do the math."

Sarah Ren, the Maverick Party's director of communications, strides up looking at her phone. "He's acting like a human being again," she says. "He can't be talking to people."

"He'll learn," Mikey says.

"We don't have much time for him to learn. This isn't prepper camp where you learn to shoot a gun and fill a bug-out bag."

Mikey sighs. "Listen, we got a human being here—I admit that. You knew that when you signed up for an independent campaign. There are some advantages to having a human being as a candidate and there are some disadvantages to having a human being as a candidate. One of the advantages is that some people like imagining a real person as president. One of the disadvantages is that a human being might talk to people like they're people."

"You see this F2F?" she asks, not looking up from her screen.

"I'll handle it. I'm going to meet Dominic at one."

"First day after launch and there's already an emergency."

"It's probably—"

But Ren is already striding across the room. The fact that she is working for the Maverick campaign is absurd. She's far too good. Mikey is a sentimentalist. He wants to save the republic. Sarah Ren just knows how to win.

In the aftermath of January 6, 2021, Mikey dropped into a deep dark hole, and Cooper had brought him out, brought him to his Rocky Mountain compound, shared his own despair and his plan, the plan to save the republic.

He still remembers the moment Cooper turned to him, in the middle of some copse of aspens on the never-ending hikes on that visit, and said, "If the country does go down, don't you want to say that you fought for her?" That *her*, with its genteel patriotism, rang like a gong in his heart.

Sarah Ren must have a heart, as a biological fact, but it's not the kind of heart that rings out. She's a killer.

Ren organized this event through her connections with Larry Kapek, the top bundler in New York. The room is what a real estate listing would describe as "an ornate Upper East Side apartment." The bland American nineteenth-century portraits and landscapes have accent lights above them.

In the living room, where the candidate and the crowd of people with $3,300 to give away had their little chat—fifteen minutes of speaking and ten minutes for questions—pictures of political celebrities cover an entire wall, from floor to ceiling. In another era, it would have been lined with the stuffed heads of elephants and zebras and rhinoceroses. But here, in left-leaning New York circles, success in life must be demonstrated by the host's confirmed presence, at one or another moment, beside Obama and Mandela and Bono and the Clintons.

The total from the event is $98,768, all toted up in ACTGray, with all the necessary information required by the FEC: the email addresses, the phone numbers. They need the contact info for legal reasons but also for future donation requests.

That is the number one rule: get the money before you give the selfie. But there's another rule that applies to American life generally: keep the customer happy. So Cooper must work the selfie line.

The selfie is the threshold act of American politics now, the primary gesture that defines those who follow. The threshold political act used to be the handshake—you went out on the street and you met people and brought them into a room together. Now, you frame yourself in other people's screens, so that they share you.

The trick is speed without hustle. If a candidate spends thirty seconds taking a picture, it's much too long. The average person has five hundred followers, so if you take two hundred selfies you've potentially created a hundred thousand impressions.

With a good handler, an effective candidate can reduce his or her time per impression to fifteen or twenty seconds, which matters because for every fourth or fifth person, there's typically one fuck-up or phone malfunction.

The selfie consultant—Mikey strains to recall her name, Emily or Emma or something—had stressed the importance of suppressing your irritation, maintaining the smiling positive mood at all times. It can be tough. Sometimes the mentally ill slip through the handlers, the hopeless and the broken pressing in. The loonies might bring whole binders of their political writings with them. They might bring bongs or action figures to sign. They might ask the candidate to make white power gestures nobody on staff knows exist yet.

With Cooper, there had always been idiots who wanted to

have him invest in their crypto plays, their online luxury travel companies. They'd seen him help businesses on TV. They wanted him to do what they'd seen him do on TV. Cooper usually gave them a card, told them to call one of his producers, who would give them the PFO, the polite fuck off.

Working the selfie line involves technique but there is talent too, the capacity to project intimacy on demand and at volume. Cooper has a terrific selfie smile when all is said and done. He looks, in pictures, like he's just shared spring break with whoever is in the shot with him, like they've all been in on a lark together.

Cooper's celebrity trained him so far, but there are rules for the political selfie that don't apply to regular celebrities. No sticking out your tongue and making hang ten gestures. No middle fingers. No pulling faces.

The selfie consultant had offered a selfie guide that included an optimal angle, tested by focus groups. For Cooper, the optimal angle is thirty degrees to the left.

Mikey can see Cooper improving. He hits that angle shot after shot now. The guy is coachable. But he's still taking too long. The Maverick Party's platform is universal basic income, the decriminalization of all drugs, and electoral reform. If you get Cooper started on any of them, he won't shut up. The midtwenties trust-fund art-school kid with the fancy scarf is listening, rapt, as Cooper reels off stats about open primaries.

The two Trinity girls are next. They're fifteen, maybe sixteen. Ren is somehow back at Mikey's side. She's probably talked to seven people in the time she's been gone. "This is dangerous," she says.

"Let's see how he does," Mikey responds.

Sometimes people press themselves against your body when they're in a selfie because they know closeness leads to the best shots on social. Cooper, as trained, uses his air hands, floating just above their shoulders so that the picture looks intimate on first glance, but if anyone wants to check, it's clear he's not touching. This, too, was an insight of the selfie consultant. That's why you hire consultants.

"Two more bundling events today," Ren notes. "I'd like to get that to five. Kamala can do five."

"Well, he's not going to do that many. Here, LA, San Francisco, maybe Austin."

"You need to talk him into doing more."

"How do you explain to a billionaire that he ought to work for a living?"

"Fifty thousand dollars an hour is a good rate for anybody. Plus, other people's money signals more organic support. Commitment, Mikey, commitment."

It's a funny word out of her mouth. Ren knows how to win. She also fucks too many people too much. That's why they can get her.

Ren's career has a pattern. She helps a candidate to power, fucking everybody along the way, then the press describes her as a bimbo until she becomes such a distraction that she has to be fired. Then there's a line of people out the door waiting to hire her. Needless to say, if Ren were a man, she would simply be the leading political operative in the country. The sex wouldn't enter into it.

Larry Kapek strides across his ornate living room toward them like a man flagging down a waiter to complain.

"You want me to do the host?" Ren asks.

"No, I'll do him," Mikey says. "He prefers men."

There are more rules to these bundling events. The candidate has to talk to the donors, but the campaign manager has to listen to the ideas of the hosts. That's the deal.

Larry's not so bad, as bundlers go. He's a seventy-five-year-old gay man who made a fortune on licensing Broadway musicals, and invested the money in this apartment, political influence, and cosmetic surgery.

Larry Kapek knows how the world works. Except that's not quite right. Larry Kapek *thinks* he knows how the world works, and he's been right often enough that a few others also think that Larry Kapek knows how the world works, but Larry Kapek only knows how the world *used to* work.

In a photograph, he looks fifty tops. Up close, he looks like a puzzle of a face with the pieces forced together.

Larry puts his arm around Mikey's shoulder, leans in close. "Hope," he says. He wants Mikey to ask him what he means, and Mikey knows that Larry wants him to ask what he means.

"Hope?"

"Hope."

"What do you mean by *hope*, Larry?"

"Hope is what's missing here."

Mikey nods. "Hope is missing from a good chunk of America, Larry."

"When I fundraised for Hillary, when I raised money for Barack, when I worked with Bill thirty years ago, what got me into this was hope. That's what people spend money on, that's what they want to give money to."

"The Man from Hope."

"The Man from Hope. Your guy is the Man from Despair."

Mikey presses a button on a tape recorder in his mind. It is the basic plot of the Maverick Party, the universal basic income, electoral reform, decriminalization of all drugs, the fact that these are the only possible responses to automation and globalization, that Cooper Sherman represents a real chance to halt the national slide into autocracy and a real chance to spread American prosperity.

Larry stops the spiel with an upraised palm. "Your policies are wonderful. I have no problem with your policies. Or, at least, I can see how your policies make sense, as ideas, and I agree with you that the time is right for big ideas. But you have to get into office before any of those ideas can be real. Am I wrong?"

"You're not wrong but—"

"Am I wrong?"

"I'm not sure we can make any of those policies happen even in office since the system is so corrupt."

"You're not wrong there either, but listen. What I'm saying is that, listen, there needs to be more of a vision to sell. A vision of American grandeur, of the opportunity this country represents."

"*Opportunity*," Mikey says like he's taking a mental note. "Understood."

"One more thing. You've got to stop cursing."

The old man has missed the point once again. Cursing *is* the point. America makes you want to curse. "Cooper is Cooper," Mikey says.

"Your slogan is 'Unfuck America.'"

"That's not our slogan. Our slogan is 'Do the Math.' The kids chant 'Unfuck America' at the rallies because that's what they want us to do. And *you* want us to do it too." Larry says nothing, so Mikey fills the space: "Look, the Republicans want to end democracy, and the Democrats can't or won't stop them. To speechify to people about 'work hard and play by the rules' is just . . . They won't believe it. They're not buying it. The first rule is to meet people where they are."

"And where are the people?"

"They know the system is broken. They all know. That's why we have a chance."

Larry pauses. His cheeks have been stretched back so far he cannot quite purse his lips, but he looks like he would be pursing his lips if he could. "You know, I think you know something I don't," he says.

"What's that?"

"I don't know. I don't even know if you know what you know that I don't know. But the world . . . this country . . ." He looks up with eyes searching to be understood. "This country confuses me."

Mikey shakes his hand. "You and me both, brother."

Larry, like everybody else, wants to go back to the America he remembers. But Mikey knows all of the old Americas are never coming back.

Everybody says that every election is the most important election in history, yet the stakes of this one won't be who controls the machinery of American self-government; they will be whether there is self-government in America at all. The question is not which America will prevail. The question is whether there will *be* an America.

12:32 p.m., 360 Clinton Avenue, Brooklyn, NY
"Real life is starting to get messed up," Zayn says, stretching naked by the window. "It's not just the news anymore."

Martha is eating her salad curled up in bed. It is delicious—crunchy, soft, sweet, sour, light, filling. Her husband is handsome and kind. She should be happy. She should be savoring the moment. She can't. There's news. She needs to eat quickly.

"It's not just like Tucker Carlson screaming anymore. It's like civilization is going down." Zayn is putting on his blue button-down. "I was crossing over Sixth Avenue today—you know, over by Fox News?—and a fight broke out."

"A fight?"

"Somebody was protesting somebody and somebody else was protesting the protesters. And as I was walking by, this, like, I don't know, sixty-year-old dude in a beard, you ever notice how the violent crazies always have beards? On both sides? Anyway, he has this thin sign, a thin little piece of wood, and it says *Compassion* on it. And then there's this other guy, and he's dressed in a suit but he looks like he's high. And they're talking and I can't even hear what they're talking about, and then the guy with the sign that says *Compassion* starts whaling on the other guy, and they fall down on the street together."

"The medium is the message," Martha says.

"I moved away fast. I never knew who was on whose side."

"Compassion has to be on our side, surely."

"I don't know. It sounds pretty Christian."

Martha is eating her salad too fast. She slows down, forking a single pickled beet. Anxiety always makes her rush. Political violence hums in the background now—that assassination of a Democratic state senator in Michigan last week, a Kentucky radical shooting out the power stations the week before that, the mass shooting at UCLA which killed a judge—but it's still weird that it would enter their lives, the little lives of Martha and Zayn.

"Who won the fight?" Martha asks.

"I didn't see."

"I put my money on compassion." Martha picks at the bottom of her bowl for the last of the candied pecans. "We'll be fine."

Martha and Zayn are having a conversation under their conversation. The fertility struggle leads to a lot of conversations under conversations.

Zayn is saying without saying that the world is chaotic, that America is falling apart, that maybe they shouldn't be trying so hard for a baby. Martha is saying that their lives aren't worth anything without a family at home.

Zayn puts on his pants. Martha puts her bowl in the kitchen sink. A classroom is waiting for Zayn in Harlem. The tip line is waiting for Martha.

1:07 p.m., Hudson Yards, Eleventh Avenue and 30th Street, Manhattan, NY

The Maverick Party staff is buzzing. Twenty-five of them are going to have a lovely evening out at the ketamine bar. Their collective trip at a "psychedelic wellness center" will all be supervised, an immersive experience with soft chairs, plenty of plants, cozy carpets, and pastel flower art. The idea is that they will all trip their brains out as a reward for the successful launch.

Mikey approves. It will make for good group bonding. He is not going though. He hates drugs, and he hates trendiness.

The offices of the Maverick Party resemble an overfunded start-up. The staff can walk out to the High Line for lunch or a meeting at the Hudson Market or an Equinox nearby. They are close to the Google offices where many of their friends work.

Mikey is too much of a New Jersey Italian to buy into the Silicon Valley bullshit completely. His long-dead marble-working great-grandfather sits on his shoulder and judges their AI guy, who believes he is never going to die, and the fully invested Priestess of the Horned Lord who used to work for Elon Musk.

But the Maverick Party is a tech play. The banner over the door reads, *Do the Math.* The real slogan had come at a Tech-Crunch forum, when Cooper declared that his mission was to "unfuck America." His plea to the engineering class to save their country—"We broke it, we bought it"—had gone megaviral.

Engineers joined in droves. The campaign unleashed their engineering.

On launch date, they released a video game that allowed players to join in with the campaign, built by the same people who created *Kim Kardashian Superstar*. To advance, you needed to make donations. They released their own deepfake of the candidate so that users could make him do or say anything. He had already been grafted onto porn, onto Hitler speaking at the Nuremberg rally, and so on. It was all attention. *Attention first* was the play. A robot Maverick army generated a shifting kaleidoscope of memes that flood socials.

Nellie Katz, head of operations, is perched on the edge of a desk before a hanging garden of plasma screens playing Fox and MSNBC and CNN. "Did Ren come back with you?" she asks.

"She's still at the event. The candidate can never be left alone. Where's Dom?"

Nellie shrugs. "I haven't seen him, but he should be around here somewhere. Do you have another appointment soon?"

Nellie's politeness and concern always surprise Mikey. He met Nellie working in New York on the Biden campaign. She is the true American thing, talent that has worked its way up. If you ask her to do something, it's done. If you ask her to plan something, it comes off. If you ask her to sell something, it's sold. She's an itty-bitty thing, five foot three in shoes and skinny as a pinkie finger, but if she were a dog she'd be a big bounding golden retriever—ladling out never-ending bowlfuls of positive energy. Maybe it's an act, but if it's an act, it's persistent and original.

The last American election is like all the others before it. The end of democracy in the United States will be perfectly democratic. It seems, on the surface, like the same drama that has played out sixtysomething times before.

The Democratic roster includes a highly successful Black woman with shallow support; a boyish Midwesterner; a brilliant antitrust lawyer who looks like a schoolteacher who graded you hard for your own good; a vaguely hippie-ish woman like your liberated aunt who brings up auras and innovative sexual positions at Thanksgiving; and the billionaire governor of Colorado who looks like the guy responsible for deciding the location of the Walmart that wrecks your town.

"What do you see?" Mikey asks, nodding at the wall of televisions.

"The Dems are in trouble," Nellie says.

"One question. Can they win? Do any of them look like they can stop the Republican?"

Nellie shrugs. She doesn't say nasty things about people. She doesn't even say nasty things about nasty people. It's her trick. It's her gift.

Then the Republican appears on Fox. Mikey and Nellie's eyes automatically turn to him. The Republican has the angry glare of a man at a golf course where the valet parkers have misplaced his car. He looks put out. Americans are responding to that look. A lot of Americans feel put out.

At this point, the Republican is facing one last holdout from the field, a Wyomingite named Beth Link. As usual, he's found his enemy's sore spot. The one shameful act of Beth Link's political career was voting against gay marriage even though her sister is a lesbian with adopted kids.

"We've got some lovely carpets here," the Republican is saying to a rally in Pittsburgh. "You know, I've known a lot of women like three-dollar Beth and they like carpets this way."

Is he calling her a carpet-muncher? Probably. The man is

an impressive bully. He knows how to put the hook in people. The Republican strategy is established now, whoever the candidate is: the thrill of bullying, the pleasure of making others smaller than yourself.

It works too. It works except that it builds a tolerance. You need more and more of the hatred to feel the thrill. Name-calling leads to street fighting which leads to shooting which leads to insurgency.

And nobody knows where the insurgency will lead.

Can the Democrats prevent the end of democracy in the United States? Can they hold back the forces that wish to convert the greatest republic in the history of the world to a squalid oligarchy overrun by political tribes devoted to each other's destruction? *But the Democratic operatives never consider the end of democracy*, Mikey thinks, *except as a trend piece in the weekend news.* Like him, they probably think about fundraising all day, every day. They are probably thinking, right now, *Is there any way to use TikTok to motivate the small-donor base?* No, he corrects himself, they are thinking, *What consultant can I hire to teach me to use TikTok to motivate the small-donor base?*

There is an item on Fox about inflation, comparing contemporary America to Weimar Germany. There is a story on CNN about the gridlock in Congress. MSNBC is running an interview with a teacher who still wears a mask in her classroom in Idaho, against the wishes of the parents.

"There's the one that's going to bite the Democrats in the ass," Mikey says.

"People hate doing what they ought to do."

"Americans hate being told to do what they ought to do."

Then their launch comes up on CNN. A small half cheer arises from the staff at their desks. There is a shot of Cooper outside the garage at 2036 Crist Drive, Los Altos, California, where Steve Jobs and Steve Wozniak launched Apple in another, earlier American era.

Nellie, who is leaning against the desk, stands up. She has been like a sailor scanning the sea. Now she is a harpooner spotting a breach in the waves.

There is Coop with their hand-picked group of appropriately diverse supporters behind him. Cooper almost looks normal, talking about the history of American innovation and the glory of its capacity for reinvention. There's a ragged lawn and a simple bungalow without the least pretension to anything except an American home. It projects normalcy. It projects tech. Cooper can wear his tech-bro fleece without looking like a freak.

It is a successful fifteen seconds of television, the result of months of planning and hundreds of thousands of dollars in consultancy fees.

Mikey looks over their fundraising app, which shows campaign data in real time. There's a legitimate surge. Their launch video has 927K views on social media. The website has 231K visits. The email list has risen by 53K. 27,341 people have donated an average of $18.12 each. The numbers are terrific.

The microdonations will be the key, the smaller the better. Cooper needs to escape the impression that he is a billionaire buying the presidency the way his fellow billionaires buy themselves a trip to space with the cast of *Star Trek*.

These numbers only matter insofar as they will help Cooper reach 15 percent in the polls. If enough polls show Cooper at 15 percent, he should qualify for the presidential debates—if the Commission on Presidential Debates doesn't change the rules because their board members are all either Democrat or Republican.

Dominic Strindberg, director of digital, strolls in with

his laptop and file folder and yellow legal pad. He came to the campaign straight from the business side of Cooper's tax-compliance software company.

"We secure?" he asks.

"We sure are," Nellie says.

Dom plops himself down in the chair, places his hands flat on the table, shuts his eyes, takes a deep inhale through his nose, and lets a deep exhale out of his mouth. With his wild hair and unkempt beard, the man is like a shaggy, skinny Muppet, if there had been an accountant Muppet. "We got offered a big donation," he says to Mikey in the low intense voice he saves for news that matters.

"How big?" Mikey asks, running a hand through his hair. The moment they have been waiting for.

"100,000 Ethereum," Dom says. Mikey and Nellie sag back in their chairs. It's not real money. "The donor wants the whole campaign to run on Ethereum. He wants the staff paid in Ethereum. A little more than two hundred million in fiat American currency."

"Who sent it?" Nellie asks.

"Anonymous donation."

Nellie and Mikey laugh an absurd laugh. It's a nondonor giving them make-believe money. On the other hand, somebody loves Cooper Sherman enough to give him two hundred million dollars to float between them.

"Do you think that's the best idea?" Nellie says, scrunching her face. "I mean, we're supposed to be the let's-get-money-out-of-politics people."

"Yeah, but our guy's a billionaire," Dom says.

"I mean, best-case scenario is it's some crypto bro who wants to jack up the price of his NFTs," Nellie says.

"Explain that to me," Mikey says.

"It's the same as the crypto movement into the art market or anything else. The value of this currency is the value that people ascribe to it. If crypto moves into politics, that means that crypto is more established. If it starts to affect politics, then its arrival is more certain, therefore their portfolio is worth more. But that's the best-case scenario."

Dom takes a note on his yellow legal pad. Dom takes notes on everything. He takes notes on his dreams. He probably takes notes on sex, and his notes on sex probably make him more effective as a lover. "First of all," he says, "the value of *any* currency is the value ascribed to it. We're not on the gold standard anymore."

Mikey can see Nellie tensing up.

"Second of all, we want to be the tech-bro candidate, don't we? That's our dream, isn't it? Massive tech engagement? Third, it would look amazing on our sheet. 'Tech candidate raises two hundred million in Ethereum.' Isn't that what we want?"

Dom and Nellie look to Mikey. He is the campaign manager. He hasn't said anything yet.

"So what's the play, Mikey?" Dom prods.

Mikey doesn't say anything. He doesn't have to. He knows enough not to say anything when he doesn't have to say anything. He lets his silence weigh on them long enough to let them know he could say something.

"The good news is that you both get to go to the ketamine bar. This isn't on you anymore."

"What are you going to do?" Nellie asks. "Do we take the Ethereum or don't we?"

"I'm going to talk with Cooper," Mikey says. "It's his call. In questions like this, we are just support mechanisms. He has to go to the valley by himself."

3:23 p.m., 360 Clinton Avenue, Brooklyn, NY Martha goes into the small den she dreams of using as a baby's room one day, and begins scrolling through the less-secure messages.

There are five different tip channels the *New York Times* employs: email, encrypted email, WhatsApp, Signal, and Secure-Drop. She can check the first four on her phone, but Secure-Drop requires a private server, two computers, and a USB key. Before COVID, the SecureDrop hardware sat in its own room in the *Times*'s offices. After COVID, the paper installed a safe in her apartment.

It's a slow day. There's the usual hate mail, death threats. There are a few conspiracy theorists who write the tip line several times a week. One poor woman sends a note from a different email address every morning, always stream of consciousness, always ugly, always about the Jews and the World Economic Forum.

One guy sends PowerPoint presentations every month or so exposing elaborate connections between Georgia politicians, Taylor Swift, and video game corporations. There's a message from him today.

On the encrypted email, there's a long description, possibly genuine, of the sexual peccadilloes of John Kerry. It's gross. It's probably not true. Either way, it's not news. On Signal there are a few uploaded documents from an Exxon insider. Martha flags those. A reporter is already working that source.

Running the tip line is sensitive and time-consuming and boring, but it is important and requires a knowledge of the internal politics of the newsroom and a story sense. The questions Martha is supposed to answer are both negligible and all-important: *Would I read this in the* New York Times? followed by, *Who at the* New York Times *wants to write about this?*

Late in a nonelection year is relatively calm for the tip line. During times when ordinary people sense they are living through history, the tip line blows up. In the early days of COVID, hundreds of videos of overcrowded hospitals filled the encrypted email. They were incredibly useful, since the hospitals had banned reporters.

When #MeToo broke, Martha must have read two or three thousand accounts of abuse—some by minor celebrities, some by the managers of the local Wendys.

On days when the public does not feel invested in the history they are living through, days like today, the tip line receives a couple of hundred messages. Ten might be worth looking at. Of those, two might end up as stories.

One of the permanent truths of media is that people think they have more news than they do.

The *Times* moved Martha to the tip line around the time they fired James Bennett from the op-ed section. She thought she was invulnerable to cancellation because she had shared in the Pulitzer Prize for the #MeToo material, nurturing actresses to violate their NDAs.

She had objected ("not cool") on a Slack channel when a young female reporter posted the emoji of a guillotine beside Bennett's name. Then her mentor, a guy named Ross Abbott, had been on a *Times*-sponsored tour of Colombia with some Upper East Side kids who wanted to put the trip on their Ivy League applications, and he used a Malcolm X quote that contained the N-word. He, too, had considered himself invulnerable, since he had won half a dozen social justice awards, including a National Association of Black Journalists Prize for his work reporting on AIDS in South Africa. Martha was half-canceled by association.

Not that she had even defended Ross—he explicitly insisted she didn't—but she had refused to join in on the ritual humiliation.

Like many people who have devoted themselves to an institution, the more it betrays her, the more she worships it. The *New York Times* employs nearly five thousand people. Before they are hired, each is vetted like a candidate for the Secret Service or the Supreme Court.

The reason journalists submit to such an inspection is because the *New York Times* is the best and the most powerful news organization in the world. Like any comparable institution—the Mormon Church or the US Marines—it runs on true believers. They believe the *New York Times* serves a purpose on this earth, and they sublimate their own lives, and anybody else's they come across, to that purpose. Martha Kass is one of those true believers. She is a true believer in exile.

Martha also knows that like any large institution, the *Times* has its moods. Internal politics morph under their own phases. Everyone follows a wave and then becomes disgusted by the wave they followed, and so there's a counterwave. She might well ride the counterwave out of the tip line with a Big Story.

There's nothing on Signal except a message from a nondefinable source: *Check SecureDrop. Confirm receipt.*

Martha's annoyed. Checking SecureDrop is a rigamarole, and she checked it already this morning. First, she goes to the safe and puts in the code and her fingerprint. She takes out the public-facing server and the USB key. On the laptop connected to the server, she uploads the message—there is only one—onto the key. She takes the key out of the connected laptop—this is called the airdrop—and plugs it into the secure viewing station. Once she has read the message that means the end of the American republic, she will restart the computer.

The audio is faint, rustling. If she had to guess, it's probably voice memos on an iPhone in a pocket, amplified by software after recording. The men's voices sound slightly intoxicated, like they are reaching that point of drunkenness between joking and sadness. They are almost, but not quite whispering. The recording begins midconversation:

"The American military will have to decide. Sooner or later. The voters are too crazed with hatred. They want a civil war and they'll have one if we let them. You know, I don't think the voters want to decide anymore. They want us to take over. And let's be honest, real honest here, the US military is the only institution left in the United States that isn't overrun by careerist frauds. We're the only ones the people trust. It's natural that we decide the presidency. We may have to suspend the Constitution. Let's say—"

"I don't do 'let's says' . . . The world as it is is fucked up enough for me."

"American democracy is ending, and you don't want to look it in the face? That's what fucked us in Iraq and Afghanistan, you know. We didn't want to play 'let's say.' We wanted to stay optimistic and positive and concrete. Now Iraq and Afghanistan are coming home for us. We need to prepare. We need to get out in front of this thing."

The other voice grunts.

"I'm talking situational awareness here. I'm talking basic planning. I'm talking simple moral questions. Basic. Do you dance with the fella that brought ya?"

Fifteen garbled seconds follow, possibly an audio failure.

"The reason I know what's going to happen is that it's the worst thing that could happen, and the worst thing that could happen keeps happening, and that is this."

"Mitch, shut the fuck up. I'm serious."

"I am serious as pancreatic cancer. Now you be serious."

There is a deep sigh of acquiescence.

"The Republican wins the electoral college but loses by ten million

votes. Widespread violence ensues across the streets of American cities. The current president wants to impose order. The maybe future president wants to take over. Martial law. It's going to come down to you and me and about a dozen others. The future of this country is going to come down to military intervention. Even if we don't want it. But we should want it. American democracy is ending, and the US military, the institution we have been charged with leading, is the only one that can prevent the outbreak of total chaos. It's an abrogation of duty not to talk about it."

There is a pause of forty-one seconds.

"Just talking here?"

"Just talking."

"Talking. Nothing more."

"We're just talking here."

"I'd follow the oath to the Constitution."

"Bullshit. Cop-out. Nobody knows what the Constitution means anymore. There's my Constitution, there's your Constitution, there's our Constitution. There's their Constitution. There's his, hers, and its Constitution. You'll have to choose a side. That's what we're talking about here. If there were a functioning Constitution, we wouldn't need to talk about this."

"Just talking?"

"Just talking."

"We'll go Republican. Of course. But I'll tell you, the first thing we have to get rid of is Black Lives Matter and the Oath Keepers. That's what we didn't do in Afghanistan and Iraq. Not early enough, anyway."

"Exactly."

There are more garbled sounds, then silence. Martha is sitting in her living room. Outside there is vague traffic. She will remember exactly where she is now for the rest of her life.

Two currents run through her. The first is a vague hope

that maybe this is nothing. The second is the throbbing knowledge that it isn't nothing.

She listens to it again. What she hears is the plot of a military coup, a conspiracy by senior military leadership to overthrow the political system as it has existed since 1776. She's not sure what else it could be.

Journalists see mostly what everybody else sees. Martha has seen the slow erosion of her country's democracy like everybody else—the 2000 recount, the perversions of the electoral college, the stacking of the Supreme Court, January 6, the end of *Roe*. Sometimes journalists see what everybody will see before they see it. In her living room, surrounded by the sounds of Clinton Street, Martha is seeing the future fall of the American republic, what it will actually look like, the people who will actually do it.

By the third time she listens, she knows. Who will stop them? Who will stop the military from taking over the country? Whoever is speaking on that recording is right: the military is the only force the American people trust.

The only power that can stop them is a public outcry. And there can only be a public outcry if the public hears.

This is the Big Story. The reason Martha knows it's the Big Story is that she's not going to give it to anyone else.

3:25 p.m., Eleventh Avenue and 30th Street, Manhattan, NY
Only Ren and Cooper are in the back of the black car. They look faintly crumpled. Fernando the body man must be elsewhere. Ren steps out of the car and slams the door before Mikey has a chance to enter. Mikey tries not to see what he's just seen. It was only Ren and Cooper in the back of the black car. That's what he tells himself.

"Tell me about the F2F," Ren says, looking at her phone.

"What? Oh, somebody wants to give us two hundred million dollars in Ethereum."

She looks up. "What's the problem?"

"They don't know what they're doing and we don't know who they are."

Ren's face crinkles. "Those aren't problems. They sound like our kind of people." She adjusts her skirt. "I take free money. Don't you?"

Ren opens the door of the black car. Coop looks slightly less crumpled. The man is Botoxed, fake-tanned, with thinning dyed hair. On screen, he looks like the lead alumnus of a powerful fraternity. In person, he looks like the old guy at the nightclub.

It doesn't help that Cooper has his post-selfie face on. The sheer force required to maintain positivity and intimacy during these fundraising events drains him to a state of complete expressionlessness. It might look, to an outsider, like he's scowling, but Mikey knows it's just fatigue.

"Mikey, oh Mikey, when the fuck can I stop doing this shit?" Cooper asks.

"January 1."

"How far away is that?"

"Thirty-eight days. You made, like, nearly 200K already today."

"You know that I make a hundred thousand dollars every twenty-eight minutes."

"Soon. Soon you'll be able to stop. These events are flywheeling. They take on their own momentum. This is going to take off, go viral. Besides, there are the media people. Celebrities. Rose McGowan is going to be at the next one."

Mikey knows that Cooper is just complaining to hear himself complain. Cooper knows he has to do these events because the money raised at them, as well as the gathered crowds, make for good stories, and good stories are what they need.

"So what's the situation?" Cooper asks, rubbing his hands with the eucalyptus lotion he always carries on him.

"An Ethereum guy wants to give you two hundred million dollars. The equivalent of two hundred million dollars. In Ethereum. One hundred thousand Ethereum."

Cooper nods, and his eyes go clear. Large sums of money bring him to attention. "What's his play?"

"We don't know and we probably won't ever know, but if I were guessing, there are a couple of options. The most likely is that it's some crypto bro making a play to increase the value of Ethereum through social exposure. The first thing he mentioned is that he wants the staff paid in Ethereum. That's not legal."

"So he doesn't know about political campaigning."

Mikey nods. "The other option is that it's somebody who sees you as a disruption to the political process and wants to jack your presence up to hurt the United States of America. Like the money the Russians gave to the California separatists."

Cooper looks out the window. A homeless man, ragged and sharp-eyed, stumbles by with a lost face.

"What's the upside-downside?"

"The downside is that you don't need it, and dark money is probably the single most toxic force in American electoral politics, since whoever this guy is, we can be quite sure that he is giving this money for his own interests rather than the interests of the American public, and that the corruption that this money represents is, in both the long and short term, the decay that is stripping away the legitimate function of representative democracy in the US."

Cooper is laughing now. "I love it when you talk dirty to me. The upside?"

"It's two hundred million dollars."

Cooper doesn't have to think too long. "I just whored my ass for fifty thou and a few social media impressions."

"And besides, it will make you look like the tech candidate."

"Go talk to this guy and make sure it's not an obvious trap."

"Meeting him soon."

They sit for two blocks in the pleasure of not speaking.

"You know, I have this dream," Cooper eventually says. "Or it's not even a dream, it's like a movie that flashes through my head sometimes. There's a swimming pool full of shit, and I'm diving down to the bottom looking for the plug, and I think I have the plug, but I can't pull it up."

"We're going to come up covered in shit either way," Mikey responds. He knows what nobody in this business can bring themselves to know, the rule without exceptions: all political careers end in failure.

5:23 p.m., 360 Clinton Avenue, Brooklyn, NY
Mitch. That's all Martha has. She has the name Mitch. Whoever was talking on that recording mentioned a Mitch. It's a clue. It's a start.

Martha has hustled all afternoon. She has sent the leaked Exxon document to the head of the environment vertical. She has sent a clip of a fire in the Bronx to the City desk. Now she needs time to think.

The audio message isn't just a question of a story. It is a question of her career. The message is a career-maker if she can shepherd herself, with this bit of hot news, out of the backwaters of the tip line into the full light of real reporting again.

Somewhere in her head, the last scene of *Three Days of the Condor* is always playing, the scene where Robert Redford, in a magnificent navy peacoat and his best ever hair, confronts a shadowy CIA operative outside the *Times*'s offices, and Redford, like a scruffy bird god, says something along the lines of, "They have the whole story," and the bad guy, the secret agent, the representative of the powers that be, responds, "How do you know they'll print it?"

There are a couple hundred Robert Redfords coming to Martha every day. Martha takes the flood of American suffering and all she can do is maybe pass on a tip to a reporter who maybe will write a story.

She calls up Ross, as she has done every time she faces a career choice.

Since his cancellation, Ross lives like a lord in exile, in a massive house on Cape Cod full of federalist furniture. He now goes on long walks with his depressive hypochondriac wife. He fought against distortion his whole life, but in the end, the distortion swallowed him. He lives with it. Everybody is pretending to live in an America they remember.

"Who's the most powerful man in the world named Mitch?" Martha asks without preliminaries. This is the kind of question you could only ask Ross, and it is the kind of question Ross loves to be asked.

"There's a lot of Mitches in this world," he says. "Mitch McConnell?"

"It's not Mitch McConnell," Martha says.

Ross thinks a bit on the other end of the line. "There's a Mitch relatively high up at NATO but he's British, so he can't be really powerful."

"These are Americans."

"*These*." Ross is already trying to piece together the story for himself.

"These," Martha confirms.

"So Mitch and some other guy or some other guys. What are you talking about? What is this?"

Martha says nothing.

"So we're going to assume that we're not talking about multiple Mitches, but Mitch with other powerful people. Political?"

She doesn't answer, so he answers for himself.

"Who isn't political anymore? Fucking Chick-fil-A sells homophobic chicken and Oreo sells trans-positive cookies. Political but not political-political then. Maybe. Military? Possibly? This is getting brazen. What is this, Martha? What are you talking about?"

Ross once taught her an old interviewer's trick: Never say anything. Let the awkwardness build. Shut up and let the subject fill the silence. She uses this trick against her mentor. That's the beauty of the trick—it works against people who know it works.

"Mitch Middleton on the Joint Chiefs of Staff. Mitch Rischoldi from the CIA."

Martha writes the names down on a pad. "One more," she says.

"Three's a trend, huh?"

"That's the job."

"Mitch Roan at State?"

"Most powerful Mitch?" she asks.

"Depends what you want: to kill somebody, to destroy a country, to torture somebody? I suppose it would have to be Middleton. Joint Chiefs of Staff. Buys the light bulbs and pays the power bills for the greatest military force in the history of the world."

Martha sighs. "I gotta confess something."

"Don't do it to me." There is a faint begging in Ross's voice.

"I gotta."

"You're serious?"

"I gotta."

"You're going to leave me here and call me up and ask me, 'Who's the most powerful Mitch in the world?' and then not tell me why, and then I do it and you leave me hanging? You're going to do that to an old man?"

"I have to."

"You know how this works, don't you, Martha?" Ross says.

"I know how it works," she responds in shame.

"The next time—"

"This is probably nothing, Ross, and when it's nothing, I'll tell you."

Disgruntled silence fills the line.

"All I can tell you is that I'm not going to invite you to my dinner party," Ross finally says.

"Is it a fancy dinner party?"

"I'm not going to tell you."

"C'mon, tell me."

"It's going to be the fanciest dinner party. All the best people are coming. Maybe Mitch will come."

"Which Mitch?"

"I'm not going to tell you."

Journalists are easy to understand. Their motives are simple. They want the story. Everything else comes after. Some want everybody to know they have the story. Some want to have the story that nobody else has. Some want to have the biggest story. But they all want the story. Sometimes, they don't even want to *tell* the story.

Hell for journalists is not eternal fire. It's knowing there's a story and not having it.

6:33 p.m., 1029 Vermont Avenue NW, Washington, DC
Balfour is waiting at Stan's for a man whose name he can't remember. It's one of those J names, Joshua or Jonah or something.

Balfour has ordered a gin and tonic, which at Stan's is a tall glass of iced gin with a small carafe of tonic on the side. You pour the tonic into the gin as you drink it. An unappreciated lime lies discarded on the table.

Balfour's drinking is starting to show, in red patches on his cheeks and in awkward balloons around his middle. Stan's is forgiving of such evidence, especially in its darker corners.

Balfour is watching a video on his phone when the J kid enters. The kid is very pale and copper-haired. If he was any whiter, it would qualify as a medical condition.

"You see this?" Balfour hands over his phone. It's a scene of a masked man walking out of a Walgreens with sacks of high-end makeup while a security guard watches.

Jackson, that's the kid's name—Balfour remembers at the last minute that his name is Jackson—looks on, uninterested. He says nothing.

"It's brilliant, isn't it? Who got the idea? You just walk into a store and take the stuff. The bosses tell the security guards not to stop you because the risk of you suing them for millions is so much higher than the nine hundred bucks worth of cosmetics you're stealing, and the government has so crowded the prisons that they can't afford to jail you for petty theft."

Jackson fidgets, takes a manila envelope out of his briefcase. "I saw that. San Francisco."

"It's spreading everywhere. You have to respect it, don't you? Americans always find a way. You think, *You can't rob that Walgreens, there's a security guard.* But some guy is out there thinking, considering, weighing the possibilities, sifting through the corporate structure, calculating what motivates who, where the gap in the armor is, and he comes up with a plan: just go into the shop and take it. It's brilliant."

"Feels like the collapse of Western civilization to me," the kid named Jackson says.

"Why don't you get a drink?"

"No thank you."

Balfour watches to the end of the video, then clicks his phone off. "I can see why you would feel like it's the collapse of Western civilization," he says. "The breakdown of private property. Young men taking things that don't belong to them without consequences. But surely even you can see that the history of Western civilization is a lot of young men figuring out ways to take things that don't belong to them without consequences."

Jackson pushes the envelope over.

A waitress appears, masked. "What's your poison, honey?"

Jackson waves his hand in front of his face. "I'm just here and gone."

She nods and wanders back to the bar.

Balfour takes a look at Jackson. He looks at the kid's khakis, his blue shirt, his crisp, frightened face, angry for no good reason. Jackson's jaw is clenched as if he's about to say something nasty but can't figure out what to be nasty about, or who to say nasty things to.

Balfour opens the envelope and teases out an image. "You're kidding."

"What?"

"Cooper Sherman?"

"What's the matter?"

"You're sending me up against Cooper Sherman?"

"Is that a problem?"

"Yeah, I got a problem in that I don't see what the point is. He's a third-party candidate who will either blow up in three months or take more from the other side than us."

"They're afraid of some numbers." The "they" in this case don't need to be named. The shot callers, the right-wing media owners, the tech libertarians. The donors.

"What numbers?"

"Someone is giving him two hundred million in Ethereum. Look, you're being upped. This is strategy, not operations. You have a budget."

"I do not . . ." Balfour shrugs. What's the point of explaining? "Were there any direct instructions?"

"No. Do what you do. Complete freedom. They want long, continuous stories, stuff they can spin out. Look, it's only until the debate. Once he can't get 15 percent, we'll move you back."

"Back to what? Back to Georgia—going to the houses of election officials and telling them that their families are in danger if they don't certify the way we want?"

Jackson looks down, then looks up. "Honey Badger don't give a shit."

Balfour empties the remaining contents of the envelope onto the table. "I mean, what do we even have here?" He flips through the pages. "Some sex stuff in Detroit. Who cares? Financial curiosities around a couple of IPOs. You know the American people don't give a shit about this stuff anymore, right? 'Grab 'em by the pussy'? Remember that? He still won."

"Make them give a shit."

"You little Harvard motherfuckers know about as much about personal destruction as you know about fornication."

"I went to Duke." And with that, Jackson stands up and walks out. Of course he went to Duke.

Balfour pours a finger more tonic into his glass. The other

customers do not look his way, even though he's the only white man in the place. They know about confirmed drinkers. Once upon a time, he thought of himself as a journalist, an objective observer, or at least an observer who resisted other people's distortion, but then the time for choosing sides arrived, and he chose his side, and now he is an oppo man, little more than a narrative assassin, a tool other men point to shoot. The line between tilting a story and outright deception blurred long ago. Now he knows beforehand what others will figure out later. Democracy is on the way out. Who will control the aftermath?

Balfour swallows half the gin and opens the file again. The beaming face of Cooper Sherman is bright with hair dye and teeth whitener.

He chose to do oppo because he's excellent at oppo, the best at oppo, far too good to be doing oppo on a third-party candidate who is running for office the way other billionaires take up collecting yachts or art.

If he has to be a tool, he will be a precision instrument. It should not be too difficult to destroy Cooper Sherman. The man will probably destroy himself first.

7:13 p.m., 159 W. 54th Street, Manhattan, NY

Mikey and the envoy from the Ethereum donor meet at Faces & Names, a bar at the foot of one of the new brittle skyscrapers just below the south side of the park. A large surrealist portrait of Christopher Walken looms over them in matte-green and gray.

The man with all the money looks like a graduate student in physics dressed up for his dissertation defense. He is wearing a white linen suit that may never have been worn before. He has tidied up the facial hair on his goldfish-round face, but it's clear that once home, this neatness won't last long. His gaze is flat. He isn't scared but he is out of his depth.

Mikey shakes the hand which is as moist as if it had just been washed. "Pleased to meet you . . ."

"Alex."

"Alex . . ."

"Alex McLuhan."

The name sounds made up to Mikey. He can always look it up later. "Any relation?"

"To Cooper Sherman?"

"No, to Marshall McLuhan."

"Oh, yes," Alex says, surprising Mike. "He's a distant cousin. Third, I think."

"Marshall McLuhan said that the third world war would be a guerrilla-information war in which there were no combatants and no civilians."

"Yes. He did."

These geeks have no capacity for small talk. The bartender drifts over behind the bar and Alex orders a cranberry juice and Mikey orders a bourbon on ice.

"So, Alex, I guess I should know if we're talking about *your* money here, or somebody else's money, or . . ."

"It's not my money. And I'm here under a very specific set of instructions, from which I'm not permitted to waver even in the slightest. I hope you can accept these conditions, given that we're talking about a hundred thousand Ethereum."

Mikey smiles. "That must sound like a lot of money to you," he says. He spins the coaster sitting in front of him at the bar. "We're talking the US presidency here. Whose money is it?"

"That is one thing, among many things, that I'm not allowed to tell you." Alex looks at his phone.

"What can you tell me? Can you tell me if your friend's American?"

"I can't really tell you anything about him or her. He or she has a hundred thousand Ethereum he or she wants to donate to your campaign," Alex says. "He or she wants to make all the payments in Ethereum. Like to the staff or what have you."

"Would it be accurate to say that your client—"

"He or she is not a client. I'm just speaking on his or her behalf."

"Okay. Can I ask you what attracted him or her to the Maverick Party?"

"Um, I'm not really sure I can say. Not because I'm hiding anything. I just never asked. It never came up. The whole tech vibe, I guess. The whole not-being-one-of-the-other-two-parties thing."

The bartender brings the drinks. Mikey takes a sip of bourbon. Alex takes a gulp of cranberry juice.

"So here's the thing, Alex. You're not really going to get much for this money. You see, you can't tell us what to do, and even worse, we can't tell you what to do. You're asking for the staff to be paid in Ethereum. Well, it wouldn't be our staff. It would be yours. After this conversation, we can't really speak again. I take it your buddy has never made a major donation to a party before."

"You want him to give two hundred million with no say in how it's spent?"

Alex looks down into his drink in embarrassment. Mikey smiles despite himself. It's a *he* and Alex is no spy.

"It's the law. It's the dumbest law in the history of the United States, but it's the law. The reason we can't talk after this is that *Citizens United* says that you can give as much money as you like to a Super PAC, but you can only give $3,300 to us. So after this conversation, you've got to set up a Super PAC and then we can never speak again. This creates a structural problem. We will have all the intel, we will have the polling, we will have the AI, we will have the market-segmentation analytics. We will know what to do. We will have the strategy. *You* will have the money."

"So we work out a strategy now?"

"If only it were that sensible. Strategy changes. We're in the early days here. Anything we came up with here now, at this bar, wouldn't be worth a thing by next week."

"So when the strategy changes, you just secretly call us?"

"No. People go to jail for that. Actual custodial sentences. Usually at a more local level when people get sloppy, but no. We will never speak to you. Not even in a crisis."

"So how do we communicate?"

"Well, first of all, you hire a Super PAC manager—we'll give you a list—and she'll know how to read our signals. And we keep everything public. You can act on information that's public. So, we send out an email blast saying, I don't know, *We're going to concentrate our ads on x, y, z counties in New Hampshire.* The Super PAC manager will read that email blast and know what to do. Then we unsend it."

"You know we have people—" Alex begins.

"Yeah, we can't use them. Like, for advertising, we will have done the testing, the focus groups, and we'll make the footage. Then we'll release video of the candidate, you know, walking by a mountain stream or in a hard hat at a construction site or whatever, over some messaging service. It will make its way to YouTube, but there's nothing we can do about that, and then the campaign manager will use it for the ads. You see? But we will have nothing to do with it."

"What if my friend has his own ideas and wants to contribute them to the campaign?"

"We're doing, like, three or four events a day. If your friend wants to come to one and give out his 3,300 bucks, he can tell Cooper just what he thinks. He can sure tell *me* what he thinks. But in person, please. And it is best, for everybody, if *we* orchestrate strategy."

"Too many cooks."

"Exactly. And there's one more thing," says Mikey.

"Go ahead."

"Media buys for political candidates, by law, have to be set at the lowest available rate. But not for Super PACs. Again, the person you're going to hire will understand all this. But it's important to be early in certain markets, so you want to move fast with this money."

Alex looks somewhat taken aback with all of this information.

"Do you need me to go over any of this again?" Mikey asks.

"Yes, please."

Mikey describes the Super PAC system again, the forced separation, the direction without direction, the way to keep lines of communication open when they're illegal, all the private Kabuki required to make dark money work legally, to assuage the idiotic conscience of Anthony Kennedy when he decided to destroy his country by flooding the political system with unregistered, uncontrolled money. The Supreme Court required all this flimflammery to justify turning their electoral system into a luxury marketplace.

"I don't mean to offend you," Alex says after texting the details to himself, "but this is the stupidest fucking system in the world."

"Dude, this *is* absolutely the stupidest fucking system in the world. We want to change it. We're *going to* change it." Mikey tries to say it like he believes it.

Alex considers the ice in his drink. "But he can definitely say it's an Ethereum-backed Super PAC."

"I think that would be great for the campaign. I think that makes us look, you know, tech-savvy."

Alex nods. Mikey understands the play. It's a crypto guy trying to pump up crypto by attaching it to disruptive political trends. He's relieved: it's not the Chinese government.

7:29 p.m., 360 Clinton Avenue, Brooklyn, NY
Martha has figured out by now that it's not Mitch Rischoldi from the CIA, and it's not Mitch Roan at State. But Mitch Middleton has never given a public speech and the other voice is equally private.

She hears a rustling at the front door, and it's Zayn. "You here again?" she asks.

"Picked something up." Zayn brings in her favorite, Peruvian chicken with rice and beans and fried plantains. He kisses her on the top of her head just like at lunch.

It must look to Zayn as if nothing has changed. But *everything* has changed.

"You feel pregnant?" he asks.

She feels pregnant, but not with child. She has audio of senior members of the Joint Chiefs of Staff describing how they'll negotiate the end of the republic. Even though the message arrived on SecureDrop, and even though the sender took every available precaution of secrecy, she will figure out who sent it, and she will talk to that person.

Journalism exists, it functions in the world, because everybody wants to talk about themselves. Nobody wants to be secret, not really.

Everybody is in a movie in their own head, and everybody feels that if they could just be the narrator for a scene or two, they could turn themself into the hero. Journalists sell recognition without selling, and the world is their customer.

Martha knows that somewhere deep in the apparatus of the state, somewhere in the Pentagon, there is a man or woman who doesn't want to be known but wants to be known. And she will know them. And she will tell their story to America. And America in its outrage will save itself. She believes that. She tells herself that she believes it. She believes it because she has to believe it.

Under the fire of her new mission smolders an ember of new fear. This story is important enough to be dangerous. Whoever sent those recordings is playing, very much, in a world where political murder is normal. She feels the danger on her skin, as sudden as the onset of rain. She is being watched, by people who kill some of the people they watch.

She won't tell Zayn, not now. He doesn't need more fear.

10:23 p.m., Bedford and Barrow Streets, Manhattan, NY
A text message from Cooper: *This almost looks like a real campaign.*

On the Slack channel, Ren sent a GIF, a scene from that Soderbergh movie *The Limey*, of Terence Stamp slightly spattered in blood, shouting, "Tell him I'm coming! Tell him I'm fucking coming!"

Nellie sent some numbers: their launch video at 2.13 million views, the website with 932K visits, the email list at nearly two hundred thousand, 96K new Twitter followers, and, most impressive of all, 57K donations averaging $19.47 apiece. The donor demographic could not be better, weighted to states with high numbers of independents, like Minnesota and Colorado, and to professionals in the tech industry.

All the good news has elated the staff. They are off to their ketamine journey in high spirits. Under Mikey's instructions, everybody is to put away their phones. He doesn't know what ketamine-texting looks like but he can't imagine it would help a campaign.

He probably should have joined their adventure, though ketamine has no appeal to Mikey. It's too trendy. He always comes to things late. Money is better than drugs anyway.

Money is the message. Their message is starting to register. Their message is starting to register because it's true and everybody can see it's true. Each generation is poorer than the one before it. Nature is more withered and torn every year. Chaos gains every year along the fronts of order. The old solutions no longer work. The American people are starting to get exhausted by their own hatred. They are starting to grow desperate for futures that don't involve their children going to war or living in the basement.

Mikey savors the market buying what he is selling—a subtle bone-deep exhilaration. You can do market research. You have your thesis. But when it works out, it's still surprising. So little does work out in this world.

He walks north through the Village. He sees a mother clearing away dishes in a semi-basement kitchen filled with old wood and an oversized antique chandelier. He can hear the scraping of a child practicing a violin from an apartment above. A teenager smokes a cigarette on a stoop. Americans are going about their business. They eat meals. They experiment with drugs. They nag their children. They hope that real life—the ordinary life of love and its difficulties—will survive the juggernaut. But the hope is fraying, threadbare. That's what the bundler from this morning could not understand. Hope is sitting on the shelf, spoiling for no buyers.

The election approaches. Elections are now to be feared. The political condition of the United States is so toxic, and the electoral system so degraded, and the information networks so distorted, that the suspicion of a great shock coming has morphed into a common expectation. The catastrophe is forming out of view, stirring in the abysses, but it is on its way. Mikey knows what others do not. He's an insider. Inside knowledge is the addiction of people in politics. But you don't need inside knowledge to see that the country is falling apart. Like everybody else, he can't see it coming for him.

Mikey Ricci's mind races with numbers and next steps. Two hundred million in Ethereum and 15 percent in the polls. This election matters more than any other in history. It isn't just what they always say. This is the year when what they always say happens to be true. It is the American election to see if there will be any more American elections.

His phone buzzes. It's Dom. The message reads, *F2F*. Mikey's phone buzzes again, this time Nellie: *Suicide on staff*.

Fear pours over Mikey like a bucket of hot slop. He's suddenly sticky with panic. Mikey doesn't have to guess who. He knows. And, for the first time today, he has no idea what to do.

January 7

FIRST QUARTERLY FUNDRAISING REPORT

(378 days until)

Mikey wakes up in the director of communication's bed to the sound of politicians calling for murder. He wonders if his career is going to end today.

Six weeks after the suicide, the police report on the death of Maverick staffer Katie Danjou will be released today. Mikey had come over to Ren's office last night to talk over scenarios of the fallout, and she'd dragged him into a sexual liaison of upsetting innovation.

He can't tell, at first, if Ren turned on CNN to wake him and hustle him out the door, or if it's been on all night and he just happened to wake up to the chaos. On the television over the desk across from the bed, the Republican is speaking to a rally in Michigan: "They killed us, you know that? Every time you look at a Democrat, what you need to know is that they're happy we're dead. And the police are on their side. The police are on their side for now. But we're going to change all that."

The crowd hoots and hollers. They have that WWE energy, halfway inside the real world and halfway lost in a fantasy of cleansing joyful violence. Somebody's going to get their ass kicked.

"To those people who are on our side looking for revenge, all I have to say is: don't. But you know, I am also going to say that I understand if you do. And I understand that you do. And I understand *why* you do."

The crowd roars. They're the good guys, the guys who won't play by your fucking rules.

"And when I am in power, everyone on our side is forgiven. The day of the inauguration, pardons for everyone."

Mikey rolls over. His underwear is somewhere in the twisted sheets. Personal chaos, political chaos—what's the difference anymore?

At a Republican rally in Tulsa on Christmas Eve, a stanchion collapsed, killing six instantly. In the subsequent stampede, seven more people died. Over fifty were injured. The story in the mainstream media was that the Republicans' event-planning business had cut corners and failed to put in the correct papers, an opinion shared by the Tulsa police. They charged the Republican campaign with negligence. Fox News claimed it was an act of sabotage.

Meanwhile, Mikey and Cooper had been out talking about goodwill between all Americans, and rebuilding trust through a new party, and how our similarities are more important than our differences.

Mikey hears Ren's gleeful shriek from the bathroom. The remote is somewhere in the tangled sheets. He turns the volume down. He had planned to slip out undisturbed, before she woke up. But he can't quite see how an unacknowledged exit can be managed now. It would be more convenient for everybody, but it can't be managed.

The sex with Ren was just as weird as everyone said it would be. She played the horror movie *Saw* on the television, and watched the whole time with the volume all the way up. It was horrible, unforgettable.

Ren walks out dressed in what she was wearing last night, high heels, black skirt, red blouse. She throws her phone on the bed. "We're safe, Mikey."

"Safe?"

"The police are no longer investigating the suicide of Katie Danjou. Just heard from my boy in Chicago."

A delicious relief trickles down Mikey's neck and spine. Six weeks ago, Katie Danjou, a volunteer in the Chicago offices of the Maverick Party, had been found dead in her apartment after overdosing on Tylenol PM. She had been fired a month before. She'd left no note.

The suicide of a junior staffer who'd just been fired from the campaign could, in any other year, have sunk a candidate. Even if the campaign hadn't caused it, the fact that one of their staffers committed suicide would have pointed to bad judgment in hiring somebody who was mentally ill, and if you avoided that trap, there was still the basic smear: *Turmoil in the campaign.*

But Ren proved her worth. Ren told journalists that the campaign couldn't comment because it was unethical to write about suicide in general. She referred them to the American Psychological Association's guidelines on suicide awareness, which describe the Werther effect—the fact that reporting of suicides leads to increases in the suicide rate. Ren said the campaign would not comment out of ethical considerations and out of respect for the parents' grief.

And it worked. A few far-right sites ran conspiracy theories, but they ran so many conspiracy theories that the Katie Danjou suicide barely registered. No one had figured out the real story.

It helped that her Insta and Facebook pages showed signs of breakdown. *Despair can be tasty if you suck on it long enough,* she had tweeted the day before she overdosed. On fucking Tylenol PM.

Ren grabs the remote and turns the volume up. "What we are seeing here is exactly the kind of violence that leads to civil war," Brianna Keilar is saying, "and which defines societies transitioning out of democracy into autocratic forms of government. What are we supposed to do as Americans? This election grows ever more important as it increasingly feels less like a process whereby we select which candidates we want to be our leaders, which candidates we want to represent us, and more like a process in which we pick the system of government we want to be governed by. You know, my whole life I've thought of *Democrat* and *Republican* as brand names, if you will. Now you get what it says on the package. A vote for a Democrat is a vote for democracy. A vote for a Republican is a vote for a republic. And what they mean by a republic is—"

Ren turns the television to the movie channel. *Saw* is theirs for another fourteen hours. She fast-forwards it to the scene of a young man who wakes up in a draining bath in the dark with his terrified voice calling out: "Is someone there?"

Ren unclasps her ruby-cluster earrings. She unzips her skirt along the side.

10:01 a.m., 360 Clinton Avenue, Brooklyn, NY

Martha still cannot quite believe that she is in a position to have private meetings with the editor in chief of the *New York Times*. She feels, waiting for the Zoom meeting to begin, very much the little girl from Scranton who worked as editor of her junior high school paper. She feels how a Catholic in a state of sin must feel when granted an audience with the pope.

Malcolm Tanager appears, putting in his earbuds. The man is entirely poised, even on a Zoom call. Behind him, a bookshelf filled with presidential biographies and a grand marble fireplace divide the background. Room Rater gave it a ten out of ten last time he was on CNN.

It is not quite a private meeting. There are two others on the call, the managing editor, Melissa McClung, and the legal adviser, Tamara Washington. They are there as institutional observers. The question before them is what to do about the leaked audio that came into the SecureDrop server and which hinted at the outlines of a possible coup.

Tanager is a precise, shirtsleeved, elegant, somewhat tweedy Black man. His movements have the precision of a surgeon. Even picking up a pen or taking a sip of coffee is undertaken with deliberation and the sense of a task desired, conceived, and executed. The editorship of the *New York Times* is aging him rapidly. His hair grows whiter by the month. Rapid aging is in the nature of the job. His life is a constant barrage of impossible situations. He never relaxes because he can never afford to relax. He is a man who is not permitted any mistakes and who will be punished for the mistakes of others.

Martha has spent the morning trying to figure out if a meeting on Sunday at ten a.m. is a good sign or not. They had rescheduled the meeting so she could recover from the IVF procedure. One of her embryos is currently in the lab, preparing for transfer. Sometime later today, Janet the fertility doctor will call with the time for the implantation.

A meeting on Sunday could mean that Malcolm's eager for her to start, or it could mean that he wants to clear her off the agenda, or, most likely, it could mean nothing: the man is so busy he probably just takes meetings as they come.

She remembers when her cognitive behavior therapist would tell her, in moments of deep anxiety, to repeat, "What if it all works out? What if it all works out?" But that mantra has worn out over years of everything not working out. She has a new one that she repeats several hundred times on her morning walk. "Things could not be going any better. Things could not be going any better." She has said it enough that she almost believes it.

"How did the procedure go?" Malcolm asks.

Martha mumbles something about how they won't know if

any of the eggs are fertilized for a few days. Panic flutters like a bright bird in the back of her throat. What if Janet calls in the middle of the meeting? Would she take the call?

Reminder: Things could not be going any better. Things could not be going any better.

It's a bold question for Malcolm to ask. Male bosses are not supposed to ask questions about the reproductive health of their female staff.

"You know, Allison and I had to try three times before we got Sam," Malcolm says. "That was back in the Middle Ages though. IVF is so much more advanced now. How are you feeling?"

Is his concern genuine or is he trying to figure out if she's weak? Is he a colleague expressing support or is he a coach trying to figure out if she's game ready?

"Great!" she says. "Terrific!"

"Wonderful."

Malcolm looks down at his notes. Martha can almost see him check off a box in his head: *Small talk completed.* He has been effective with his confidence, establishing intimacy and trust in under two minutes. Journalists must possess the ability to manipulate conversations to their own ends while maintaining the illusion that they care about the other person. It is a core skill.

"So I guess the first thing I should ask," Malcolm begins, "is have there been any more messages from the source, over the tip line?"

"No. I've tried writing back, but nothing."

"Nothing."

She shifts in her seat. She wishes she had chosen a better background than the kitchen. "Nothing so far."

"Okay," Malcolm says. "Listen, we're not going to run that audio."

Martha tries to stop herself from blushing with the hot mixture of embarrassment and foiled ego. "Can I ask why?"

"There are two reasons, and I want to be frank about them. The first is the sourcing. We don't have any. The second is the possible catastrophic effects of a story of this magnitude without the sourcing."

Martha nods. "It is a story with a lot of magnitude."

"It is."

"I mean, I have to be honest, Malcolm, this is information that the senior levels of the intelligence services and the Joint Chiefs of Staff are preparing for a possible civil war, and are preparing to take over the functions of government. That seems to me, you know, the kind of thing the American people should know about. I would want to read about it. I would want to read about it in the *New York Times*."

"Now, I don't think what we have here constitutes the Joint Chiefs of Staff preparing for a civil war," Malcolm replies. "We have one single tape with voices who don't identify themselves, almost certainly recorded illegally, discussing one military scenario."

"And that scenario involves negotiating an end to the Bill of Rights."

Malcolm takes a deep breath. "Can I tell you an old-man-journalist story?"

"Please," Martha says. Now she knows her story has no chance.

"I was a cub reporter in Boston, and I met this kid, I met him at Biddy Early's. And he told me a story. Career-maker."

Tamara and Melissa have stopped whatever they were doing to listen. They must have heard Malcolm's story before, but journalists love stories where other journalists screw up.

"The kid's name was Larry, and he was one of those Boston guys who starts drinking himself to death around twenty-five, and I was also one of those guys then, before I met Allison, so we were in this community of drinkers, Larry and I. Running around, you know. We're watching the hockey game one night. It was that game that went into fourth overtime, and a fog descended on the Garden. And Larry starts sobbing. Just sobbing into his beer. And so I ask him what's going on, not as a journalist."

"As a friend," Martha says.

"Not even. As a human being. Anyway, it was his coach," Malcolm continues. "On a triple-A hockey team. Huge beloved figure in Boston. Abusing the kids, it turns out. Fourteen-, fifteen-year-old boys were his thing. And this kid I was talking to, Larry, he hints at what happened to him."

Malcolm takes a thin, precise sip of water. "Anyway, I do my job. I wheedle the story out of him. Friend or whatever, well, you know. It's a story. He goes on the record. I take it to the powers that be. I more or less force my editor to run it. Threaten to quit and so on. We run it."

"It didn't work out," Martha says.

"Coach denied it. Team supporters found some mental-illness episode in Larry's teenage years. Every single one of Larry's teammates backed the coach. Larry was accused of blackmail and worse. He ended up hanging himself in his bathroom."

"Jesus."

"And that's not the worst part," Malcolm says. "The worst part is that nobody could run a story about that hockey coach again. When they did catch the guy, when a few dozen hockey players did find the guts to point the finger, it was eleven years later. Eleven years of systematic abuse."

Martha does not know what to say. "What are you telling me?"

"This business is not just about what's true or false. It's not just about what's right or wrong. A story comes in its time."

"Do you think you should not have run that story?" Martha asks. "You think you should have let that coach go? Stayed silent? What are the choices here?"

"I should have had the *whole* story. I should have had every corner nailed down. I should have thought about how the story would play out. I should have recognized that a story walks around in the world."

Martha racks herself for a way out, some possibility that she can keep this thing alive. "What if he writes back?"

"Oh, if there's more, then we'll have to reconsider everything. If he writes back, then we'll talk about it. We will definitely talk about it—but Martha . . . Martha, I want you to think about something."

"Yes, Malcolm?"

"We're not the only people with SecureDrop. This man, he probably leaked it to us *and* the *Washington Post*, at least. Probably the *Wall Street Journal* too. And why haven't any of them run it?"

Martha nods, in an imitation of thinking.

"A story comes in its time," Malcolm says again.

10:22 a.m., 1216 18th Street NW, Washington, DC
The young man who is about to change history has the right place but the wrong time. The wrong time makes him think he has the wrong place.

The poster in the window of the door of the Open Bar says clearly, *Salsa Brunch.* The young man is not dressed for the weather. He is wearing a windbreaker and ripped jeans.

He remembers the profile he read online. "The justice is a dedicated salsa dancer and never misses the Sunday salsa brunch at the Open Bar in Washington." Did he screw things up again? Had he misunderstood? Was it canceled or something?

The young man's name is Lucas Coyle. His name is meaningless now. Everybody will know it in twenty-four hours. Until three days ago, he lived with his mother in Taos, New Mexico. He is unemployed. He is twenty-one years old. Everything he owns is in his pocket: the $857 in cash he took out of the bank account he closed, a gun that he built from a 3D printer during a class at a community college.

A beefy Latino with a goatee and a ponytail, and big round shoulders under his black leather jacket, is manning the door. "Can I help you?"

"Salsa brunch?" the young man says.

"You coming to salsa brunch?" The young man who is about to change history doesn't look the type, with his scruffy chin and his ragged clothes and his awkward bad-haircut whiteness.

"I'm supposed to meet someone here."

"Salsa brunch is at two o'clock," the man in the black leather jacket says.

"That doesn't sound like brunch."

"What?"

"Brunch is supposed to be between breakfast and lunch."

A shrug. "The time is the time, man."

The world never knows who walks in whose shoes. The beefy man, and the few locals and tourists on the street, do not know that they are part of a historical drama, and that this mundane scene, Sunday at the shops near Dupont Circle, will be described minutely in books and recreated as a key scene in the great drama of the American republic.

The young man knows what the world does not yet know.

11:17 a.m., Zion Episcopal Church,

128 W. Central Park Avenue, Davenport, IA

The key, Balfour knows, is not to look at the Danjous, not to shift, even vaguely, in their direction.

He is already out of place in the Zion Episcopal Church, a bland postwar modern Midwestern church built for people who wanted the stability of a god without all the fruity nonsense. The interior is white. Tacky textiles hang down from the altar, displaying on one side a raven and on the other a dove. God loves quilting in this place.

Balfour wears his linen suit, and he is the only one in the building wearing a suit at all. He doesn't own khakis and a blue shirt, which is the uniform of the men here. They do not receive, he imagines, very many new congregants.

If he even looks in the direction of the Danjous, everyone in the room will know why he is there. They probably have their suspicions already. But if they knew, they might act.

For the people of this congregation, the first fact of their religion is that God was born in a barn. Balfour is practically ethnic here, but then again, in this room, which doesn't even admit the frippery of stained glass, a clove of garlic would be ethnic.

The Danjous must be in their early seventies, Balfour thinks. Mr. Danjou has his arm around Mrs. Danjou, as their friends and neighbors come to comfort them in the rawness of their loss. Mrs. Danjou looks like she is about to weep openly, like she is embarrassed that she looks like she's about to weep openly.

Is this how average Americans mourn? The girl has been dead six weeks. Balfour has never cared for or been cared for the way these people care for their daughter. He's not sure of the protocol or standard practices.

This is an American community. As the world falls apart, they are taking care of their own. Mr. and Mrs. Danjou are their own, and they are with them for Katie's suicide.

Now that the service has ended, the fifty or so worshippers at the Episcopal church are shaking hands and chatting. Balfour has positioned himself at the back so he can watch the Danjous without watching them. There are coffee and bagels in the basement, and he needs to see where the Danjous are headed. If they join the coffee klatch, he doesn't know what he'll do.

Balfour is desperate. His bosses are starting to grow calm. So far he has nothing except a large expenses bill. Fortunately, the Danjous are not staying for coffee and bagels in the basement. Balfour waits half a minute and then follows them into the cold Plains light of the parking lot.

They're getting into a red Toyota truck.

"Mr. and Mrs. Danjou," he says.

They look up like deer.

"I'm sorry. I don't mean to intrude. I knew Katie in Chicago and I just wanted to tell you how sorry I am for your loss."

Mrs. Danjou gasps and sobs and buries her face in her hands. Mr. Danjou stands behind her, consoling her with his hands on her shoulders.

> *10:57 p.m., Hudson Yards,*
> *Eleventh Avenue and 30th Street, Manhattan, NY*

Everyone in the campaign will eventually figure out that Ren screwed Mikey, if they don't already know, but Mikey and Ren agreed that she would go in first and he would come in later so that their screwing doesn't become the subject of the day. Cooper hates lateness. Mikey takes the reputational hit out of residual gentlemanliness.

The team has already gathered around Cooper's treadmill. He walks an hour and a half a day without exception. Nellie and Dom are sitting against the unused desk, notepads in hand. Their compliance consultant, Raj Thakor ($25K flat fee), has taken a seat in the Aeron chair beside the treadmill with his MacBook Air open on his lap.

Off in a corner, checking his phone, is Nadav Bertelsmann, the new head of security hired in the wake of all the new threats coming in since the success of the launch. He is six seven, bulky, with the build of a lineman, and he does triple service as Cooper's driver and training partner. Nadav is ex-Blackwater. The rumor is that he's killed somewhere between five and ten people. He never smiles. His hands are always crossed in front of him. He is perfectly attentive at all times but never hears or sees anything. The job of security is to be completely unobtrusive so that everyone can forget that running for office in America means that thousands of people want to kill you and have the means to do so.

On the screen over Cooper Sherman's head is this map:

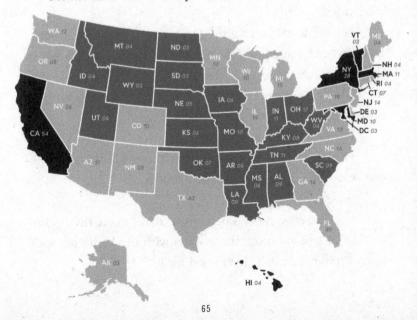

"Mikey, you late piece of shit," Ren says, "do you have any sense of decency or shame? The country is waiting for us."

"Sorry," Mikey says.

"This is a little bit important here, Mikey. Path to victory," Cooper says. "Go on. It's good this motherfucker is late because I need all this explained to me again. Start at the beginning, Dom."

"As I was saying," Dominic continues, "the American system for presidential elections is not one system, and we, as disruptors, cannot think of it as one system. We can't think, *Hey, we're going to win over the American people, voter by voter.* That's just not how it works. We need to think in terms of electors in the electoral college, and those electors are not all equal—"

"The way to get to electors is voters though, yes?" Cooper interrupts. "I mean, I know there are differences between the popular vote and the electoral college, but we're talking marginal returns here, no?"

Cooper and Dominic inevitably return to the language of business when they speak. Mikey likes it. It's refreshing. It's clarifying.

"Let me work backward," Dom says. "Thirty-three states have laws enforcing faithful electors. Seventeen states don't. In those seventeen states, the electors can vote for whoever they want. And that means that if we take those states or even portions of those states, we have some leverage."

"The other ones aren't free."

"The other ones swear an oath that they will abide by whoever wins the popular vote in their state."

"Gotcha."

"Now the good news is here: these states where the electors tend to be free are often those states with the highest proportion of independents. That's good for us."

"We can get to a victory without California and New York?" Cooper asks.

"Forget them completely. You're not running in those states. You are running first of all in Colorado and Minnesota, then Washington, Oregon, Nevada, Arizona, New Mexico, and Georgia. These are your backbone. These are the spine of an independent America. And then there's Florida and Texas. They're how you win."

"Fuck," Cooper says. "I hate Florida."

"Can I ask some questions?" Ren says.

"Shoot," Dom replies.

"So we play for Texas and Florida to win, but those itty-bitty states, these independents, if we win them and don't win the whole shebang, can we negotiate with their votes?"

"Look, it's never been done before," Dom says. "But yes, we can. In theory."

"So if we don't *win* win, we can stop others from winning, right?"

"That's definitely right."

"And then we would have them by the balls, and Cooper here could have them give him anything under the sun."

"That's a rough sketch, Sarah," Dom says. "But yes, with these free electors he could extract concessions in exchange for those votes, and those concessions might include actions that would otherwise be unpalatable."

Mikey needs to speak up here: "Let's not worry about that. Let's worry about winning this whole thing."

Everyone in the room knows that a certain amount of vagueness is required to drive an independent campaign. There are plots within plots. They have to play for the win in order to play, but there are many other paths that fork out from a partial victory.

The assumption has to remain unstated: every electoral vote Cooper wins is a token for trade. He could trade for a cabinet position for himself, or for promises of electoral reform. Those promises could work. It might give a Democratic or Republican president cover from their own party to do the right thing and save the country from its own insanity. There are several possibilities worth fighting for.

"All right," Cooper says, "I want this map seared into everybody's mind. This is our way forward. We have two tiers of votes we need to pursue. The first is these independent states with free electors. The second is Texas and Florida."

"Meeting one is over," Ren says. "Meeting two is now on. Raj, this is you." The consultant startles up in his seat. "What's the embarrassing shit that's going to hit us from compliance?"

"Uh, I don't know about embarrassing," Raj says, "but you're fully compliant."

The subject of their second meeting is the first quarterly fundraising report. By law, they have to release their numbers, and their numbers are staggering. They have raised $17.8 million in a quarter with an average donation of $22.37. This is a win, a huge win. But nobody will know it's a win unless somebody says it's a win. Who is that somebody? Who to leak it to? How?

"You get what Ren is talking about?" Cooper asks Raj.

"Not entirely," Raj answers.

"There's a whole aesthetic to this filing," Ren explains. "It's for a small audience but you've got to get it exactly right. Because the clowns who give a shit about this clown nonsense are a bunch of cruel clowns. These clowns are fucking nasty. They're the kind of clowns you find in a Stephen King novel, looking up from the sewer at you."

"Pennywise," Nellie says.

"I want to be precise here," Raj says. "I think that's my value add. I can tell you without any doubt that the filing is compliant with FEC law, and it's fully legible. I'm not a political consultant, I don't understand the optics. I think you might need somebody else for that."

"What we're worried about, Raj," Nellie says, "are stories like the time Joe Biden spent twelve thousand dollars on paella or the time John Edwards spent four hundred dollars on a haircut or the time Bernie Sanders used Amazon when he's been preaching against using Amazon."

"Is there anything off brand in the filing?" Cooper asks.

"What's the brand?" Raj says innocently. Everyone else laughs.

"The rich guy who doesn't do rich guy things," Dominic says. "Tech baron who hates tech barons. Big guy who helps little guys build back their businesses on TV. Innovator. Savior of the republic armed only with common sense. American patriot who has seen the brokenness of the American system."

Raj raises a spiderlike hand to his forehead. He is a human computer computing. "I don't think so," he answers at last.

"Why do you have to think about it?" Ren asks.

"There are private jets. There are the expenses of this office which are not insignificant." Raj gestures around. "There's, like, New York stuff. Suites at the Equinox. But I think it's all pretty normal. I mean, everybody else is doing it. You know about it anyway."

"What do you think, Ren?" Mikey asks.

"Go with it," she says. "If we're fucked, it will only be a negligible fucking. It will be just the tip."

"Thanks, Raj," Nellie says.

Cooper turns up the speed on the treadmill while Raj collects his papers and leaves. Cooper only lets his inner circle see him sweat.

"What's next?" Dominic asks.

"We're going to leak it today," Mikey says. It's his call.

"Are you sure?" Cooper says. "I don't want to get bigfooted."

Politicians hate, more than anything, being bigfooted. To be bigfooted is to have the attention that is rightfully yours taken away. You're in the green room at *Jimmy Kimmel*, and everyone's making a fuss about you, but then Barack Obama walks by and all the cameras follow him. That's being bigfooted, the wave of your story overtaken by the bigger wave of a bigger story.

The fundraising report could so easily be bigfooted. If somebody has a better fundraising story than theirs, their story will be lost. The money only matters insofar as it's meaningful, and the meaning of the money now needs to be carried across the line into medialand. It requires delicacy and confidence, like an egg-and-spoon race.

"Two points," Mikey says. "The first is that we really don't know what the fundraising numbers are. I hear the governor of Colorado is doing well. It looks like he had the best quarter of his life, but I think he'd already have leaked it if that was true. And he has to exceed expectations."

"Can we really not know how much the others have raised?" Cooper asks Ren.

Ren shrugs. "Can't separate out the lies they're telling themselves from the lies that serve their interests. Best to know what we don't know, rather than pretend we know what we don't know."

"Second point," Mikey says. "There could be some new story that drowns us out, though it could just as easily be next week as now."

"Politico?" Cooper asks.

"No," Nellie says. "Insidery. Pure clowns. The most clown-ish of the DC clowns. Clownishness embodied."

"Correct me if I'm wrong," Dominic says, "but a story about a quarterly fundraising report is only going to be of interest to the political and media clowns, and Politico is the major source for those clowns. It's the clown bulletin board. Isn't that where we want to be?"

"Dom's right," Cooper says. "This shit is for the clowns, and all the clowns read Politico . . . *Politiclown*," he adds, pleased with the coinage.

"We're going to get those clowns anyway. Those clowns are going to be lined up," Mikey says. "We got a narrative changer here. We need a clown who all the other clowns steal from."

"Maggie at the *Times*?" Cooper says.

"She hates your guts," Ren says. "Hates reality television politics. Hates your hair. Hates your teeth. Thinks you could get the Republican elected. Thinks you're a clown who doesn't even know he's a clown."

Cooper laughs. He loves being insulted by Ren. "I did not know that."

"I want to try the *Times* though," Mikey says. "That junior guy. Trevor something."

"Trevor Harrison," Ren says, not looking up from her phone. "If you've got contacts at the *Times*, use 'em, because I'm not using mine. Not for this shit."

"That's smart. Keep your powder dry," Cooper says. "I guess we'll need it later."

"I know somebody I could try," Mikey says. "Anybody have a contact for Martha Kass?"

"Sidelined," Ren says.

"Is she?" Mikey asks.

"MeTooed."

"I thought she *was* MeToo," Nellie says.

"MeTooers MeToo other MeTooers," Ren says to Nellie,

as if explaining to a child that dogs pee to mark their territory. "The left shreds itself."

"She's out of the *Times*?" Mikey asks.

"Shit detail," Ren says. "I forget which one. Somewhere well out of the matrix of real power. You fuck her?"

"Yeah," Mikey says. "Back in college."

Nellie and Dom are somewhat embarrassed, but Cooper's impressed. "Mikey fucked a clown," he says.

Ren shrugs. "Worth a shot."

Cooper turns down the speed of the treadmill. "Give Martha whatsername a shot. If you fuck it up, we'll go back to the Politiclowns." He's trying out his new word, but nobody in the room is willing to take it up.

12:15 a.m., 360 Clinton Avenue, Brooklyn, NY

Time is a narrowing corridor. Martha has no baby. Martha has no story. When will her time come? Will her time *ever* come?

For an hour, Martha has been writing angry emails to her mentor Ross. She writes out her anger and then deletes the message.

She's writing and deleting her anger so that she doesn't dump it on Zayn. Never go to your spouse for career advice. They don't know what you should do. They don't want you to succeed. They want you to be happy so that you're less work for them. They don't love you for your ambition.

A story comes in its time? What kind of bullshit is that? I've been stuck in the farthest outposts of the empire for not kowtowing to the new etiquette. Are we reporting only the shit that everybody already knows? I find THE MOST IMPORTANT STORY IN THE WORLD and

She erases the text. She knows what Ross would say—*Pity party*—and he would be right. She starts typing again:

A story comes in its time? Do you know what he means by that? He means that there's a risk for the Times. It's like the Weinstein story. Everybody, and I mean everybody, knew about Weinstein for decades, but he advertised on the Arts pages. Once the Arts section started dying, they could have a go at him. The right thing to do became cheaper, and that's why

She erases the text again. What's the point of sending any of this to Ross? He knows it all. Besides, that's not what the unsent emails are about.

How did ordinary life get so hard? It's not like she's asking to be queen. She wants a family and a job. Somehow having a family and a job is "having it all." Having it all means having a life.

Everything in America is a struggle. Health care. Education. Work. Every front a battle, and you marshal your connections and your contacts and your initiative and your money. And most of the time it's not enough.

She scrolls through the tip line's anonymous emails to distract herself. There are already seventy-six messages this morning, not including SecureDrop, and she will have to deal with them, even in her dejection.

Right at the top of Signal, from a string of numbers, *A story comes in its time?*

She almost believes it's a message from Ross, like he's commiserating. She hasn't spoken to Ross. She hasn't spoken to anybody. She checks the string of numbers against the string of numbers in her file. It's the same string of numbers that sent the audio clip. It's the source.

Her throat constricts, and her hand rises to her throat. She does not know on what ground she has been standing.

Everybody knows they're living in a surveillance state, but everybody forgets they're living in a surveillance state because nobody can stand to live in a surveillance state.

1:15 p.m., 9045 New Liberty Road, Mays, IA
Balfour has to remind himself that he's not in danger. He shouldn't be. A couple of elderly Iowans invited him back to their acreage for lunch. It's not the kind of situation that tends to get you killed. Balfour has to remind himself of that general tendency. He probably won't be killed.

The lunch has been exotic in its banality. The kitchen is clean and country. They sit on uncomfortable wooden chairs around a well-rubbed round table, eating tomato rice soup and grilled cheese.

On one wall is a series of family photographs in black-and-white, sturdy men in fields, women holding children in place. On the wall behind him is a needlepoint sampler that reads,

God give me work
Until my life does end
And life until my
Work is done

Balfour's work is lying, and it's a job that comes naturally enough to him, but lying can be exhausting, and right now he is on the extreme edge of the lying profession. He is fabricating information about a woman he has never met in front of her parents. All he knows about Katie Danjou is that she dropped out of a political science PhD at Northwestern, that she worked briefly for the Maverick campaign, and that she suffered from bipolar disorder.

He's been vamping, filling, telling stories he's made up about her confronting a professor over an ethical lapse, and her working at a soup kitchen he invented. This is the stuff parents want to hear, he figures. This is a high-wire act of lying. His net is his truck outside. He left the keys in the ignition. He would have left it running if he could.

The Danjous are in such grief that it makes their reaction hard to read. The father says nothing, spooning his soup to his mouth mechanically. Only every now and then does he look up, with a deep, examining gaze, a poker gaze. The mother is simply in rapture, like a child at a fair who is overwhelmed by a magic show. Any story of her daughter will do, any at all. She will burst into tears or she will beam with joy, and it doesn't matter much what he says.

Balfour knows he has to take his shot sooner rather than later. As Mrs. Danjou clears away their bowls and side plates, he opens the crack of his intentions ever so slightly: "I miss her. I really do miss her. And I don't know about you, but I just think it was really horrible what the campaign did to her."

A plate slips from Mrs. Danjou's hand and shatters on the floor. Mr. Danjou rises to comfort his wife.

"Gosh, I'm sorry," Balfour says. "I didn't mean to . . . ."

"It's all right," says Mr. Danjou. "You just go sit in the living room." The old man, his arm around her shoulder, leads his sobbing wife upstairs.

Balfour finds a broom in the cupboard and sweeps up the shards on the ground. It is the least he can do. Then he goes and sits in what he assumes is the living room.

There is an old hi-fi and a sectional in front of a fireplace that has not been used in years. The room is colder than the rest of the house. He considers leaving. He can't leave. He needs a kind of answer. He needs to take the chance that he'll learn what happened between Katie and the Maverick campaign. Even a chance at a scrap of information is worth the risk. It might lead to something if it's not the thing. Besides, he might get lucky. He's not in any real danger. He repeats to himself, *The keys are in the truck's ignition.*

Fourteen minutes later, Mr. Danjou comes down the stairs with a guitar case. "I'm sorry about my wife," he says, sitting across from Balfour. "She and Katie are the same. Sensitive. Too good for this world. Too loving." He places the guitar case on the floor, opens it, and takes out a shotgun. "They feel too much, and it means that people take advantage. Do you mind?" He starts to clean his shotgun with a pink shammy.

"Not at all."

"I'm hunting this afternoon," Mr. Danjou says. "I didn't plan to. But sometimes you just have to kill something."

"Mr. Danjou . . ."

"I despise politics myself. I never understood why Katie would want to be around such people. I mean, you have to understand, this was a little girl who could do anything. Honestly. You've never seen anything like her when she was eight, nine years old. She could learn anything in two days—a math function, a piece on the piano, the periodic table. She just had that kind of brain. It could do whatever it decided to do."

"I know."

Mr. Danjou begins loading the shotgun from a box of shells in the guitar case. The shells clank into place. "I don't know what's going to happen to this country," he says. "I suppose some people are going to die. My father died in a Hamilton bomber over Hamburg. Now this gun," he holds it out for an inspection, "this could easily kill a man. But I'm only loading it with bird shot. This wouldn't make a hole through a soft target, moving or otherwise. It's for quail. It won't kill you, it will just pepper you up nice."

Balfour sits perfectly still, like a stain.

"Katie died because she wanted to make the world a better place, and she realized she couldn't. Maybe that's a sign she couldn't grow up. But it tells me something. Do you want to know what that something is?"

"Yes," Balfour says. His mouth is dry.

"I don't know who you are but I know *what* you are, and I know that Katie would never have known you or anyone like you. In short, sir, we have no community of interest."

Mr. Danjou places the shotgun across his lap. He places his hand over the trigger guard.

> *1:31 p.m., Cathedral of Saint Matthew the Apostle,*
> *1725 Rhode Island Avenue NW, Washington, DC*

Lucas's last meal is the peanut butter burger off the secret menu at Shake Shack. He came to the Cathedral of Saint Matthew the Apostle to eat it. The door was open. It is close to the Open Bar.

The Cathedral of Saint Matthew the Apostle probably has a rule against eating in the church, but Lucas is in a time beyond rules. He wolfs down the peanut butter burger. He saw it on some *Buzzfeed* video. It is tasty. Lucas has never seen the point of food. It would be better if everything came in pills.

A priest in a robe that makes him look like a *Star Wars* alien is giving a tour to a man in a blue suit and red tie. Lucas wonders if the man in the blue suit and red tie is worth killing. Probably not. He is probably a functionary, and the functionaries don't matter, only their functions.

"And we have the red mass here, usually in September or

October," the priest is saying. "And usually all the justices attend, regardless of their religious affiliation. Of course, at the moment, many justices are of the faith . . ."

One less tonight, Lucas thinks.

In the warmth of the church, with the grand organ, the mosaics in gold and blue of angels and crucifixion, the red marble, the hatred that burned so hot in him in Taos sits like a glowing ember in his chest. The ghost gun in his pocket is him. Plastic, deadly, anonymous, untraceable, built to specifications found on the Internet. The president, the real president, promised to forgive him, him and all like him.

Not that they need forgiveness. The real president is just stating the obvious. They are at war. He is a soldier. It is a new kind of war. He is a new kind of soldier. The leftists planted that railing that led to all the death. They would stop at nothing, so he could stop at nothing.

The priest walks back up the aisle. He looks anxiously at the young man who has just eaten a burger and fries in his church.

Lucas relishes the warmth. He will stay just another half hour. He checks his Timex. The attraction of churches, he thinks, is that they have no clocks on the walls, like casinos.

2:15 p.m., 360 Clinton Avenue, Brooklyn, NY
For two hours, Martha has been texting with the source. Sometimes he writes back right away. Sometimes ten minutes or more will pass. Each time she thinks her story has vanished forever.

A story comes in its time? the source texts
He just means I don't have enough.
That's not what he means. He means he's scared.
He's scared because we don't have enough and he's right, Martha

texts, and then adds: *I assume you faced the same problem with WaPo.*

I only tried the Times. The romantic in me I suppose. Three days of the Condor.

We will print it, or run it online, if you give us the stuff.

What stuff do you need?

Everything you have. You. Meet with me. Blow the whistle.

I'm afraid that is not the kind of person that I am.

You're the kind of person who can listen in on secure Zoom chats between journalists.

Five minutes pass before the source texts back: *That is closer to the kind of person I am.*

Meet with me.

This is why people hate the media.

Why's that?

Because you make shit up and call it the truth, and then when the truth is handed to you on a platter, you don't like the smell or the taste.

Martha texts back: *You're too grown up and this is too important for that nonsense. People hate the media for the same reason they hate lawyers.*

What reason is that?

The world needs us.

I need you?

Let me help you get what you need.

You have no idea what I need

No. But I'm American and you're an American, and America needs what you have. Democracy needs what you have.

The source doesn't write back for seventeen minutes. He probably won't write back. Not today anyway.

Martha's phone buzzes. Unknown caller. This is it. The source is calling.

She takes a deep breath and answers. "Hello?"

"Hi. Is this Martha Kass?"

"You know it is."

"This is Mikey Ricci."

Is that the name of her source? She knew a Mikey Ricci. No, wait, Mikey Ricci from college. Why the hell is Mikey Ricci calling?

Martha and Mikey slept together for a week in college, as their third year was winding down after exams. She had picked him up, among their mutual friends, after a baseball game, and they hadn't left her bed except to go to a steak joint to fortify their blood with iron. Otherwise they had broken up their time with bowls of cereal and cigarettes she had rolled for them from a pouch of Drum tobacco. They had only seen each other a few times since college, but they had been cheerful times.

"I hear the bioluminescent plankton's in the harbor again. Just wondering if you want to go in my canoe," Mikey says.

The memory is like a scene from science fiction, the time they took mushrooms and paddled into Narragansett Bay as a blossom of the bioluminescent plankton flushed up from the Gulf of Mexico, and they brushed their hands in the water that lit ghostly green to their touch. How had life ever been so beautiful?

"That was amazing," Martha says. "Which of us got the mushrooms? Do you remember?"

"Oh, you were the dealer, you were the one with the connections. I did manage to procure the canoe, though. Remember?"

"No one could forget that. You knew about the plankton, you knew that they lit up when you touched them. How long do you think we spent out there?"

"No idea. I mean, the mushrooms skew your sense of time in the first place, and then the colors in that bay . . ."

"It was brilliant, wasn't it?"

The onset of their fond memory has delayed the obvious question: why on earth would Mikey, whom she hasn't seen in years, be calling her?

She can remember, a few years ago, in some meetup with old girlfriends for margaritas, before COVID, when people still met up with old girlfriends for margaritas, a girl who had also slept with him in college mentioning that he'd drifted into political consultancy.

"Where are you at these days?" Martha asks.

"I'm working for the Maverick Party. You still at the *Times?*"

"Yeah, still here, and Zayn and I are living in Clinton Hill."

Mikey doesn't mention he's in Manhattan. He might have to suggest a drink then. He doesn't want a drink. She wouldn't want one either.

"I'm calling to ask your advice about something," he says. In midlife, relationships morph into power, real connections convert into alliances. It's the most natural corruption in the world. "I have this story and I'm trying to figure out how to play it."

"I see." Martha suspects that Mikey never asks for advice. Back in college, he assumed that he knew better than anybody else. If he is asking for advice, he probably needs a favor.

"We've had an epic fundraising quarter. Our best ever. We obviously want the best placement for the story. And the info isn't out yet, so we want to give it to somebody. And we were thinking somebody at the *Times.*"

"Maggie," Martha suggests.

"Maggie hates us."

"Right. Your guy's a celebrity politician. Going to bleed off Democrats and get the Republicans elected. You want a kid."

"I want to leak it to you guys. And who should I leak it to? Do you guys have, like, a tip line or something?"

Martha laughs. "I *am* the tip line."

"You are the tip line."

"I am the tip line. I have the fucking SecureDrop servers in my apartment."

"I should have known that."

"Don't worry. Just like you, the luckiest guy in the world. You call an old friend to figure out how to send a tip to the *New York Times* and she happens to run the tip line."

"I have always been lucky with the women who've entered my life."

"The guy you want is Harrison. He's young enough that a stud like you can easily work him. I'll hook you up. He probably even *wants* your ridiculous fundraising story."

"You sound good," Mikey says.

"I am good. Did that reality TV star you work for really raise so much money that it amounts to a story?"

"That's what I'm here to tell you, or to tell Harrison anyway."

"American politics is even crazier than I thought, apparently," she says.

"It always is, isn't it?"

5:37 p.m., I-80 East

The first beer calmed Balfour down. The second beer is cooling him. His dad, that prick, always told him there were one-beer roads and two-beer roads. That was Maine. But driving to Detroit has to be worth at least a six-pack of Coors.

He could tell his bosses he'd been shot at. They'd like that. And he'd just make some shit up about Katie Danjou. Rumors she'd been fucking the candidate. They probably wanted him to make it up, so he would.

The opposition pre-research had pointed him in the direction of MTR, a sex club in Detroit. Apparently, the less current and educated members of the Republican establishment assume—because they're still cosplaying the eighties—that the American public gives a shit that a Silicon Valley executive attended some swingers club in Detroit.

So he is driving toward Detroit. Balfour hates Detroit.

6:29 p.m., 1216 18th Street NW, Washington, DC
A steady stream of immigrants is coming out of the Open Bar doors. The young man who is about to change history shivers in the cold and watches. He missed his chance when the justice entered the salsa brunch, and so he has had to wait for her to exit the salsa brunch.

The immigrants are families, two or three generations. They are dressed to dance. They are laughing. Many are innocents who nonetheless must die in war so that liberty and justice prevail. But they're not actually innocent. They came to take the country away.

He checks his watch. Two nine-year-old girls in red dresses skip along the street and then through the door. He can faintly hear the hot high music whenever the door opens, even from the corner across the street.

These are families. He has no family. He has no family anymore. Why should they be special because they have families?

A black Yukon pulls up. This is it. He sees the bar door opening behind the Yukon, and it must be her.

He moves across and up in one smooth movement.

She is being helped by a large Black security guard. Her owlish eyes look up, more curious than anything. He's only ever seen a photograph of the woman in her robes, and here she is wearing a long gray sequined affair. Somebody's abuela.

He lifts the chunk of plastic and clunkily fires. Her head snaps back.

He fires and hits her heart. Again, to the heart.

Then seven brutal stings, and darkness.

> *6:57 p.m., Hudson Yards,*
> *Eleventh Avenue and 30th Street, Manhattan, NY*

Mikey lovingly refreshes Twitter. There are the tweets he has devoted the past three months of his life to. They're on the *New York Times* feed, and it could not be better.

> *Breaking: Cooper Sherman raises a staggering amount of money in First Quarterly Report. $17 million.*

> *The billionaire, who is self-funding, has traction in states with high levels of independents.*

> *A real contender who could upend the 2024 dynamic. This is now a three-way race.*

> *Story to follow.*

There are 2K retweets and 47K likes, numbers that send Twitter tingles up Mikey's back. But when he looks up from his phone, wanting to share the triumph, he's alone.

Across the office, twenty of the staff are standing together, watching the bank of televisions. Stragglers are drifting in from their workspaces. Mikey drifts with them. Nellie is working the remote. She ups the volume on CNN.

"The assassin has been killed," Wolf Blitzer is saying. "We have no information on his identity or his possible motivations at this time. For those of you just joining us, Supreme

Court Justice Susannah Gutierrez has been shot and killed as she exited a restaurant in Washington, DC. She has been pronounced dead at the scene."

"Go to Fox," Mikey says.

Nellie clicks. The flinty face of John Roberts somberly communicates the party line: "Justice Susannah Gutierrez has been taken from us in an act of senseless violence. She was a tremendous jurist, a pioneer, and a wonderful colleague. Our prayers are with her family in this difficult time."

"Did you know her?" Nellie asks Mikey.

"No. Did you?"

"I knew people around her. Somebody's grandmother." Nellie begins to cry. Several others on staff are beginning to cry.

Mikey's phone has started buzzing and flashing. His period of mourning is over. He must strategize now. "What's our next two, three days like?" he asks.

Nellie brushes her eyes. "Media appearances for the quarterly report. You want me to cancel?"

"No need," Mikey says. "They'll cancel. They're already canceled. There is no news except this for forty-eight hours."

"What do we do?"

Mikey considers. The first goal of a campaign is resource management. The top resource is the candidate's time. "Call Cooper. Tell him he's got a half day off. All of today and tomorrow morning. Tell him to unwind, decompress, and build up his energy."

Nellie picks up her phone.

"Wait. I'll tell him. How many in-person bundling events can you schedule twenty-four to seventy-two hours from now?"

"Two, maybe three."

"Three is better than two. Four is better than three. Also, Nellie, bring in the senior team for an operational meeting.

Tell all the field agents that for the next forty-eight hours their only task is to get their field offices in order. They may as well use this time to oil the machinery."

CNN and Fox are showing the same footage, lifted from You-Tube. The assassin's corpse lies mangled on the street. A shocked crowd records the corpse and the crowd recording the corpse as the police arrive. How soon will he be a martyr? And to whom?

Ren calls and Mikey answers, walking out onto the street.

"We're fucked," Ren says.

"I know."

"Flight to safety."

"I know."

"Do you realize there's going to be fucking confirmation hearings in the middle of all this?"

"Let's not get ahead of ourselves, Ren. This is a classic forty-eight- to seventy-two-hour news cycle."

"Don't fucking kid yourself, Mikey. Kid me but don't kid yourself. It's going to polarize all the partisans. The president might even stack the court. I would if I were him."

"Okay, we have a story in response. We want to limit Supreme Court justices to eighteen-year terms rather than life-time appointments, and we're right. We say there's insanity on both sides, and we're right. We're the only people who can solve the underlying structural issues, and we're right."

"*Underlying structural issues*," Ren sneers. "What a great fucking turn of phrase. You should be a politician. Let's put that on the bumper stickers: *Solving underlying structural issues.*"

"Ren, listen—"

"Nice work on the quarterly financials," she says, and hangs up.

Mikey is standing on a Manhattan corner without a clue. His phone vibrates with a text from Cooper: *Death bigfoots us all.*

11:15 p.m., 360 Clinton Avenue, Brooklyn, NY

Martha has already processed eight different videos of the assassination of Susannah Gutierrez. No one recorded the shooting itself, but everybody took their phones out the moment after, and the *Times*'s video team is planning on reconstructing the shooting by stitching the clips together. It should look incredible.

In the two shots of the justice that have reached the tip line, her face is bloody and two holes near her heart leak out stains. The videos are brief. You have to slow them down to see the gore. Her security detail whisked her away so quickly.

The images of the assassin are longer, because he lay on the ground longer, because he was obviously dead. His young body, in ragged clothes, bleeds from multiple holes. His oddly peaceful face seems to be smiling in most of the videos.

Martha sits at her computer like a woman at a sorting line in a recycling plant. She ships any clips of any kind to a reporter. She junks the conspiracy theories that arrive at an average rate of five a minute.

But Martha doesn't mind all the photos, all the clips recording the murder from all the angles. And Martha doesn't mind all the turgid nonsense flowing from the never-ending sewer of American political rage. She knows that a man or woman, deep in the corridors of American power, is recording the reactions of the Joint Chiefs of Staff and senior members of the intelligence community, and that she must somehow obtain those clips.

Her story still has a chance. She still has a chance to emerge from the tip line. She needs more audio, and she will get more audio.

A story comes in its time. The time is coming.

February 7

IOWA CAUCUSES

(348 days until)

B y the time the taxi pulls up outside the sleek glass and wood of the Target Center in downtown Minneapolis, Mikey has managed six hours of the most delicious sleep of his life.

Sleep may not even be the word for the oblivion that swallowed him. In the back of the cab between Davenport and Minneapolis, his consciousness shut down. No dreams troubled him. Six hours passed like a handclap in silky emptiness. He woke up like a computer that's been turned back on.

"You a musician or something?" the cabbie asks as Mikey uncrumples five hundred-dollar bills for the fare. Back in Davenport, they had agreed on a four-hundred-dollar fee but Mikey is grateful for the sleep. The man looks almost exactly like Robert Duvall. He'll be telling this story for years—the time a crazy fare flagged him down on the street in Davenport and paid him four hundred bucks to drive to the Target Center in downtown Minneapolis. For an extra hundred bucks, a fair enough price, Mikey makes himself the hero of the story.

"Do I look that cool?" Mikey says, handing over the money. He unballs the jacket he used as a pillow from the corner, and smells his armpits. He will have to do.

"I'm trying to ask myself who takes a cab from Davenport, Iowa, to the Target Center at, like, one in the morning. A musician's manager? I would have asked you, but you passed out, brother. I've never seen a man sleep like that."

Mikey could have flown in one of his boss's helicopters,

but he took a cab because it was the only way he could find the time to sleep. In a hotel room, someone could knock on the door and expect him to get up.

"I'm with Cooper Sherman," he says.

"That independent? The, uh, the, uh, Maverick Party. He's a bit like a rock star, isn't he?"

"We're expecting twenty-five thousand tonight. This is our fuck-you rally. This is our statement that we're bigger than the Iowa caucuses."

The cabbie is counting his money, and couldn't care less about the Iowa caucuses or political rallies or the spillover. He's a real person, not a politician. And even the politicians don't care all that much about the Iowa caucuses.

In a political game as arcane as the American presidential system, Iowa caucuses stand out as uniquely silly. They are democracy at its most anachronistic. They look cute, what with the white people meeting out in the open, waving their hands in the air, voting like kids voting on what movie they're going to watch at camp.

The caucuses are a good introduction to the whole ridiculous business of a campaign. They exist for no good reason. They don't make any sense. Nobody wants them to exist. The Democrats have tried to shut them down. But the Republicans, to keep their rural base happy and because someone has to go first, have kept them going. Now the media show up mainly to describe the divide between urban and rural America and track who's drawing crowds. There's not a lot else to talk about.

Mikey looks at where the hell he has ended up. It's dawn in Minnesota in February. The arena is like the most beautiful Target in the world. Already a dozen volunteers are hovering near the entrance, like parents outside a kid's hockey game. They should be let in. The advance staff should already have let in the volunteers. How many other screw-ups is he going to have to deal with today?

Then there's the candidate's health. Cooper has come down with a serious flu. When Mikey left him the night before, the man was throwing up *Exorcist* style. The sane thing to do would be to cancel the rally for tonight. They can't do the sane thing. The Maverick Party is not a sane campaign.

To the side of the volunteers, on his own, not part of the team, stands a ghostly old man in heavy boots and a heavier coat, with a face Mikey remembers. But Mikey can't remember how he remembers the old man's face.

The thought that he might be an assassin flashes by, though Mikey dismisses the flash. This is a dangerous time in American politics. There are plenty of ghostly old men who look like assassins hovering on the margins.

The Maverick Party has staffed up on security because of a surge in online threats.

9:33 a.m., Park Tower, 400 N. Tampa Street, Tampa, Florida
Nine thirty in the morning is a terrible time to plan the destruction of a man. No one who understands oppo would pick such a banal and punctilious time. Balfour's previous boss wouldn't have scheduled anything for nine thirty in the morning.

When he was working for that guy, everyone would bring whatever dirt they managed to scrounge up to the conversation pit, a floating carnival of the grotesque that coalesced only with all-night pushes to blow an enemy away. Balfour could still think of himself as an intellectual in those days, or at least a man engaged in some kind of narrative contest.

In this anonymous office building, he can't pretend to be in any other business than the business he finds himself in: opposition research.

It's a room for focus groups. No doubt the last time anybody filled this room, they were telling some junior marketer how six different versions of honey mustard made them feel happy or sad on a scale from one to five. The room even has a one-way mirror. Whoever is sitting behind that mirror no doubt wants to think of reputational assassination as another product to market, but selling hatred isn't the same as selling honey mustard.

Working for idiots is one of the costs of doing business in politics. You must suffer fools gladly.

Balfour examines his dreary colleagues. There are two other sets of oppo consultants around the table. He could oppo them without leaving the room. They are predictable humans, despite their lousy trade, pirates without flair.

A midthirties man and woman in sleek banker wear came probably from some high-end research division of a multinational consulting firm. They whisper over their leather-bound agendas, signaling ersatz professionalism with every breath. They have never been journalists, obviously. They're just the fourth tier of Ivy League kids. Their presence in this room they no doubt consider a mark of profound personal failure.

The other two are more idiosyncratic: a walleyed, obese man and a kid with red hair and a huge Adam's apple who looks like the right place for him is at a comic book convention. They are dressed in gray suits with white collared shirts ill-fitted to their necks and inelegant red ties—your classic think tank idiots. They probably have degrees in classics and a great deal of rage about how the world turned out.

That's the thing about character assassins—they're just not quality people. You don't use good iron to make nails.

In front of each person at the table sits the oppo book on Cooper Sherman. Every significant politician in America has such a book written about them. Experts gather everything shitty a candidate has ever done, every dubious decision, every friend that turned out to be sketchy, every child who came out damaged, every compromise that turned out to be fraudulent, every man or woman they ever sat next to at a party who ever made an anti-Semitic remark—and they're all collated and printed in the form of a book. Balfour has seen more of these oppo books than anyone alive probably, though he can't have seen more than fifty or so.

American politics would work so much better, Balfour has always thought, if there were a public library where you could go and read the oppo books on all the politicians in the country. But that is not how the information systems work. There need to be secrets in order to reveal them.

The book on Cooper Sherman is substantial, 737 pages long. Balfour flips to the table of contents.

Top Hits
Lawsuit by Early Investors
Sexual History
MTR Club
Silicon Valley Connections
IPO of CompliSoft
CompliSoft Scandals and Improprieties
Lobbying and Donors
Real Estate Holdings
Travel
Clergy Endorsements
Staff Members
Fundraisers

Key Themes
Ethics and Corruption

Offensive, Radical, and Controversial Comments
Sexual Activities
Lack of Expertise in Law and Government

Personal Details
Background
Childhood and Family
Sexual Activities
Personal Political Donations
Voter Registration and History
Property Records
Businesses and Organizations
Criminal and Traffic Violations Record
Unsatisfied Vendors
Divorce

They put "Sexual Activities" twice, Balfour notices, in addition to "Sexual History" in the "Top Hits." Obsession is the hallmark of the repressed. But Balfour can't complain. It's his work they're highlighting.

Jackson, that little shit Balfour met at Stan's, comes in and sits down, clearly pleased with himself. The young man is living his dream: to be one of the players in the great game. The denim shirt and khaki pants he's wearing may as well be the uniform.

"Thank you all for coming," Jackson says. "And I hope you've had a chance to look over the fruits of your collective labor. All we're here to do today is to look over the book and talk about the smaller possibilities and the juicier moments. We just want to squeeze what we can out of this."

Behind the one-way mirror, there's a faint crash. Somebody must have dropped the pitcher of water they always have behind one-way mirrors. The big shots don't want their own attack dogs to know they're being watched.

A vast desire for a tequila sunrise permeates Balfour's being.

9:37 a.m., 360 Clinton Avenue, Brooklyn, NY
The *New York Times*, like the United States, provides itself with an annual public gathering, a chance to pretend to reckon with the problems it faces and to indulge in self-congratulation.

The importance of the annual State of the *Times* meeting is to tell the best journalists in the world, the men and women with the most developed bullshit-detectors available, that despite their capacity to recognize bullshit, they must, like everybody else on the planet, chew and swallow and pretend to enjoy what the world serves up to them. The State of the *Times* permits the more studious *Times* journalists to know which ideas are on the menu and which trends are popular with the management. It allows whoever cares to see what buzzwords are coming. One year they tried out "solutions-oriented journalism." Another year they tried "trauma-informed journalism." They are just alibis, of course. The *Times* is like a citadel that protects its journalists by conferring status and being one of the only profitable papers left. The *New York Times* is not in financial trouble but it considers itself, more or less, a synechdoche for journalism and so must address solutions that it doesn't happen to need. Everyone else needs a system for fixing journalism because it can no longer be fixed.

The imaginary solutions give everybody a distraction from the death of the industry and the darker fact behind the death of the industry—the reality that Americans don't want reliable information anymore. They want confirmation of their biases and rage.

Everybody at the *Times* has to attend the State of the *Times*, but most can get away with a check-in. There will be more attendees than usual this year. They will want to know what Malcolm is going to say about the election. The shape of the election coverage determines the shape of the whole year.

Most of the others will half listen, doing their own kind of Timesology: who is in, who is out, what the family wants, what those who are in power want, how the tides of power are rolling, who can distinguish the outlines emerging out of the fog of the successor ideology.

Martha pays close attention for reasons of her own. To escape from running the tip line will require a complex understanding of the internal conditions of the paper. To emerge from the labyrinth, you must understand the labyrinth. To understand the labyrinth, you must see it from above.

She is scheduled to have an egg retrieval in two days, and before then she needs to finish a piece of actual journalism: the compiled audio from her source detailing how the US military is planning to deal with the chaos of the election.

For the past month, Martha's source has given her the most scandalous audio in the history of the United States. Stitched together properly, they show the plans of senior military leaders to take control of the country. They have a constitutional means of doing so: the electoral mechanism of the "contingent election."

Martha hasn't yet told anyone at work what she has gathered. Today she has to figure out one thing. Will the *New York Times* run this story if she brings it to them?

> *9:41 a.m., Target Center,*
> *600 First Avenue North, Minneapolis, MN*

The amateurs are too trusting. They need better security, since he's been allowed to wander the enormous concrete labyrinth by telling everyone he's met that he's with the campaign. Maybe that's a Minnesota thing, the basic trust. The campaign's private security handles the bodyguards for the candidate, but for a rally this size, the local police deal with the public. Apparently, the local police aren't too worried.

They probably should be. It's not just the death threats against Cooper which have been rising in direct proportion to his popularity. The political violence is ramping up generally. In mid-January, a standoff with a 3 Percenter faction in Oregon led to the death of three FBI agents and the arrest of over 350 partisans, including several local Republican leaders. The Republican candidate described them as "political prisoners" on Fox.

Nobody ever believes the violence they read about is coming for them.

Still, Mikey's found little else to complain about. The green room has been prepared to the correct specifications, with a case of Ramlösa, a bowl of unsalted mixed nuts, Gatorade, and a bowl of apples, bananas, and mangos. There need to be more tables in the waiting area for the merch, for the voting registration, for donations.

They've made another classic rookie mistake as well. The signs for the crowd to wave have all been correctly laid out on the arena grass for inspection by the advance team, but they're one-sided. The political signs at a rally like this need to be double-sided. The drone shot will otherwise show a bunch of blank signs.

The main problem—and Mikey doesn't know what to do about it—is that it's so goddamn cold. The temperature is near zero. It's hard to stand out in that cold, and after Cooper gives his speech inside, he plans to stand outside for the selfie line, greeting the crowds who couldn't get in.

Cooper will want a hat, or at least earmuffs, and he can't have either because nobody votes for a man who's wearing earmuffs.

Nobody votes for a man shaking from cold, either.

Nobody votes for a man with the flu. Cooper has come

down with a serious flu. It's not outside the realm of possibility that the Cooper Sherman candidacy will end this evening with Cooper throwing up and passing out in front of twenty-five thousand people.

Mikey is lost somewhere in the underbasement, in a corridor so long it's like an experiment in perspective, its end an optical illusion, when he sees Nellie walking toward him. He can relax. She'll show him the way out. Beside her is a six-foot woman in high heels and a black silk pantsuit, tight in her manner, excited, unfamiliar, thrilled to be there. It must be the chief volunteer. Mikey has been sure to remember her name: Tristra Robinson.

They walk toward one another for what feels like minutes. They are laughing awkwardly by the time they're in each other's presence.

Mikey basks, momentarily, in the sensation that Nellie brings him, the assurance that everything is going to work out combined with gratitude. A world with women like Nellie Katz cannot be all bad. He's lucky enough that they're on the same side.

"This is our superstar," Nellie says to Mikey, introducing Tristra. Tristra is a yoga instructor and part-time physical therapist. She's overdressed for the occasion and underprepared. She's not a professional.

But Mikey can't bring himself to be cynical. This woman, who is not independently wealthy by any means, has suspended her life and her business to make this rally happen. She believes so much in Cooper Sherman, what he represents to her country, that she has given over three months of her life to this single event.

She raised the money to rent the arena. She organized three hundred volunteers. These volunteers are Uber drivers and schoolteachers and bartenders. Their time is valuable to them. They are there because they believe in the United States and they want to fight for its future.

Cynicism toward Tristra and her people would be stupid. Their idealism is real. All the kids setting up tables in their *Unf*ck America* T-shirts are there because they want to unfuck America. The moment is humbling. Mikey remembers why he started in politics.

All flacks are soured romantics. They play at cynicism to justify the grandeur of their life choices.

"How are you getting on with the advance team?" Mikey asks.

"We're getting on like a house on fire," says Nellie.

"I've screwed up so much," Tristra says. "I'm so, like, embarrassed by how many things I've got wrong."

"No, you're great," Nellie says.

"It looks amazing to me," Mikey says. "I've been over this place for an hour, and there's only a few tiny things. The reason we have an advance team is to go over the little things that there's no way you could know."

"The signs on one side," Tristra says, mock-burying her head in her hands.

"There is one thing we do need to discuss," Mikey continues. "Is there any way we can heat the candidate during the selfie line when he's outside? For reasons better left unexamined, the American people will not tolerate a candidate in a hat."

Tristra laughs a barnyard laugh, healthy and open. They raise them right here in Minnesota. "Coop is going to be cold then."

"If he wears a hat, he looks weak. If he doesn't wear a hat, he looks stupid."

"Maybe he could try earmuffs," Tristra suggests.

"Earmuffs are worse," Mikey says. "What I'm wondering is if there's any way to heat the walkway. Like, when they do rock acts here, do they have those propane heater things or . . ."

Tristra guffaws again. "I don't think so. Nobody usually plays Minnesota this time of year. It's too cold." She finally notices that neither Nellie nor Mikey are laughing. Her mouth curls over itself. "I'll look into it," she says.

"We'll look into it," Nellie says. "I'm sure we can figure out something. But, Tristra, you should tell him."

"Oh, right," Tristra says. "There's a gentleman from Iowa to see you. He says it's important. He's down the hall."

"It's Katie Danjou's father," Nellie says. She is making it clear that she isn't responsible for the old man's presence. You can't expect amateurs to tell bereaved parents to get lost.

Mikey suppresses dull dread. The man with the face like a face he remembers.

9:57 a.m., 360 Clinton Avenue, Brooklyn, NY
Martha listens to the audio for the three hundredth time.

"They have a name for that. It's called a coup."

"Call it whatever you like. I'm sick of losing wars for being too stupid to plan." The voice speaking is an administrator for the Joint Chiefs of Staff. *"It seems to me that if we learned anything from the past seventy years of spilling our blood and wasting our treasure on civil wars in the rest of the world, we can learn one goddamn lesson for our own."*

"And what's that?" The second voice, as far as Martha can figure out, is the undersecretary of the Department of Homeland Security.

"Stop this shit before it starts. Break these assholes. I want to round up the Oath Keepers now. I want to put them all in black sites now. And I want to crush Black Lives Matter too."

"The lefties crush themselves pretty fast on their own."

"Not fast enough."

All in all, the messages Martha has culled from her sources

come to four hours of audio. She is planning to play two clips for the editor in chief.

"*What if the election isn't decided by January 20?*"

"*Buddy, you know as well as I do that according to the Presidential Succession Act of 1947, the Speaker becomes the president. There's, like, ten million rules around the succession of the chain of command. You can't expect me to know them all. It's like asking how my car works. I don't know, but I know how to drive.*"

"*What happens when it breaks down?*"

"*I call in a mechanic. So, long answer is the same as the short answer: somebody's going to be president, and I'm going to serve him just insofar as it agrees with the law.*"

"*Listen to me. Listen . . .*"

"*I don't like hypotheticals, Mitch. We'll throw ourselves off that bridge when we come to it.*"

"*What if the old Congress refuses to seat the new Congress?*"

"*What?*"

"*That happens January 3. Will you insist?*"

"*Insist on what?*"

"*Will you insist they seat their duly elected congresspeople?*"

"*We're not going to insist on anything.*"

"*So you're going to allow a putsch.*"

"*Mitch, fuck off.*"

A clip from a few days later follows:

"*Who says we have to intervene?*"

"*History says. I say.*"

"*So we maintain basic order and follow the procedures.*"

"*Ever hear of a contingent election?*"

"*What are you talking about?*"

"*A contingent election is the mechanism the Constitution put in place if the results of the electoral college don't identify a clear winner. Which could happen. Which will happen. You admit that?*"

"Sure. Not impossible."

"So every state delegation gets one vote for president in a contingent election. Alaska. New York. Wyoming. California. Fifty states, fifty votes."

"Cakewalk for a Republican."

"Exactly. The Republican wins without winning. And the US military is at the service of someone who is not fairly elected."

There is a pause.

"If that's the system, that's the system. What's our role? I think our role is to keep America together, to defend the capacity of its institutions. The Republicans have the system gamed out so they're most likely to provide stability. Democrats can't do it. They're too weak. They don't have the guts. But whoever we take needs to know that it's time for us to be in charge for a while, just until this country cools down a bit. They need to understand that before we let them take office."

"But the Republicans are the ones who are ripping apart the institutions . . ."

"The Republicans in every possible scenario win a contingent election. That's why we have to throw ourselves behind the Republicans. So that we can pretend, for a little bit, that the military and the electoral system are aligned. The American people need to be able to pretend . . . That's how we don't call it a coup."

"It's still a coup."

"The first rule is never call it a coup."

Later, in these series of conversations, others are brought in, and they speak in hushed voices. The administrator for the Joint Chiefs of Staff is talking again. This time there's a faint tinkling in the background, which could be a bar or wind chimes on a mostly still night.

"I am increasingly uninterested in the sordid details of what you call the constitutional requirements. The public's faith is already broken. How can you fuck up something that's already gone? If the Constitution worked, we wouldn't be having this conversation. I swore an oath to the Constitution, but what did I swear to? Remember Iraq? Remember Afghanistan? The only way to win at counterinsurgency is not to play."

"At the very least, we're going to need plans to control the country in January and possibly afterward, and possibly for an indeterminate amount of time."

Here, a more senior voice comes on the recording.

"The conditions you're describing, Mitch, you believe this is a legitimately conceivable outcome?"

"More than that. I consider an undecided election and political violence—"

"What do you imagine the situation with political violence would be?"

"The result of the delegitimization of political norms is always the same. Spikes in violence. This seems likely to me. The most likely outcome."

The darker voice pauses and seems to speak out of a textbook: "The purpose of the military in insurgent conflict is to provide enough space, not defined by violence, for conflict to be resolved."

"Pardon me, sir, but we're talking about the same thing. Who's going to provide that space? Who's going to control it?"

10:27 a.m., Park Tower, 400 N. Tampa Street, Tampa, FL

"Tell us about the sex club," Jackson says cheerfully.

Balfour wakes up from a somnambulant boredom. For the past hour, he has been listening to the corporate researchers rehash their dubious spins on Cooper's corporate purchases and sales. The think tank boys had started going over Sherman's Twitter feed, overenthusiastically parsing some pro-trans remarks, and he drifted off.

Jackson has so enjoyed his stint at the head of an office table, like a real grown-up doing real grown-up things.

"The sex club stuff is all in the book," Balfour says. "I wrote it all down."

"Can you stand up and give us a summary?" Jackson says.

Balfour snorts. He does not stand up. But he's being paid, so he summarizes: "Well, our candidate attended a sex club in Detroit in the early 2000s. It is called the MTR Club."

"It still exists?"

"It's a thriving institution among the sexually depraved of the Motor City. A couple run it. They're grandparents but still fuck a half-dozen people on the weekends. MTR is three stories and a dungeon. On the top two floors are rooms that you rent for orgies. On the ground floor is a swimming pool with people fucking around it, and then little scene rooms for different acts with different people. Good American screwing, men and women and the in-betweens trying to get to the bottom of desire."

"Gay stuff?"

"It's a straight club but, you know, nobody's paying much attention to what you're doing with who."

"Underage?" Jackson asks.

"Not possible. The people who run this club are religious about the membership roll and the hygiene. That said, for sure they have unicorn nights, and for sure Cooper attended."

"What's a unicorn night?"

Balfour sighs heavily. He is bored with how much he is titillating these puritans. "A unicorn night is when young single women and middle-aged married couples show up and they have threesomes. It's by far the most popular form of swinging. Novelty for the old marrieds. Safety from danger for the girls."

"This is great," Jackson says.

"No, it isn't."

"This is great. We can really hit him with this. We can play into the Comet Pizza stuff, the pedophile-ring stuff."

"No, you can't. It won't work."

"Why not?"

Sometimes the stupidity becomes too much to bear. "You don't understand oppo at all, do you? Okay, I'm going to explain it to you because I'm a professional, and I find the amateurishness of these proceedings to be upsetting. So the reason the sex club won't work is that they're *cheerful* in that sex club. They're completely unashamed. They're doing everything privately but in the open. So you go into the club. It's run by a long-married couple and they offer you milk and cookies. They happily show you around the dungeon in the basement that has glory holes and bondage chairs. It's not embarrassing to them."

"Americans aren't going to vote for somebody who fucks a bunch of strangers," Jackson says.

"Americans will vote for a rapist as long as he's not embarrassed about being a rapist. The job of oppo is to turn strength into weakness. Rule one: strength into weakness. Swiftboating is the beginning of wisdom in this practice. Everybody already thinks of Cooper as a freaky-deeky Silicon Valley libertine pig. Saying he is what you already think he is doesn't hurt him. None of this shit, nothing in this book, is going to derail him. We have nothing here and we'd better admit it."

Jackson is turning red. Balfour's rant is humiliating him in front of whoever happens to be behind the one-way glass. His first response to the revelation of his own ignorance is rage. It's a common reaction. "I don't think we're useless," he says.

"The effect we're searching for is of a bubble popping. This shit"—Balfour picks up the oppo book—"is irrelevant. Wonky real estate transactions? Who cares? Sex in a club with his wife in attendance? They're going to *admire* him for it. You have to identify the best part of your opponent to destroy him. You have to acknowledge why people love him, then sour that love.

So why do people love Cooper Sherman? Why are twenty-five thousand people going to show up to see him give a speech in Minnesota tonight?"

The room is silent. The other researchers are looking down at their hands. Balfour addresses his next remarks to the pane of glass behind which the big shots are sitting. "People love Cooper Sherman because he's honest and unashamed and he doesn't hold with the old pieties. You need to smell out his hypocrisies and all I can smell are ours. Now, I will be in the bar if anyone who knows anything about reputational destruction wants me."

11:41 a.m., Target Center,
600 First Avenue North, Minneapolis, MN

The chaos is building—laughing mobs of kids moving tables, old ladies ticking boxes on agendas, husbands of activist wives joking while they await instructions—when Mikey finds Mr. Danjou sitting like a judge at a rave. He sits quietly with his decency, a man on a mission, a man rocked by grief to the point where the ordinary comedies of life no longer register.

Mikey shakes his hand and leads them both away from the nonsense. The only private spot he can find, though, is a locker room.

"I wanted to talk to Mr. Sherman," Mr. Danjou says, sitting down on the bench.

"Can I be honest with you, Mr. Danjou?" Mikey responds. "That's not going to happen. Not today anyway. This is a machine with a lot of moving parts, and he'll arrive at the last minute and fit in and he probably won't be here for longer than a couple of very intense hours. But anything you have to say to Cooper, you can say to me, and I will pass on anything you need me to pass on. I'm his . . ." Mikey looks for the words that Mr. Danjou will understand. "I'm his right-hand man. Whoever talks to me is talking to him."

"This looks like quite an operation."

"The real problem is the weather," Mikey says, smiling, trying out a rural bit. "The cold. You got any advice on how to solve the cold?"

"It is going to be very cold tonight," Mr. Danjou says, unsmiling, "and I'm Katie Danjou's father."

"I'm sorry. I knew Katie in Chicago. We were all just devastated. She was one of the good ones."

Mr. Danjou extracts a folded piece of paper from his jacket pocket. "I've been hounded," he says.

"By the press?"

"By the press, yes, but by other agents who don't offer a clear framework for their desire for information. These are the men I despise. I've been hounded by jackals, if that expression makes sense."

"It does. From what I know of this business, it makes perfect sense."

"I have spoken to none of these jackals, and I am never going to speak to any of them, but I would like something in exchange for my silence. I would like an explanation." He hands over the piece of paper. It is a printout of an email Katie had sent to Cooper's personal email address.

Dear Cooper Sherman,

Hope is a funny thing. Is it the shadow of the sun or is it the sun that makes the shadow? In the end, and right from the start, I didn't desire hope so much as I craved an end to despair. The campaign made promises. I heard them. I heard them right down to the womb: the future has to be more than an abortion.

The note is so Katie, down to its lack of signature, like she had forgotten who was writing while she wrote it. For her, intelligence and sensitivity were the same. Her feelings grew over each other in denser and denser layers as the world became more complicated. Her heart and mind had become wildernesses. Mikey looks up and the old man's eyes are brimming.

"I suppose you're asking yourself, *How can I get rid of this old man?*" Mr. Danjou says.

"Poor Katie."

"I need two things, and you owe them to me. I need you to show that message to Cooper, and I need to know what it means."

Faintly overhead, they can hear Cooper's helicopter landing on the ceiling of the building. "I will do the first," Mikey answers, "and I will try with the second. I'd like to be honest with you, though. It seems pretty mysterious. I always found Katie quite mysterious. She was mysterious to me, anyway. She was so sensitive to the world, so intelligent, and this world is brutal. But may I ask you, genuinely, do you think we'll ever understand why Katie did what she did?"

"I don't need to understand," Mr. Danjou answers. "But there is a reason for her death I have not seen, and I need to look at that reason."

The old man must know he's asking for the impossible. Mikey does what he can, what he must. He shakes the man's hand, and tells him he'll do his best.

12:21 p.m., 360 Clinton Avenue, Brooklyn, NY
The call from an unknown number arrives just as the State of the *Times* is breaking for lunch.

She has learned a great deal, but not very much from the State of the *Times*. That is always the way with official lines of communication from the organs of the *New York Times*. The publisher told them the business is strong, for a twenty-first-century journalism outfit that has undergone a model shift over the past decade. The *Times* is a juggernaut. The *Times* has over ten million subscribers. That's what they all wanted to hear. Such numbers cover a multitude of sins.

Then Tanager came on to announce a recalibration of the organizational structure. There are now to be four "fields of emphasis": beats, breaking news, enterprise, and framing. This is just a new way of carving up the old carcass, trying to preserve something of the old decencies in the middle of a wild new system.

Beats will stay beats: City Hall, real estate, the grinds that feel important and *are* important, but which nobody reads.

Breaking news means more livestreaming, more videography, more elaborate packaging for the 130 million–plus readers a month.

Enterprise means Pulitzer-hunting: big shit that makes the readers feel good about themselves if they can manage to read it, and makes editors feel virtuous for defending in meetings, and sometimes, sometimes, explodes and gives the paper not just a story but a reason to exist.

"Framing the news" is the new way, which will not survive, of doing what used to be called opinion writing. They can't call it opinion writing anymore because everybody is entitled to an opinion. "Framing the news" is the latest jargon to distract from the basic contradiction of wrestling the *New York Times* into social medialand: its existence is based on freedom of expression, but freedom of expression has fallen out of fashion.

All the fiddling is camouflage, anyway. The newsroom showed up for one single remark. It came after the usual banality about how, even though everyone always says every election is the most important election in American history, this election *is* the most important election in American history. "That importance, and the unique information environment in which this election takes place, demands a unique approach," Tanager said. "The *New York Times* is going to take a truth-based approach. We've always operated with a wall between hard news and opinion. That wall no longer makes a lot of sense. We can no longer be stuck in what-about-ism. We have to be conscious of our effects on the world. And while this will primarily alter 'framing the news,' it will saturate the whole of the paper. When a candidate lies, we're going to call him or her a liar. This is a question of consciousness of what we are doing, and of the power biases that underlie all claims. We're going to stand up for what we know to be true. We've always pursued the truth. Now we're going to be *clear* that we're pursuing the truth. Truth will be the new metric." The new buzzword: truth.

And now Martha is looking at an unnamed call. There are two possibilities for the unnamed. The first is her source. The second is the nurse from the fertility doctor's office calling to confirm her appointment.

It's neither. It's her fertility doctor, Janet.

"I'm afraid I have some bad news," Janet says. "There were three grade A eggs, but they failed to develop into blastocytes."

These people who will never be people. These people who would have been her people who will never be people. "Why?" she asks softly.

"There are many possible reasons, and we basically won't ever know what it is in this case. They simply weren't viable."

"Adoption time," Martha thinks and says out loud.

"Not necessarily, Martha. No. As we've discussed, up to 50 percent make it to the blastocyte stage. I know you're disappointed, but it doesn't mean . . . It doesn't mean any more than itself."

"I guess we'll set up a new appointment."

"Talk to Zayn and we'll do that."

Neither of them mentions the seven thousand dollars implied by that appointment.

Janet hangs up. Martha isn't hungry. She will have to do the rest of the State of the *Times* thinking of all her foiled eggs. She feels wounded but untouched, unworthy even of failure. She does not have time to cry before her next Zoom call, a breakout room on breaking news she has to attend because of her role on the tip line.

4:21 p.m., Target Center,
600 First Avenue North, Minneapolis, MN

Over the course of the day, a surreptitious energy has been building, like the arena itself has been swelling. The volunteer crowds have been growing, and the media have been filling the back of the hall with their cameras. The people in the building believe they are in the most important building in the world.

Whenever Mikey sees Nellie, it seems like she is conjuring the whole building's energy. Her small, scrappy body radiates unquestioning optimism, and as if by some kind of electricity jump, every person she meets receives a bit of her power. On his way to check in on Cooper in the green room, Mikey runs into her as she is jogging toward some last-minute emergency. "It's a joy to watch you work!" he shouts.

"Unfuck America!" she calls back giddily. "Do the math! I'm an eighteen-wheeler slathered in bumper stickers."

"Ride that highway, good buddy."

Outside the green room, Terence the speech consultant is pacing back and forth in the hallway, lifting his hand to his mouth like he's pretending to smoke. The night before, the plan had been to send Terence back to New York, but consultants are like burrs on the campaign trail: nobody can remember where you picked one up and they're tough to pick off.

Not that Mikey has a problem with Terence (never Terry). Terence is unusual for a consultant insofar as he's useful. His background is off-Broadway. Terence teaches politicians how to perform the role of human beings.

"Mikey, you know I can't intervene, but I think *you* need to intervene," Terence says. "They are self-focusing him. The candidate needs to be other-focusing right now, and they are self-focusing him. What did you hire me for?"

"We hired you because you're the best, Terence. Now tell me what happened, and be precise and be brief."

"The guys you hired to write the speech itself are in there. And they are giving him advice." The word *advice* is spat out. "They are telling him which words to use and which words not to use. They are laying mines down along the path he has to walk. And the man is not well. He's thrown up at least twice today." Terence grabs Mikey by the shoulders to make his point. "Advice ruins everything. He must be other-focused."

"Advice is bad," Mikey replies.

Cooper has two problems as a public speaker. The first is that he tends to speak too fast. In one disastrous public event, they clocked him at 7.2 words per second. He drifts too. He loses eye contact, and he doesn't engage with the questions.

These failings can make him look, at times, robotic. Terence trained Cooper out of this stiltedness with several exercises. In one, Cooper had to tell a story using only his eyes and his gestures and no words. There was also a game with Legos. After every sentence Cooper had to put one piece of Lego on top of the other. It slowed him down. They solved the eye-contact problem by making Coop catch a wiffle ball after being asked a question and then throw it back after he had answered. Incredibly, these exercises worked. After his lessons in humanizing muscle memory, Coop looked like a guy talking to his friends, even on massive stages. Terence's fee was maybe the best money they had spent, and they had spent plenty.

Mikey finds Sarah Ren outside the green room. She doesn't look up from her phone as he arrives. "Which one of the speechwriters do you want to fire?" she asks.

"We get to fire both?" It's the most cheerful news Mikey's heard all day.

"They're both talking critically to a guy who's thrown up twice today and is about to give a rally to twenty-five thousand people."

"Both of them are talking?"

"Both of these motherfuckers are fucking dumb as hammers."

Mikey thinks for a bit. "I guess I'll fire Jill Lowith. I hate her. I hate her guts."

"If you hate her so much, let me fire her. They'll be picking bits of her ego out of the New Jersey swamps."

"Oh, if you hate her too, you fire her. Who does that leave me? Chris Siblin, right?"

"No loss there," Ren says. She looks up, breathes in through her nose and out through her mouth. "This is just what I want to do today. Kick the shit out of a speechwriter. Sweet."

The green room smells of vomit that's been cleaned up. Splayed out on a military cot is the candidate, who looks like he's just been hit in the stomach. It doesn't seem possible that he'll be able to walk to the bathroom on his own, much less speak to twenty-five thousand people in a few hours.

The two writers are leaning in over Cooper, whose skin has a faint tinge of gray-green. "I'm not sure *unfuck* is the kind of word you want to be punching," the one called Chris is saying.

"*Unfuck*. It's a negative. It's a neologism. It's dirty. All of those could be alienating," the one called Jill adds.

"And, like, it's okay with the base, but the truth is that the base, you've already got them. We're in Minnesota. We want Minnesota nice—"

"Hey, Chris, can I talk to you?" Mikey interrupts.

"Oh, sure." Chris looks up. His face is round as a dish, and it gives him an aura of astounding naivete. He looks like a child playing the donkey in a nativity play.

"Bring your coat. Let's go for a smoke outside."

They go down first, then across a narrow passage, and then up two flights of stairs. Over the course of the day, running errands, Mikey has become familiar with the concrete bunker labyrinth. The emergency exit doors have their alarms disabled. Mikey pushes through, and they're standing outside, in the flat cold light of Minnesota February. Crowds are greeting one another, preparing to go in.

A taxi arrives and drops off four middle-aged women in Cooper Sherman gear. Mikey holds the taxi door open, and gestures for Chris to climb inside.

"What's going on?" Chris asks.

"This is going to take you to the airport," Mikey says. "We don't need your services anymore."

"Hold on a minute. Hold on. You hired me a week ago."

"We don't want you anymore."

The speechwriter looks poleaxed. "Cooper likes me. You need me. I can help you."

"Cooper won't even know you're gone and I can buy a hundred like you with a phone call. Keep the receipt for the cab, you'll be fully reimbursed."

Mikey walks with the crowd back into the arena. The Minnesotans for Cooper are jubilant, like they're on their way to a big picnic, or a football game where they know their team will win. Mikey slips by security—a nod from Nadav—then underground, and up to the green room again.

Cooper has just undergone another session of dry heaves. The lights are dimmed. The volunteer Tristra is sitting perfectly still in a far corner of the room. She sits perfectly still the way a parent sits perfectly still while doctors work on a terminally ill child. Ren is on the phone with the campaign doctor, whispering about various medical options. And Nellie is putting a moist towel on Cooper's head, humming.

7:41 p.m., 360 Clinton Avenue, Brooklyn, NY
"What do you think the *truth-based* approach means?" Martha asks Ross. She's doing the dishes after dinner. "Weren't we truth-based before?"

"No," Ross says, "not at all."

"What were we then? Based on lies?"

"We were fact-based. We brought facts to people and let them generate their own truths."

That's not what Martha wants to hear. "So this is a big deal."

"It is a big deal. They're picking a side. They've decided that in a state of post-truth, they can't just leave it up to people anymore. They have to pick a side without picking a side."

"You're telling me something."

"I'm telling you that you now work for the Democratic paper of record. But you knew that."

There's a pause while Martha figures out what she already sort of knew.

"It's not even their fault," Ross says. "This is the world that's arrived. They'll fight for Democrats, and for the institutions they serve. It's not their fault that the truth has become inseparable from who is speaking it."

"They'll never run my story, will they?"

Ross breathes heavily on the other end of the line. There's the sound of a dog entering the room. "You know what a journalist is?" he says. "A journalist is a spy. A journalist is a spy for the masses. The first journalists were spies in courts reporting for foreign kings. Then a few bankers. The Medicis. The Rothschilds. They ordered private reportage. Then it was for merchants generally, then it was for everybody, for cabdrivers and housewives and gangsters and saints and duchesses and the boy who cleans the boots, so they can know what the price of rice will be and what the fanciest vacations are and which television shows are cool and who sleeps with who in the White House."

"Where does that leave me?"

"Every journalist who is worth anything is a traitor. You betray sources to serve the reader, and only a very low kind of journalist has any loyalty to the bosses. That's what I'm asking you to remember. Remember that treason is the best part of you."

She hasn't told Ross about her failed embryos. She hasn't told Zayn about their failed embryos. Her position in the world is slipping, and she can feel the rocks under her feet crumbling, giving way. Ross is right. The time is coming for treason.

She's behaved, and where has it led her? To nothingness, to a tip line. She can see what will happen when she brings the story to her editors, how impressed they'll be, how they'll celebrate the work, how they'll find reasons not to run it.

The story of how senior figures in the military and the intelligence services are planning a coup doesn't serve the interests of progressive politics and it doesn't support American institutions in their time of crisis. At the State of the *Times*, Tanager may as well have announced that the paper will never run a story like hers.

Still, after she finishes the dishes and her conversation

with Ross, she returns to her computer and sends the files to Tanager, under the subject heading: *Audio We Discussed*. It's her job, after all. She has to give them the chance. She owes them that much. And for a moment, Martha allows herself to imagine the headlines.

JOINT CHIEFS OF STAFF PLAN FOR INSURRECTION

JOINT CHIEFS OF STAFF WILL TAKE CONTROL OF COUNTRY

JOINT CHIEFS OF STAFF BELIEVE IN LIKELI-HOOD OF CIVIL WAR

Under all of them the byline, *Martha Kass*.

She still hasn't told any of this to Zayn. It might exacerbate his despair. It might make him want to stop trying for the baby. There is a reason under those reasons. She doesn't want to have to admit to him what she's about to do.

> *7:43 p.m., Target Center,*
> *600 First Avenue North, Minneapolis, MN*

"Topeka bodega topeka bodega topeka bodega topeka bodega," Cooper is saying. Mikey and Cooper have been chasing each other around the green room throwing and catching wiffle balls. Cooper has his shirt unbuttoned and Mikey can't stop giggling. Above them, as random as thunder, comes the boom of twenty-five thousand strangers cheering.

The opening act was Stipe Miocic, UFC fighter and volunteer firefighter. Now Jesse Ventura is talking about Minnesota as a state for independents. The laughter is huge. The applause is even huger. Ventura is killing. He always does.

Nellie has been watching Mikey and Cooper play catch like an amused au pair. The message comes to her headset and she passes it on: "Showtime."

Mikey towels down Cooper's sweaty chest, and they throw on his shirt and jacket, and they pin the mic to his lapel and then tuck the cord into his jacket pocket and head up through the backstage area.

Cooper stops Mikey on the stairs. He puts his hand on Mikey's shoulder, and Mikey taps his fist gently on Cooper's chest. "You've got this." Then there's the hot first staccato beats of "Call Ticketron" from Run the Jewels, and the crowd is howling "*Kumbaya, bitch!*" as Cooper strolls up beaming into the spotlight, the blinding illumination of the world's attention.

Mikey heads down, underground, to the control center. Above him the roar of the crowd permeates the air, the stomping of tens of thousands of feet. Just before Mikey plunges down the corridor, he hears the opening line: "They told me I'm not supposed to swear." There's a huge laugh, then Mikey is alone, all sound swallowed by concrete. He makes his way underneath the arena as secretive and determined as a Jesuit on a mission. The sounds of the wider world, the muffled ecstasies of the crowd, are distant. He is too far underground to hear them climbing up and down stairs used to sluicing tens of thousands of thick Minnesotans.

Nellie is monitoring a bank of screens in the control booth.

"How we doing?" Mikey asks.

"Look at this drone shot." Nellie is flush with happiness.

The shot passes over a massive crowd all waving Maverick Party signs toward Cooper's beaming face. The cold makes the air clearer, emptier, and he appears defined, imperturbable, feeding off and feeding into the great wave of mass love. It's going to look amazing in ads.

Cooper's speech is majestic, rapturous. "The reason I started down this path," he is saying, "the reason we began the crazy adventure that is this campaign, is that I see what you see. The system isn't working. The country works but the system doesn't. This great country, the most productive country in the world, a country built on openness and frankness, is turning into a country where only guys like me have a shot, where everyone wants to close down the other guy, where our words have been caged in shame. Enough. Enough. It's time to take a risk, because in politics, just like in life, the real risk is *not* taking a risk."

Thirty-six seconds of applause by Mikey's Timex.

"And let's be real honest here. Okay, we got one party that has stopped believing in democracy, and you got another party that isn't willing to do what it takes to defend democracy. And, you know, as I used to say on television, do the math."

The crowd begins to chant, "*Do. The. Math. Do. The. Math. Do. The. Math.*"

"This won't do anymore, man. This isn't going to work out."

Nellie is holding Mikey's hand, gripping it, twisting it. "You feel it?" she asks.

"I feel it," Mikey answers.

They are feeling the rush of the crowd's ecstasy overtaking them, spreading through them from this arena to the world. Their ideas are better. Their ideas are registering. It has become obvious that the system, as it is, isn't working. Universal basic income will spread prosperity to all. The decriminalization of drugs will lead to the demilitarization of the police. The Maverick Party is a spiritual proposal: You don't have to hate anyone. You can refuse to throw yourself into the punch-and-counterpunch brawl of American politics in its decline. Nellie and Mikey can feel their reach extending. They can feel the onset of power. They share the rush flowing simultaneously into and through them.

"We need to be clear. We need to be clear about our successes as much as our failures. The problem isn't the American people. The problem isn't the American spirit. We are, today, as much as we ever were, a nation of strivers, a nation of liberty lovers, of fighters for a cause. We're the country of innovators. Why can't we innovate our system of government? We're riding into the twenty-first century on a dying mule."

The crowd laughs at this lame joke. They now await his cues.

"And I'm going to tell you something. The moment we get a system that works, we will be untouchable." Cooper coughs.

Somebody from the crowd shouts out: "Say it!"

And Cooper looks toward the voice, smiles. There's enough time to throw a wiffle ball. "You want me to say it?"

There are a few more shouts.

"Nah, I can't. There's a fine." He's still smiling.

More people in the crowd are calling for him to say it.

"All right, you know what? I'm going to say it. The time has come to unfuck America!"

The roar overtakes them all, and it overtakes Mikey and Nellie in their booth. Maybe they're going to win. Maybe the republic isn't going to end. Maybe they're going to build a new America out of the Maverick Party. And there is nothing like American politics for ecstasy, a crowd overwhelmed by a vision of themselves and their country, and by its never-ending dream that a new world is possible.

March 5

SUPER TUESDAY

(321 days until)

9:21 a.m., 1-88 West between Chicago and Tampico, IL

Super Tuesday is roughly the time the great slumbering mass of the American people starts to notice the fact that there's an election.

Politics never entirely disappears from American life anymore, a perpetual toxic fog everyone must walk through every day of every year. But it is in bright fresh mornings sometime around mid-March that the general nonsense miasma of American politics begins to condense into a choice, and politics moves from the regular season to the playoffs. This is the season in which the love and hatred and fear and hope that rise out of ordinary people in their sense of country take on the outline of a fight, and the trained elite minds of the country shift their energies from raising money for political purposes to spending money for political purposes.

The game is on. The stakes are on the table. The political question becomes the American question: what are my side's chances, and how do we win this thing?

At this point, the Republican is leading in the polls with somewhere around 39 percent of the national popular vote. The Colorado billionaire is the leading Democrat but stands at an almost equal 38 percent in a head-to-head.

Cooper Sherman is at 15 points in the polls, and gaining, and that means the media have started attacking him. The *New York Times* ran a series comparing Cooper to Ross Perot. The *Washington Post* went after old business ties in Cooper's early days at the tax-compliance software company, finding a disgruntled early partner who had an ax to grind and suffered from mental health issues. The Maverick Party is starting to seem real, siphoning off votes from the centers of both parties, and the edges too. They are starting to scare people.

Which is why Mikey is on his way to prep Cooper's interview with alt-right YouTuber Andy Ponds in Tampico, Illinois. An alternative campaign needs alternative media. Mikey is driving toward an audience of two and a half million, with five hundred thousand social media followers. Southern Illinois is far more beautiful than it has any right to be, even in March. The stubbly grasslands, dusted with snow, have an archaic sadness to them, interrupted only by whitewashed clapboard farmhouses.

"Are we going to your hotel or to the castle?" the driver asks. The young man, blond and scruffy under a *1619* baseball cap worn ironically, looks up in the rearview mirror. His eyes are close together like a possum's.

"The castle?"

"Sorry, that's what we call the studio, or the house where the studio is."

"It's that big?"

"Oh yeah, man, it's like ten thousand square feet. There's a chicken coop. There's a half-pipe in the basement. There's everything you could possibly want or need."

"I guess the castle," Mikey says.

"You got it."

Tampico, Illinois, was famous, until recently, as the birthplace of Ronald Reagan—but now its claim to fame is being the home of Ponds's studio. Andy Ponds put himself in the middle of nowhere as a show of power: *Look how far famous people will come for my attention.*

Ponds is alternative both ways. He began as a vlogger at

Occupy Wall Street, and then morphed over the Obama and Trump years into an anti-woke anti-vaxxer. He is attuned to American anger the way that certain ferns are attuned to pockets of light on a forest floor, and the Maverick Party needs voters who are willing to reject both sides of the American catastrophe. They need young men like Andy Ponds whose fear and loathing have doubled back. That is the mood of the present.

The American people want from their political system what reasonable people in all Western democracies want from their political systems: the chance at a job and a decent life, to face the ordinary problems of love and money in peace, and to be told that their country is special, that their country has a destiny in history, and that therefore *they* are special and have a destiny in history.

That's what they want. But they don't vote for what they want. They don't think about what they want when they vote now. The American people vote against what they *don't* want.

Fear and loathing are much more reliable vote-harvesters than vision and hope. Fear and loathing rouse. Fear and loathing win—the fear that the system which defined you and sustained you will be upended; loathing for all that has been denied you. Politics has become a way to take revenge on life itself. Americans expect so much from their nation. They dream their country should be a shining city on a hill, so they are outraged and flummoxed when it proves to be a city of gray stone and concrete, run by people whose solutions are partial.

"Hey, this castle," Mikey says to the driver, "how many people does Andy employ at this moment?"

The blond scruffy beard turns quizzical. "About fifty. A little more. Thirty are writers. They have to write five pieces a day for the website. The rest of us are support. Drivers. Lawyers. Accountants. So on."

"Fifty people. Jesus Christ. It's like its own station, its own newspaper."

"Media empire," the driver says. "That's how Andy thinks about it."

"He's not wrong."

Now that the mainstream media fears them, these alternative media outlets—YouTube streamers, podcasts, TikTok channels—matter more than ever to the Maverick campaign.

"How often do you do this trip, man?" Mikey asks.

"Every day, man. Every single day somebody comes to see Andy in the castle."

They drive south, deeper into the cornfields. Southern Illinois is the South, though it is technically in a blue state.

The strangeness of America, as usual, is its juxtaposition. They were just in Chicago and now a painted Confederate flag disgraces a barn wall. Mikey is driving from one fear and loathing into another.

10:22 a.m., 360 Clinton Avenue, Brooklyn, NY
The tip line is all conspiracy theories in the lead-up to Super Tuesday. The Colorado billionaire has accumulated a string of sexual assault allegations, one from a waitress in Dubuque, another from a hairdresser in Chicago.

There are at least a dozen notes describing the assault in Dubuque, but they use the same language in various places, so it's probably an organized campaign. Still, Martha forwards the notes to the investigations team, with a message pointing out the similar language.

The Black female Democrat is a secret member of the Illuminati and has been involved in making matzah with children's blood—a few dozen astroturfers have sent lengthy disquisitions outlining their uncovering of this ritualistic practice. These messages could only ever be of interest to scholars of blood libel. The *New York Times* has no scholar of blood libel on staff.

The pleasant Midwestern candidate has, according to several sources, been involved with high-level negotiations with an alien lizard race to exchange planetary sovereignty for technological development. A woman who writes the tip line at least once a week even uploaded a contract, complete with alien script and English and Chinese translations. It's shiver-inducing. Martha doesn't think too much about the psychology of the conspiracists. The insanity is so general that the paranoid style is banal by this point. But the alien contract is new in its detail of expression, and she sends it around to a few friends for a laugh.

One of the friends to whom Martha forwards the alien contract is Melissa McClung, recently promoted to executive editor, who calls her right away. Melissa used to be on the disinformation beat, so Martha knew she would find the contract at least half-amusing.

"What will your role in our new transplanetary order be, Melissa?" Martha asks.

"Sorry, what?"

"When the alien overlords come for the earth, what are your plans? You saw that fake contract I sent you from the tip line about how the Democrats have made deals with alien invaders?"

"Sorry, Martha, I didn't."

"Oh, that's embarrassing. Well, check it out. It's amazing." Hold on, though. Why is Melissa reaching out if it's not about the alien materials?

"I'm actually calling for something else," Melissa says. "Malcolm asked me to talk to you about these audio clips from high sources."

"Okay." The sudden tingle of imminent defeat flutters

up Martha's back. It must be what a gambler feels when he starts to see he's about to lose more than he can afford. Melissa wouldn't be calling if it was a yes.

"So, it's a pass," Melissa says. "I know that's not the answer you're looking for."

"How can it be a pass?" Martha asks, laughing at the absurdity.

"Look, these are Malcolm's reasons, not mine, but basically he doesn't like the anonymity of the source."

"Deep Throat was an anonymous source. The Pentagon Papers came in anonymously."

"I know that. You know that. Malcolm knows that. But the feeling at the top is that this just isn't the right time."

"What does that mean?"

"I'm just telling you what Malcolm said."

"Malcolm said it isn't the right time?"

"I mean, he didn't say this in so many words, but if we're going to make an assault on the military leadership, on the last institution in the United States with any level of political trust, we need to have it cold."

"I have audio. I have their voices."

"I think Malcolm just doesn't want to give red meat to the extremists without more reporting."

Martha doesn't hear much of the rest of what Melissa has to say, because she knew, without exactly knowing, that rejection was always going to be the result. The story will never be fully baked enough for the *Times*.

Editors can always reject a story because it "needs more reporting." It's convenient and it puts the blame on the writer. How can anyone object to being asked for more information? But it's just an excuse. This story is simply too dangerous. It doesn't fit their protocol. And Tanager's not wrong. The story will lead to blood on the streets. The streets are already bloody. Tanager doesn't want to be responsible for breaking the back of the republic, degrading the last institution anybody trusts.

But that doesn't change Martha's situation. She is sitting on the biggest story in the world, and she is with the biggest outlet in the world, and she can't run it.

Instantly, with her phone still in her hand, she knows she's going to leak it. She'll have to find somewhere else to run it. She'll have to find another way to inform the American people about the end of their republic.

How? Who?

10:29 a.m., 2480 2600 North Avenue, Tampico, IL
The future of media is a McMansion outside Tampico, Illinois. Andy Ponds's compound looms over deserted fields, big enough to serve as a resort. A massive electric fence ringed with barbed wire surrounds the compound. A sign reads:

No Trespassing!
We Don't Call 911
This Property Is Protected by the Second Amendment

"Jesus, you weren't kidding. This *is* a castle," Mikey says.

"The fence isn't actually electrified," the driver says.

"You have a lot of people trying to climb over the fence to get to Andy Ponds, do you?" Mikey says it as a joke, but it's no joke.

"Yeah, we do. I don't think Andy likes the security, but there have been a few incidents. People sneaking in with security personnel and so on. There's a lawsuit."

They pull up into the gravelly walkway. It's ten thirty in the morning, so nobody's up yet. The quiet is startling. The castle has the feel of a well-maintained frat house rather than a farm. The show itself runs from eight to ten p.m., and usually anyone who does a show that late needs to stay up into the middle of the night while the adrenaline and cortisol ebb.

"What are you here to talk to Andy about?" the driver asks.

"We're with the Maverick Party."

"Oh yeah, Cooper Sherman? Love that guy. I think I'm going to vote for that guy. Love the crypto angle."

"That's great."

"And I guess Super Tuesday. You're going to talk about Super Tuesday, I guess."

"It will probably turn into a Super Tuesday watch party in the end."

The driver leads Mikey through a side door into a sprawling subbasement that serves as a green room. There is a full bar, with a few hundred bottles of whiskey behind it. A jumbled collection of couches encloses a pool table. Off in a corner of the room sits a drum kit. Behind that, in a locked display case, are the guns: a gold AR-15 and a Revolutionary-era breech-loading rifle stand out among the dozen of them.

The decor is what you might expect if a twenty-two-year-old was suddenly given ten million dollars. There's a Klingon weapon on the wall that's the height of tackiness, as well as a seventeenth-century katana descended from the hands of some magisterial samurai family, through various catastrophes of history, to this rural Illinois basement.

Mikey can see a room at the far end gleaming in white. He walks over to have a look. It's an enormous skateboarding half-pipe. "How old is Andy?" he asks.

The driver looks curious. "I have no idea. He must be, what, thirty-five or so? When was Occupy Wall Street?"

"2008."

"So he would have been around twenty then, I guess."

"Right."

In this dark, cheap, plastic castle in southern Illinois, Mikey will have to find a corner to work. He is there to prep the interview between Cooper and Ponds, but Ren has promised him access to the Cooper Sherman oppo book. Today, Mikey knows, is a turning point. After Super Tuesday, they will know who the Democratic candidate is. After they read the oppo book, they will know the scandals they will face. By tonight, Mikey should understand who the enemy is and what weapons they possess.

The real scandals will come soon. Mikey can feel it. The season of political scandal is organic. The temperature reaches a certain level, the crocuses bloom. A politician reaches a certain level of prominence, they unload the book on him. Every politician carries within him- or herself the seed of their own destruction, what we might call the shocking truth of their lives. But nobody knows what is shocking until it shocks people. The market decides what matters when it comes to scandal, and the market is fickle.

Certainly scandal is not what it used to be. George H.W. Bush earned a week's worth of shame after he checked his watch during a debate. Then he lost. Trump was caught stating that the correct way to treat women is to "grab 'em by the pussy." Then he won. The first scandal registered; the second scandal didn't. The question that every politician's life poses is whether their particular shocking truth will be viewed as a reflection of ordinary human failing or taken up for ostracism as a scapegoat for the country as a whole.

The primal political joy—the source of tribal togetherness—is exclusion. But the basis of that exclusion is never rational.

Mikey goes to set up his laptop near the couches, but trips

over something on the ground by the drum kit. It's a bandolier loaded with shotgun shells. "Are these your bullets?" he asks the driver.

The driver laughs and says he doesn't know who they belong to. That's American politics during this election, Mikey thinks. There are bullets on the floor, and nobody is sure whose they are.

Would Ponds shoot Cooper if he had the chance? Mikey wonders. They'll all find out tonight.

12:21 p.m., 46342 Clear Ridge Road, Big Sur, CA
Balfour splurged. After his spectacular flame-out in Tampa, he went to Vegas.

If you want to connect with the real America, with America at its most honest and genuine, the best place to be is at a craps table in Vegas. Craps is a game of authentic solidarity. It was at the craps table that Balfour received his first message from Max Sevre. He marked it as spam without a second thought. It had to be a scam. There could be no reason for a billionaire tech lord to be writing him.

Weeks later, he received a text: *I think my emails are going to spam. This is Max Sevre and I'd like to meet with you.*

Balfour went back into his emails and found half a dozen messages. Whoever was sending him the emails was doing a good imitation of the tech billionaire. As a joke, Balfour wrote back: *My initial consulting fee is 30K. You should have my PayPal reference.*

Then the money showed up an hour later. Balfour still didn't believe it was Sevre until the private jet picked him up at Harry Reid Airport and flew him, over the course of a bottle of Krug, to a compound in Big Sur.

Sevre is the leading right-wing tech billionaire, who, despite his gay-orgy lifestyle and his infamous experimentation with drugs he has designed in a private lab, has risen to be on the board of many of the most important Republican institutions.

A couple of beautiful young men in white shorts meet Balfour at the plane door and shepherd him into the main building.

A smiling nurse behind a reception desk greets him. "Mr. Sevre is expecting you, Mr. Balfour. His treatment is about to end, and he can see you then."

"I didn't know Sevre was sick."

She smiles condescendingly. "Oh, he's not sick."

"I don't know what you mean."

"This is a radical life-extension lab."

"I thought this was Mr. Sevre's home."

"It's become a home to him. We deal in mitochondrial renewal."

Balfour vaguely remembers a story in *Wired*: Sevre, among his vast businesses and political entanglements, is a leading amortalist. He believes he can buy his way out of death.

While Balfour waits, he looks up the story on his phone. Sevre is only a reference in a single paragraph: "The most serious of the 'anti-deathists' is Max Sevre, tech billionaire and conservative activist. He owns and operates a longevity campus with a single patient: himself. He pioneered the use of the diabetes medication Metformin and cell-scraping to reduce senescence caused by mitochondrial decline. He fights intellectual as well as physical decline. A team of personal mental coaches create a 'very difficult' problem for him to solve which uses a different neural pathway every day." *Money is wonderful*, Balfour thinks. *It allows the generation of so much astonishing waste.*

Twenty-seven minutes later, the secretary-nurse leads him down the hallway. They pass a room filled with bass pumping and men laughing and a wafting tongue of marijuana licking the ceiling out of the door. The hallway opens into an enormously bright room, half-blinding.

As Balfour's eyes adjust, he is awed by the sudden beauty of the Big Sur coast. It's paradise. It might be the single most beautiful corner of the earth, lush California luxuriating down to the Pacific.

Max Sevre is staring, snug in a lounge chair like a 1930s recovering dictator. He's wearing a flat cap, and there's a woolen blanket draped over him. His face is scrunched in the daze of either recovery or ecstasy. A teenage boy is bringing him a cold lemonade.

There's another chair ten feet away. Balfour seems expected to sit in it, so he does. On a small table beside him is a large tumbler of scotch and ice. Beside the tumbler is a small plate of kalamata olives. Balfour picks up the scotch and takes a sip. It's heavy on peat, an old esoteric malt.

Minutes pass. The billionaire closes his eyes to breathe, squirming. Then he reaches over for a sip of lemonade and pulls himself up in his chair. "You think pushing the sex club angle is a mistake?" he eventually asks.

The whiskey is truly impressive. Sevre must have figured out, or hired someone to figure out, exactly what would give Balfour pleasure. It's like a perfect Christmas gift from a man he's never met. "I *know* it's a mistake," he responds.

"You think it's a mistake because people don't care about old moralities?"

Balfour shrugs. "Not exactly."

"What is it, exactly?"

"The basic fact of oppo is that it's not the mud that breaks you. It's where it sticks."

"Can you put that in terms of a falsifiable thesis?"

Balfour isn't sure what the question means, but he takes a stab at answering anyway. "You can't attack people on the basis of their already-established weaknesses. You have to attack them on the basis of their strengths. Everybody has their weaknesses. Everybody knows everybody has their weaknesses. The public can easily forgive people on their side for their weaknesses. It's the failed strength they can't forgive."

"The souring."

"Exactly. You want the public to sour on a candidate. You don't need to convince your own people to hate the other guy. You need to convince *their* people to hate *their* guy."

Sevre shuffles in his seat and moves his arm above the blanket. His skin is slightly red and flaky. "I'm afraid I don't have enough influence to stop them from playing the sex club angle. What do you think the fallout will be?"

Balfour chews his bottom lip. "It will probably help him. More importantly, it will make him harder to hit later. You only get so many shots at a guy. Each one that doesn't land means a whole bunch of people who won't listen to you next time. I personally think it will help his image, especially among non-college-educateds. How many guys wish they could talk their wives into orgies at a sex club?"

"I want you to be my personal retainer," Sevre says.

Balfour laughs. "What does that mean? Samurai shit? I'm just an oppo guy."

"Do you understand why Cooper Sherman needs to be destroyed?"

"Frankly, I don't. I mean, he's taking just as many votes from them as from you. He's small potatoes. He's a third-party candidate. I mean, what the fuck am I doing here?"

"Cooper Sherman is dangerous because he's an engineer. He's a real person."

"The Republican candidate isn't a real person?"

"He very much is not a real person. He's plastic and red dye no. 3. He's mustard gas and vaporware. He's as real as the light between a projector and a screen: only there if the dust catches it. And we could make government stop existing. Those are the stakes here. Do you understand that?"

"Not fully."

"The engineers are the real power now, as is our right, as is our destiny. That's why the world hates us. Everyone talks about conspiracies. You know what the real conspiracy is? Democracy. Democracy means mediocrity. Sheep built democracy, out of fear. Fear of talent. Fear of the builders. Fear of the creators. They need us but they hate us. We have a real chance this election to end the administrative state, so that we may live by what we will for ourselves."

Balfour takes another sip of scotch. The aftertaste carries forever, beyond the horizon. "If you want to destroy Cooper Sherman," he says, "you must make him seem old and chaotic. Befuddled. His strength is that he is of his own time. He's not out of touch. You have to make him look like the world has passed him by and he's living in the past."

"Can you do that?" Sevre asks. "I think it's better if we just do this ourselves. You don't murder a man by committee."

"I'll need money."

Sevre smiles a yellow smile. "Money is a tool you no longer have to worry about."

Balfour is in another country now. His profession operates on a single thesis: all politicians are liars and thugs, and the winners turn their lies and thuggery into truth and strength. How else could a family of bootleggers, who used voter fraud to win the presidency and then started the Vietnam War, become icons of American innocence? The American people want pretty speeches so they can pretend they have earned the easy money. They want sermons of equality so they can go on imagining they deserve total impunity.

The man in front of him wants to take it all the way, though, all the way to the end. Can you defraud the suckers so completely that you become the truth? Can you bully yourself past all limits?

2:41 p.m., 2480 2600 North Avenue, Tampico, IL
The castle has been a decent spot to work, it turns out. Mikey takes a corner of the couch near the guns, and sets up his laptop for the Zoom calls of the day. Dominic wants to clarify the ad spends for the dark money, and Nellie is preparing the email blast for the people with the dark money to lift info from.

As he Zooms on the couch, the castle slowly rouses. Various kid writers stumble down from their bedrooms for coffee or pills, chat about how shitty the Democrats are and how the left is destroying the country, then charge back up the stairs to fulfill their daily output of five angry posts.

The longed-for email finally appears. Subject: *Ren fucking delivers.*

The attachment is a Word file: *Cooper Sherman book.* She's found the oppo book.

Mikey pops opens his Slack channel and downloads the file. They will know now how far their enemies have been able to see into the dark labyrinth of the candidate's life, what flaws they have found to exploit.

Mikey takes his phone outside into the fields to read the document. It's like the response to a university application: whole futures ride on what's inside.

Which scumbag sold you this? Mikey slacks Ren.

No price. They know, Ren slacks back.

What do they know?

They know that I'm going to survive all you motherfuckers.

Sarah is right. If everyone in American politics were put in a cage, she would be the one to walk out alive.

The Word document is 737 pages. The table of contents is divided into "Top Hits," "Key Themes," and "Personal Details." The longest section is the financials, but Mikey knows they don't matter. There's nothing there that can harm them. The American people expect nastiness from people in business. Whatever the oppo researchers dug up on the early years of Cooper's tax-compliance software company might be considered at worst fudging your expenses and at best a demonstration of the toughness required to lead the country.

Mikey goes straight to the Top Hit marked "Staff Members," the section on disgruntled staff. They've found six, which isn't bad. He flips to the page set aside for Katie Danjou. It's just one paragraph:

Katie Danjou committed suicide before the launch of the Maverick campaign on November 23. The newspapers did not report her suicide in compliance with the psychological health report. She had longstanding mental health issues before joining the campaign. There was no contact between her and the candidate. These facts insulate Sherman himself from the fallout. But the campaign showed a) lack of judgment in hiring her, and b) lack of compassion in firing her. Danjou's father still feels like major questions about her suicide have been unanswered.

The tension release that floods Mikey is like a long-overdue piss.

These guys ain't got shit looks to me, Ren slacks.

Any surprises in financials?

Nah, I mean he was something of a piece of shit in the nineties tech boom. That shock you?

Not going to shock anybody.

Mikey scans the section on wokeness. Cooper never could shut up on social media, but he's a celebrity. He's already been through this shit half a dozen times. He tweeted something about support for the Freedom Convoy in Canada, and he tweeted something that was pro-trans. The researchers must have been confused. But that's the point, Mikey knows, it's confusing.

The architects of the culture wars don't do nuance. They need evil in its most digestible form: social justice warriors or fascists. They can't really rile themselves up to a position that's slightly complex. Ultimately, they're too reductive to make a stink out of Cooper.

And in the districts where the Maverick Party is close enough to be worth attacking, they're going for his lack of experience. Which is beautiful. They don't seem to realize that calling him inexperienced is calling him an outsider, which helps with the right people.

They got the sex stuff, Ren slacks.

I see that.

Mikey hasn't checked the chapter on sex. He flips over to it. They do indeed have all the names and dates from the Detroit sex club. They've spoken to the many freaks Cooper screwed there. An effective opposition researcher has done their job at MTR.

It's nothing, Mikey writes.

You sure?

This is the thesis of our campaign.

Early on, when he had been discussing the campaign on

long walks around Cooper's Colorado ranch, Mikey learned all about the man's sexual past. He had worked out his plan then. Mikey's thesis is that a sex scandal can only help a candidate. If you don't lie, if you aren't ashamed, if you're adult about the whole matter, it will increase your appeal.

Scandal is no longer a barrier to a candidate's success, Mikey believes. It's a requirement. Scandal generates attention. Attention generates engagement. Engagement generates power. It's a gamble, but in a third-party candidacy you have to gamble.

A producer, a frazzled twenty-year-old in sweatpants pulling on a vape pen, is standing in front of him with a sheaf of papers. No doubt releases of various kinds.

Mikey shakes his head. "Sorry, we don't sign anything, but the good news is that you can ask him whatever."

The producer shrugs. "Basically, our plan is a Super Tuesday watch party."

"Sounds right," Mikey says. On his phone, for some reason, there's a text from Martha Kass: *I'm going to call you in an hour. Pick up a random number.*

He texts back: OK *weirdo.*

4:21 p.m., Hotel Meridien, 1197 Atlantic Avenue, Brooklyn, NY
Martha walks over to the Hotel Meridien on Atlantic Avenue to make the call. The place is an empty antiquity. Ten years ago, a staff member let himself into a woman's room and attacked her. The place has been deserted ever since, except for a few tourists who haven't bothered to inquire why the online rates are half what other hotels in the area charge.

The Hotel Meridien has kept a feature other hotels have abandoned: a bank of house phones in the lobby. That's why Martha has walked all this way. As she dials, she realizes that if anyone really wanted to trace her, they would just trace Mikey's phone. But she has no other choice. Now she must plunge in.

"Martha Kass," Mikey's voice says, "where are you?"

She has a moment of panic during which she wonders if Mikey is one of the tracers. "I'm in New York," she answers.

"You want to know where I am?"

"Yeah, sure."

"I am in the ten-thousand-square-foot mansion in Tampico, Illinois, where the most popular political YouTube streamer in the world lives. It's fucked up, Martha."

"Really?"

"This guy has fifty staff. There's guns everywhere. There's a skateboarding half-pipe in the basement. This is the future. Eventually, you guys won't exist. It will just be Andy Ponds talking to his audience of masturbating rage-aholics."

"That's funny," Martha says. "That's what I want to talk to you about. You got a minute? You alone?"

"Hold on." She hears, on the other end of the line, Mikey explaining that he's stepping outside, then a rustle and the click of a door. "Go ahead."

"Okay. Can I have your word that this will stay with us?" She is aware of how old-fashioned she must sound. She is from a world where men and women give their word.

"Yes, definitely." Mikey is from that old world too. She's relieved.

"I've got a story about a coup I want your advice about. So, let's say, hypothetically, that I had a source coming to me from within the Joint Chiefs of Staff and senior levels of the intelligence community discussing a coup."

"A coup?"

"They have a way to do it without calling it a coup. They

have this mechanism for taking over the country. It's called a contingent election. It will look like democracy. It will follow the Constitution. But it won't be democracy. And I have it on audio. It's the most senior leadership in this country outlining various scenarios. Who they would accept. Who they would not accept. They want to impose martial law. They want to crush the Oath Keepers and Black Lives Matter. They're willing to support whoever will let them do that. To prevent a civil war breaking out."

"They openly discuss this?"

"Openly. They don't want Iraq and Afghanistan to happen here. So they're talking about military checkpoints in cities. They're talking about arrests for sedition or plotting sedition. They're talking, on recordings, about suspending the Bill of Rights. "

"So when is the *Times* running this?" Mikey asks.

"They're not. They think it's too dangerous. They think it would be a media intervention in domestic political life. They're telling me some line about not running pieces from anonymous sources—but what about Watergate? What about the Pentagon Papers? They've taken up this mandate to support political institutions, and, well, look, it's embarrassing. But they're not going to run it."

"And nobody else has it?"

"Apparently not, Mikey. I mean, I don't know, but I haven't seen it anywhere."

Mikey lets out a long sigh. "And you're asking me . . ."

"If you were me, what would you do?"

"Leak it on alternative media. Send it to me and I'll leak it on alternative media. No one will ever know it came from you. You don't have a choice. You can't risk telling anybody else. It was foolish to tell me."

"I could kill it. I mean, I could just pretend these clips never came into the tip line."

"I don't think so."

"Why not?"

"Because you love America."

It's such a stupid answer that they both laugh. It's the stupid truth.

"I'm being watched," Martha says.

On the other end of the line, the clockwork of Mikey's strategic brain is ticking. "You can't send me anything. You'll have to deliver it in person. We'll work it out. We'll work it out."

Martha isn't sure that anything will ever work out again.

8:31 p.m., 2480 2600 North Avenue, Tampico, IL
While Cooper argues with Andy Ponds, Mikey is emailing:

Dear Mr. Danjou,
I just want to send you a preliminary report. I showed Katie's message to Cooper, and unfortunately he had no recollection of Katie. He was never in Chicago when she was there.

I'm going to talk to her coworkers in Chicago. (If there are any volunteers whom she mentioned, please pass their names on. It would be very useful.)

Her note remains a mystery, but hopefully it will mean more to Chicago offices, and I will have more information soon.

Yours truly,
M

He hits send and returns to the spectacle.

The studio is lined with guns, but you can't see any of them on the livestream. Andy Ponds isn't right-wing talk radio, and he isn't woke vlogging. He's somehow both. In the studio, he's there with his watch cap on, looking slightly cartoonish.

He has on either side of the table his two yes men. One is a hippie, a conspiracy theorist surrounded by crystals and maps of the universe. Then there's a gay farmer. These two occasionally add some insight, but they're mostly there to nod along and give cover to Ponds's political shifts as best they can.

Yet on this occasion, the yes men are lying back, silent. Andy and Coop are going at it.

"That's not it," Andy is saying in a staccato anger pretending not to be anger but simple clarity. "We have never been a democracy. That's a lie. America has always been a constitutional republic."

"What do those words mean to you?" Cooper asks.

"A constitutional republic is a way of preventing democracy from slopping over into mob rule."

"*Mob rule.* What are you, a nineteenth-century pamphleteer?"

Andy laughs despite his obvious lack of any sense of humor. "You don't love the American system?"

"Do you? Does anybody? Listen, multicultural democracy and constitutional republic are not supposed to be opposites. They're supposed to be the same thing. That's the idea behind America. Here's the problem, Andy, here's the problem. You've inherited a government so broken, you take its brokenness for granted. Why don't we do what grown-ups do? Take the best of the past and make it work for today."

"You're a fucking dreamer, man."

"No, no, no, no, no. I've woken up. These are the stakes. We all know the system is broken. You can blame who you want, and I can blame who I want. At the end of the day, the question is how to fix it."

Mikey is in the green room watching the livestream on his laptop with the producer, who is still wearing pajamas and looks like she just rolled out of bed. "He's doing well," she tells Mikey.

"It is his job. One of his jobs."

"We'll probably get the Super Tuesday results soon. But I don't think they'll matter much." The exit polls have been lopsided. The Colorado billionaire is romping home. The other candidates are preparing their concession speeches—or at least their campaign managers and consultants are.

The producer is watching the super chat metrics in real time—blue and red lines rising and falling; the algorithm that judges all that is said and done.

Andy wants to talk about a leak from *Breitbart* that has claimed to find texts between prominent Democrats celebrating the collapse of the stands at the Republican event. "They're happy, right? It's almost like they planned it, right?"

"You're saying Democrats tricked the Republican Party into hiring substandard contractors?"

Andy shrugs. "It has certainly worked out for them."

"I don't know why you need these theories, man. You don't need theories. There is a *real* conspiracy. It's called duopoly. It's two parties that call all the shots. Enough with these secret documents and Illuminati and shit. Look at the US Senate. Look at the fact that only 22 percent of Americans are happy with Congress, but incumbents have a reelection rate of 94 percent. *That's* a conspiracy."

The producer whispers into her mic: "Conspiracy's good. Keep on conspiracy."

Mikey can see over her shoulder the red line going up. "Why's conspiracy good?" he asks.

She looks up, surprised. "See this red line, that's the super chats, and the super chats spike when they talk about conspiracy theories."

The audience for Andy Ponds's show pays to have their comments pinned, accentuated—for five dollars it stays stickied for two minutes, for five hundred it stays stickied for five hours. These super chats are one of their main sources of income. With the graph, they can find the angry engagement and ride the algorithm of profitable rage. This is the new journalism.

"Wait, wait, here we go," Andy says. The numbers flash up on screen.

The Colorado billionaire has won Alabama, Arkansas, Colorado, Maine, Massachusetts, Minnesota, North Carolina, Oklahoma, Tennessee, Texas, Utah, Vermont, and Virginia. The Black female candidate took California.

"That's it then. Three-way race," Ponds says.

"All billionaires," Cooper adds.

"You think that's wrong?"

"Look, I flew here in a helicopter. I'm not going to pretend I have a problem with rich people running for office. I'm not going to pretend I have a problem with rich people in general. I do think that if you have a system where only rich people have a say about the running of the country, it's a problem."

"But you are rich."

"I am rich. And I am *actually* rich, unlike some rich people I might mention."

Mikey looks at his phone and sees a slack from Ren: *We might win this thing.*

Mikey knows what Ren is thinking. They have been blessed by their enemies. The Republican, with his bloated face engraved with anger, is a cross between a mob boss and a street preacher. He is America's abusive father, feeding the rage and fed on the rage, with all the glamour of the most popular high school bully.

The Democrat is soft, plump, with all the engrained hypocrisies of the Democratic ruling class. He flies to environmental conferences in his private jet. He talks about inequality at Ivy League schools. His faith in the American institutions is oblivious. Of course he loves American institutions, they have served him so well.

It's hard to imagine two candidates who could indicate with greater force the need for the Maverick Party. The Republican is a monster and the Democrat is willfully blind.

And Ren doesn't even know about Martha. She doesn't know that Mikey has the play of the century to make, a scandal beyond scandal.

Even without hearing the audio, Mikey knows that her story might just be the election surprise the Maverick campaign needs to become the leading party in the country. It will make Americans loathe and fear the powers that be as never before. It will make both sides want to change the basis of the system. Martha has the change button. All Mikey has to do is reach over and press it.

8:41 p.m., McBride's Bar and Grill,
673 Atlantic Avenue, Brooklyn, NY

The taste of the watery beer is just so delicious—the taste of freedom and emptiness. For her first proper drinking session, Martha has picked out a doozy of an Irish dive. A few stools over, a fiftysomething woman in a jean jacket is talking to a small stuffed unicorn. The man beside her has a nose like a Christmas light, and they are whispering together like they're plotting a bank robbery.

On the screens overhead, the Super Tuesday results are

arriving, but nobody is paying attention in this place. They'll notice the election after it's happened, if then.

A crew-cutted man in a brown suit is sitting in a corner reading a Sally Rooney novel, staring at her. He doesn't fit. The murder of journalists is normal in most of the world. In this breakdown, who can say what will happen? Who will survive?

She deserves a beer.

She can't put up with the story she's living.

She hates the infertility-support blogs she can't stop herself from checking. She hates how the story prevaricates in its ending: In one future, she is sitting on a knoll in Prospect Park laying out PBJ and apple quarters on a blanket while Zayn teaches their daughter how to kick a ball. In another future, she is sitting at her window accepting that she'll never have a baby, trying to forget all the money and all the procedures and all the struggle that came to nothing. She read a study of Danish women once that showed couples are three times more likely to divorce after failed infertility treatments. She tries never to think about it.

Her phone buzzes. It's a text from a random string of numbers, the source: *What are you doing?*

Right now I'm having a beer, she texts back.

Do you have any idea the risk I'm running by giving you this information?

I do. I know.

Bullet in the back of the head. I sent this material to the New York Times, not you, and not for you to ship to some random political hack.

The phone bank at the Hotel Méridien was obviously not sufficient. She's an idiot, out of her depth. There is no hiding. She must remember that there is no hiding. It's so hard to accept as a way of life.

Martha thinks out her next text. She has all the information she's going to extract from the source. There's only one more ask: the *Times* won't run the story if it's from an anonymous source.

You're going to have to tell me your name.

My name is death, the source texts back. *If I gave you my name, I would not be alive ten minutes later, and know this: the risks I'm running, you're also running.*

What does that mean? Martha asks.

What does that mean? she texts again.

What do you mean?

She looks up, and the crew cut in the brown suit has vanished. Panic runs through her like currents in opposite directions. She has to leak the story. She can't leak the story.

June 9

SCANDAL

(225 days until)

Balfour wakes up to a long string of texts from his boss. First he goes to the bathroom and vomits.

He must have drunk something with milk in it last night. Milk always cramps him up. His stomach clutches out the filth from his gut painfully at first, hopefully the second time, until the satisfying and cleansing third.

He has brought his phone with him into the bathroom. There is, as usual, a string of texts from Max Sevre. For some reason, Balfour has become the best friend and sounding board for the strange Republican billionaire. The man must not have many friends. But who does anymore?

Sevre must have been high on one of his super-refined Es when he wrote these, Balfour thinks, curled up beside the porcelain.

> *I'm not sure how familiar you are with the concept of Girardian mimesis and the scapegoat. I'm going to risk giving you a primer because it may help you in your work. The basic premise of Girardian mimesis is the biological fact that we learn by mimicking others. Babies learn basic emotions by registering and imitating their parents' faces. The individual fact of biology applies not just to individuals but to society as a whole. Imitation drives culture. People do things because other people do things. The imitation is unthinking, which is why collective action is always unjust. Societies need to expel anyone who does not imitate the widespread imitations.*

Groups create scapegoats whom they collectively punish. The collective punishments are the basis in all societies of their only meaningful component, the tribe. I'm sure you understand this instinctively as an opposition man.

Balfour doesn't understand, but he also doesn't care. After the main text, many smaller addenda follow:

This is why I've said before that the Maverick campaign matters. If 3rd party voting becomes something that people do, it will explode. Hatred of the other side is currently the only reason people vote for their own parties. That system seems locked and intractable. But a single crack can suddenly blind with its light.

Politicians in general are scapegoats. We give them power exactly so we can blame them for all of our sins. This is the line we must ride.

The appeal of Cooper Sherman and the Maverick Party is that they're outside of the rancor and stupidity. We must put them inside the violence.

Mission: Scapegoat.

Balfour stopped responding to Sevre's texts many days ago. The messages didn't require a response. They were not part of a conversation. They weren't instructions either. Balfour imagined them as messages tied to balloons released into the air. They all just happened to land with him. Balfour's trade demands silence. He supposes that's why Sevre could confide in him.

This morning, Balfour finds himself in a corner of rural Ohio to meet a Mitsubishi dealer. The Mitsubishi dealer is a prominent Republican donor with deep connections to the Oath Keepers. His deep connections to the Oath Keepers are more deeply rooted in movements like the 3 Percenters and others so far to the right that Balfour doesn't know their names, if they even have names. He doesn't want to know the names of the far-right movements the Mitsubishi dealer knows. The man's father was in the Ku Klux Klan, but he's less traditional in his outlook than his hooded daddy: He wants the destruction of the United States government through violence. He doesn't much care what you call him.

Balfour doesn't know any real, live accelerationists. This man does. He would agree to a meeting in person only, which is a sign that he's serious enough to fear the Department of Justice.

11:39 a.m., Gulfstream G500, between MIA and AUS
The scandal has finally broken, and Mikey couldn't be happier. He is flying with the candidate to Austin, and he is on top of the world, in all the various senses. His boss is a filthy pervert and it is going to pay off.

The American people are spending their Sunday morning thinking about Cooper Sherman's midforties sexual escapades, and Mikey's beaming with such self-satisfaction that his colleagues are growing sick of it.

The *60 Minutes* episode will run tonight at seven p.m., but they've taken the unusual step of releasing clips in advance, in order to increase the attention.

As Cooper and the team fly to Texas for an appearance on *Joe Rogan*, the Sunday-morning talk shows are playing nothing but elaborate discussions of the most sordid details. "Will

Cooper Sherman's Sex Scandal Upend the Election?" *Face the Nation* is asking. "Cooper Sherman's Sex Club Years, the Fallout," is the subject of George Stephanopoulos's show. "America's Shredded Moral Fiber," is how *Fox News Sunday* plays it.

Mikey's favorite clip from the *60 Minutes* episode—he is rewatching it over and over and forcing Nellie and Dominic to watch it with him—is when Cooper leads Scott Pelley into the sex dungeon.

Cooper is smiling. He sometimes looks, during the episode, like a naughty boy who has gotten away with something: pure political gold.

"I have to admit, Scott, we didn't come down here much. This stuff was a little too crazy for us."

"But you know what it all does."

"Oh sure, I think so. This is a glory hole, and this one over here is a Saint Andrew's cross, and that, I think, is a gibbet cage. It's sort of a gimp cage."

"But you didn't use these."

"You know, one time Vickie and I came down here to have a look, but it was too much. It was just a bit intense for us. We were mostly upstairs having threesomes."

"It *all* seems a bit intense for me."

"Hey, different strokes for different folks," Cooper responds.

They approach a low bench in red vinyl with holes in it.

"Now I have to admit," Cooper says, "I don't know what this is for. This one's new. They didn't have this one when we were here. Do you know what this one does?"

"I do not," Scott Pelley says.

"Something freaky, I'm sure."

They laugh together.

Cut to the interview room, where Pelley is playing serious: "I think most politicians, most people, would be embarrassed by having their private sexual lives exposed, especially when it's so exotic, or, I guess, extreme. Would you say that's fair?"

"You think it's extreme?" Cooper counters. "I think a hell of a lot of married Americans are into much more kinky stuff. And, you know, I believe there's nothing to be ashamed of here. It's all consensual, between adults."

"It's adultery, Mr. Sherman."

"You know, I suppose so. Technically. But honestly, my wife was with me the entire time. What was that thing President Carter said?"

"'I committed adultery in my heart'?" Pelley says.

"Right. I didn't do that. I didn't commit adultery in my heart. I might have committed adultery in the flesh, but honestly, I don't think Vickie thought of it that way."

"But you're divorced. Wasn't this club one of the reasons? Aren't open relationships doomed?"

"We divorced for the reason the vast majority of people divorce, Scott. We grew apart. Our lives started going in different directions. Ask any divorce lawyer. Seriously. We weren't that different from any other couple."

"You've asked us not to speak to your wife . . ."

"The poor woman has suffered enough embarrassment for my sake," Cooper says. "I'm running for office. My life is open for inspection. The American people are entitled to know everything about me. But this campaign isn't her fault. None of it is her fault."

Pelley does a small shuffle in his chair, taking Cooper's point but not all the way. "Still, it's not, you know, what you might expect from a politician, a tour of a sex club."

Now the stern look from Cooper. "America is in serious trouble, Scott. I think the American people want somebody to be honest with them. And we're not in a place where people can afford to care about who I slept with in the nineties with my wife. Honestly, the situation is not one that affords that kind of luxury."

"Because you're here to un-bleep America."

"Is that really appropriate language, Scott?"

They laugh again. The show is turning into a laugh riot.

"So you don't think the American people are going to care about these revelations?"

"They're not revelations. I've never been anything but totally frank about them."

"Fine, you don't think Americans are going to care about your sex life."

"Oh, they'll care. I mean, it makes great gossip. I'm sure *TMZ* will be in here for days scrounging up stuff. I mean, I asked for this. I'm a politician. The scrutiny, the opposition researchers—I knew I was bringing it on myself. People have to talk about something. But after the gossip will come serious thought, and the stakes of this election are the survival of the republic. The stakes of this election are the survival of democracy as a global force. The stakes of this election are the possibilities of total reform along every front of our society. It's even bigger than that . . ."

"*Bigger than that?*"

"Yes, even bigger than that," says Cooper. "We are on the cusp of our civilization rising to a new level of mass prosperity and renewed dignity for the individual, or collapsing into the horrors of a few secretive rulers holding all the money and all the power and all the say. Elections matter. The next four years matter. So, quite honestly, if somebody's not going to vote for me because of this sex club stuff, it's just an excuse. They're retreating into what they know, even though they know it doesn't work, and it's a path to ruin."

Mikey shuts off the interview. The rest of the half hour is more or less a pure advertisement for the Maverick Party. "We just won Nevada," he says to Nellie. "They're all freaks there."

"Explain to me why this is good," Dominic says. "I know this was always the plan. I know that this is the result of strategy. But I still don't understand why something so salacious to the public can be good for us."

"I'm not 100 percent, either," Nellie says.

Mikey has explained this dozens of times before, but he loves explaining it. It's like a chess problem he's solved that they haven't. "In the twenty-first century, attention is political currency. Everything else is secondary. And that means scandal works. That means you need scandal. Celebrity is scandal. You need celebrity."

"But this will hit our numbers," Dom says.

"Definitely," Mikey says. "Distinctly. Definitively. We will see a dip in the immediate polls. Today and tomorrow and the week after, and for a little bit of the week after that. If you go and ask people, 'Are you voting for the pervert?' they'll say no for a little bit. But those numbers will rebound and then pass where we are now. Attention is the wind. Scandal is the sail. A candidate without scandal is weaker than a candidate with scandal. Look at the politicians we've had. Look at Bill Clinton. Look at W."

"Obama didn't have any scandals."

"Exception that proves the rule. For many people in America, Obama's *existence* was a scandal."

"So what is it?" Dom asks. "Thrill of the illicit?"

"Recognition. Simple, brute recognition. *Do I know who this person is?* In a week, all this disgust, all this embarrassment, will fade behind the knowledge that everybody does some weird shit these days. You know what kind of twisted sexual deviance the average American indulges on their phone?"

"No wonder this country is so fucked," Dominic says.

Nellie wrinkles her face like a junior high school kid who's just found a used condom in the playground. "Now I have to think about Cooper in that club with someone half his age. I'm never going to be able to get that image out of my head."

"Branding," Mikey says. "Remember that scandal is inevitable. It has to be something, and it's better that it's this. They're not going to be able to hit us with anything else from here to the election. We've passed."

"Nobody ever notices the real scandals anyway," Nellie says. "Did I tell you that I found out who gave us that hundred thousand Ethereum? It was Max Silman-Hawkins." The crypto bro had flamed out three months earlier, siphoning off billions before his exchange tanked.

"It's funny," Dominic says, "that was only six months ago, but a couple hundred million seemed like a big number then."

"That's what I mean," Nellie says. "The real scandal is that it's going to cost us a billion and a half to run this campaign. A billion and a half in dark money, and nobody will ever know who bought and sold this country."

"Seems cheap to me," Dom says. "Kanye West lost that much in a day."

Kanye West had tweeted, a few days earlier, that the Maverick Party was stealing his ideas, but that he might vote for Cooper anyway.

Cooper Sherman is catching the wave of the insanity at the moment of its blossoming. The Maverick Party is touching 25 percent nationally, and starting to scare the people invested in the stability of the system. It turns out that the 49 percent of Americans who say they are political independents are actually serious. Cooper is almost certainly going to win Colorado and Michigan, provoking a series of panicked op-eds in the pages of the *Wall Street Journal* and the *New York Times* on various scenarios within the electoral college.

Their internal polling is showing they have real chances in Florida and Texas; a wide swath of voters are exhausted by the Republican Party but cannot quite bring themselves to vote Democrat. Cooper Sherman fits easily into a Texan identity. Their ad campaign there is brilliant, built on a simple slogan that has taken off: *The Maverick Party. Don't be fenced in.*

If it were up to Cooper, they would be campaigning only in Florida now. But Cooper is not in control, Dominic is. Dominic's machines are. Their central AI, Ben (after Benjamin Franklin), adjusts the schedule in real time. Though it seems random at times, its results are beyond question. The numbers keep creeping up, in the places they want and at the times they want. The AI's parameters are so complicated that no human mind can fathom their workings, but that's true of the American people too.

Their dark money has its own AI, Deb (after Ben Franklin's wife), and it bought out significant ad markets in Colorado and Michigan early. They'd gone negative early too, making veiled claims that both their Republican and Democratic opponents were pedophiles. The inevitable lawsuits could be brushed away with money. The opponent as pedophile is the one smear that sticks.

Every few days, Cooper balks, claims he's going to ignore Ben and Deb and head to Miami-Dade to fight it out. Dominic has to threaten to quit to keep him on the AI track. It's the drama of a lover's spat they have to play out. It once reached the point that Dominic packed his bags in the hotel, but Cooper stopped him and they ended up embracing in front of the whole executive team.

Now they're rolling. They're pushing on over the clouds

on the way to Austin like Vikings pushing into the northern waters. They will take all that stands in their path. The other two parties are doing what they know how to do. The Democrats are scaring their own people with visions of a Republican presidency ending democracy. The Republicans are scaring their own people with visions of a Democratic president telling them they're evil. It's the same bag of tricks: *They're coming to take away your dignity. They're coming to take away your rights. They're coming to take away your country.*

The American people are capricious. They like to make surprising political choices. The Maverick Party is surprising at just the right time.

12:01 p.m., Sardis, OH

The Mitsubishi dealer is waiting for Balfour at a picnic table in a park on the banks of the Ohio River. The Ohio River is oak and painted trilliums and wild columbine, flitted through by tiger swallowtails and monarch butterflies. The man looks like some Baptist preacher, blond and blue-eyed, dressed in white linen, with penny loafers.

If they were not there to plot the overthrow of US democracy, their meeting could be to dunk Balfour's sinning head in the cleansing waters. The cheerful good health of the far-right lunatics has been startling to Balfour ever since he began dealing with them. But he must look strange too, stepping out of a rented Ford Focus in jeans and sweatshirt, carrying a *New Yorker* tote bag. It's not like he looks the part of an agent of chaos either.

"Well met, brother," the dealer says, enfolding Balfour's hand in a ruthless grip.

"Well met," Balfour tries. It might be some white power greeting with which he's unfamiliar. He wonders, for a flicker, if he's in the middle of a sting. The Department of Justice has a domestic terrorism unit, he knows. But the DOJ would never dress up like this man, all in white, if they were pretending to be Nazis. It wouldn't make any sense. It *doesn't* make any sense. A clean, healthy, prosperous man of substance and status is devoting himself to the destruction of the system that gave him health and prosperity and status. Balfour is uncomfortable with nebulous motives.

"The thrown stone," the dealer says.

"I'm sorry?"

"You want the thrown stone," the dealer says, and then begins a long quotation, which he speaks with complete facility, faster than he could read it out of a book: "'Thou, O King, sawest, and behold, a great image. This great image, whose brightness was excellent, stood before thee; and the form thereof was terrible. This image's head was of fine gold, his breast and his arms of silver, his belly and his thighs of brass, his legs of iron, his feet part of iron and part of clay. Thou sawest till that a stone was cut out without hands, which smote the image upon his feet that were of iron and clay, and broke them to pieces. Then was the iron, the clay, the brass, the silver, and the gold broken to pieces together, and became like the chaff of the summer threshing floors; and the wind carried them away, that no place was found for them: and the stone that smote the image became a great mountain, and filled the whole earth.' You want us to be that stone thrown at the feet of clay."

"Look, we need to be clear about a few things," Balfour says. "No more text threads with Supreme Court justice's wives cc'd. No more Facebook groups. We need secrecy. We need control. We need reliability."

"We should indeed be clear," the dealer replies. "The men

I'm in contact with are free men. It's not like I'm the commander. It's not like I give orders and they take them. I point them where they might strike most forcefully to serve our struggle, and if they see the virtue of the proposal, they agree to it."

"Then I don't think this will work. I need guarantees. I need certainty of action."

"I'm only explaining my own position. You should have no worries. You have no idea how much these people want to do what you want them to do."

"Who are these people?" Balfour asks.

"The people with my guy."

"Which guy?"

"The guy who does give the orders. The guy I know."

"The guy who gives orders."

"He will order what you want, if you can provide the resources and the specifications."

Balfour has a choice to make, but he decides he has no choice. Risk is a requirement for insurrection. He removes a couple of bricks of hundred-dollar bills and the blueprints of the Joyce Center at the University of Notre Dame from his *New Yorker* tote. "Here's 250K. It's just a start. If their expenses run further, we are good for them. *I* am good for them."

"We shouldn't give them more money," the dealer says. "We don't want them buying what they can buy with more money."

"No nuclear material," Balfour says.

"Exactly."

Balfour unfolds the blueprint and points to a corner of the building. "My insider will open this security barrier here ten minutes after the debate begins. Remind them that the debates sometimes start late. They'll need a distraction of some kind."

The Mitsubishi dealer takes a Sharpie out of the front

pocket of his linen pants and circles the entrance on the blue-print where Balfour has pointed. He writes beside it, *0+10 min-utes*. Balfour can feel himself sweating and it's not all the Ohio heat.

"What you need to tell them, what you need to hammer through to them, is the need for radio silence. Only face-to-face conversations. No bragging. No Facebook. I am going to tell you, and you are going to tell your guy, and he is going to tell his people, and they will carry it. Do you understand?"

"You can tell whoever gave you this money that his service in our righteous cause will bear fruit. And he will not be for-gotten when the truth is revealed and the real history of our times is written."

Balfour leaves his connection on the banks of the Ohio River among the dappled shadows of the magnificent oaks in all their glory. He drives away as fast as he can through the overbrush that cathedrals the road.

Balfour does not know the score when it comes to the man to whom he just gave a quarter-million dollars, and it troubles him.

More mysterious than the Mitsubishi-dealer insurrection-ist is that there are many tens of thousands like him. Balfour's instinct is to cynicism, that their anger is careerism, that they are merely asking themselves, *What do I have to do to get to the next level?* After all, violence and breakdown are the world now. Every man must make his way in the world.

There is a difference, however, and Balfour feels it. He is plotting terrorism against his political opponents. Now, you could say it's only a little farther down the road than the usual dirty tricks of electoral politics. You could say it's not altogether out of the realm of what United States agencies have done in other countries. But the white nationalist preacher man he left on the banks of the Ohio is a believer. Men like him who overlap between the Oath Keepers and legitimate government have a vision and they have a plan. They want power. They want, more than power, drama, to serve as agents of revolution, to be a force in resistance to federal authority. This Mitsubishi dealer wants to be a figure in future history books.

That's the danger, Balfour knows. The most dangerous men you meet are the ones who want their names in the history books.

2:31 p.m., 360 Clinton Avenue, Brooklyn, NY

"You want a baby," Zayn is saying. "I want a baby. We have the resources to have a baby. So why aren't you going to your appointment with Janet?"

"Can you not guess?" Martha replies.

"Look, we had one bad patch. There's probably going to be others. But, you know, we can do this. We want to do this, and we can do this, and we sort of have the money to do this, so why aren't we doing it?"

"Do you know what a miscarriage is like?"

Zayn keeps silent and stares into his coffee mug. There is nothing for him to say. She has shamed him into silence, but it's a shameful silence for her too. She knows, deep in her heart, that he's suffered with each of those losses too. There is enough pain to go around.

"I know this sounds corny and pathetic, but I would do this if I could," he eventually says. "I thought you wanted this."

"I did."

"What stopped you?"

"It's not you being poked and prodded like a laboratory animal. Do you know what I've had to do? Do you know how many appointments I've been to?"

"I know, I know. How could I *not* know?"

"All you have to do is jerk off into a cup," Martha says. "This is relentless for me."

"I know it is."

"And every month it grows harder. Every month the chance of success diminishes. Every month the struggle is that little bit more futile."

"Or we get one step closer to the end."

"But what end?"

Zayn puts his face in his hands. Then he lifts his face up. His eyes are moist. "Do you want to know the truth?"

Martha doesn't answer.

"The truth is that I want to go all the way. I want to make sure that we try every option so that we don't have regrets."

It's too late for no regrets, Martha thinks. She is too late and the world is too late. She's thirty-six now and she used her early thirties in service to the *New York Times*. The chorus of "what ifs" is constant. What if, instead of devoting herself to seventy-hour weeks, she'd had a baby? What if, instead of devoting herself to a profession in decline, at an institution that ended up transferring her to a low-end job because she defended a friend, she had chosen a family?

The beautiful unborn presence she can feel not existing would probably have come to be. The best thing she can do now is go back five years and have a baby then. And what's true for her is true for her country. The best thing America can do is go back twenty years and not allow the Supreme Court to put Bush in power, and not invade Iraq, and not watch the housing market explode. Or, the best thing for the world would be to go back fifty years and stop poisoning the earth.

There is no going back.

"What is it?" Zayn asks.

She puts her head on her knees. "I guess it's the tip line."

"What's that?"

"The degradation of the world. All the horrible messages. Then the fucking stupidity of the people sending them. And I can't tell what the problem is. Is the world stupefying people? Or is our stupidity demolishing the world?"

"But we're not stupid and we're not mean. The world's always falling apart."

"Is it fair to the baby?"

"We'll never know. It is our job in times of darkness to bring light into the world."

"I don't want to bring a baby into darkness."

All this second-guessing is pure distraction, she knows. Life isn't fair and regret is vanity. The truth is that blaming yourself for infertility is a form of asserting control. The body has made its decision. The person attached to that body needs to pretend that the body's decisions, even its most heartbreaking decisions, are hers.

2:31 p.m., Lamplit Inn, 37470 Route 7, Sardis, OH

In the hotel, with a bottle of Jack Daniel's, a can of Coke, and a garbage pail of ice by his side, Balfour watches the YouTube summary of the Sunday political shows. With professional satisfaction, he sees how right he was.

The sex scandal was only going to lift Cooper Sherman. How many American men wish they were him right now? How many American women are going to have sex dreams about him tonight, like they did with Clinton, like they did with Obama? Opposition research is a graveyard for amateurs. Dabblers need not apply.

More insane messages from Sevre have filled up his phone, and he scrolls through them half-attentively:

We are in the middle of political flux. Our spiritual system is changing and our political system will follow. Our informational system is changing and our spiritual system will follow.

One way of thinking through this transition is the devolution of the federal system. The yokels think the power will devolve to the states. They are wrong. America is four cities, not fifty states. These cities are not even cities. They are just four names for various spheres of power. New York: finance. Washington: military. Los Angeles: entertainment. Silicon Valley: technology. These, like Athens or Sparta or Thebes, are more ways of life than geographical locations.

Silicon Valley is consuming all these cities one by one. Technology is eating finance and the military and entertainment. There will be only technology in the end. We will all live in a big Silicon Valley. You are among us. You are a samurai of the future builders.

I'm not sure this will serve as compensation, but obviously you were right about the Maverick Party and Coop Sherman. Everybody here knows that. Jackson has been reassigned. You are free. I'm your liege lord now.

Balfour is glad to see his professional abilities recognized, though he must admit, if only to himself, that he underrated the Maverick Party. Somebody over there knows what they're doing. They knew enough to run *into* the sex club scandal rather than away from it. Sarah Ren is a badass but she surprised him nonetheless. He thought she was a more traditional flack. She's a killer, plugged in.

He has started to study the Maverick Party now that they are his real enemy, now that he has been tasked with more than finding their weaknesses. They are having a moment at just the right moment. Their contradictions are attractive.

They're cynical in a way nobody else can afford to be—they swear, they acknowledge the reality that American institutions are broken, they've stopped pretending that the United States is the greatest nation on earth. They are also idealistic as nobody else manages to be—they believe that they can change the system, they believe that they can rewrite the rules, they believe that the United States can still be the greatest country on earth.

The other parties are old jokes wearing their exhaustion: the Republicans pretending to clean up the Washington swamp when everybody knows they are con men hoping to achieve impunity under the cover of "limited government"; the Democrats preaching hope when all they offer is the demise of the institutions a little later than their opponents.

The standard play against a third party is that it's a wasted vote. Once Cooper Sherman looked like he was going to take Minnesota and Colorado, that play evaporated.

Plan B is the fear of risk: say that they're not up to the job. Yet the age and sheer incompetence of the Republican and Democratic leadership bar that approach of attack. Maverick is the tech party. Their whole appeal is that they can make things work again. They are the IT geeks in the office whose plan is to reboot America by turning it off and on again.

Rule number one of opposition research: take the best thing about your enemy and ruin it. Balfour knows his job. He needs to make the Maverick Party look as unprepared for the coming horrors as everybody else. Saint Mike Tyson has it right: everybody has a plan until they're punched in the mouth.

3:15 p.m., Gulfstream G500

At thirty thousand feet in the air, the Maverick team is shopping. They're picking out a vice president. Picking out a vice-presidential candidate is like picking out a fur coat: if you need to have one, you try to pick the least-embarrassing choice, and most importantly, the beast must be dead.

"Which one of these D-listers can keep their mouth shut best?" Ren asks.

Dominic, Mikey, and Nellie are scrolling through the opposition books of the four candidates they're considering.

There's Liz Pope, a renegade Republican who turned on her party when they turned on democracy. Anna Sanchez, one of the first female four-star generals, who has the advantage of being a registered Maverick Party supporter. Geoffrey Alberta, a Black charter school activist in Georgia. And Roy Chowdhery, a hedge-fund manager and author of a series of best-selling business books.

"It cannot be Roy Chowdhery," Ren says. Everybody else nods instantly. Roy Chowdhery and Cooper Sherman are just too similar. Rich guys with smart mouths.

"What do you think of Anna Sanchez?" Dominic asks. "I've met her a few times and she's, um, she's . . ."

"Nice," Nellie tries.

"She needs media training," Ren says. "When she's on screen, she looks like she's literally thinking about every word she says before opening her mouth. It's awkward and we don't have a whole lot of time."

"A few things before we go on," Nellie says primly. "Anna Sanchez is a) Latina, b) a woman, c) demonstrably competent, and d) she would do it. We need all those things."

"She's not a natural TV presence," Ren says. "We're in a screened age and she doesn't pop on screen. Next?"

They review the opposition book on Geoffrey Alberta. This round of oppo, the preliminary round, is sketchy, designed to find only the most glaring flaws. In Alberta's case, the flaws are peripheral connections to anti-Semitism and a tendency to gamble online. The four of them read in silence, trying to figure out which one is worse.

"He sat down next to some Nation of Islam guys at a banquet. Is that really enough to disqualify him?" Dominic asks.

"Tip of the iceberg," Ren says.

"What do you mean?"

Mikey explains: "This is just a preliminary oppo report. What Ren's saying is that if our hacks can find this shit out so quickly, what will they find when we give them real money and they take their time?"

"Yeah, but there's no evidence he himself has ever said or done anything anti-Semitic or even worked for anybody who has said or done anything anti-Semitic."

"You might be right," Ren says. "I don't know." The sudden humility shocks the others. It must be a ploy.

"Less likely," Mikey says. "They're pretty good at finding out that shit."

"He's good-looking enough," Ren says. "Put Sherman and Alberta together, you got a whole new season of *True Detective*."

They turn to Liz Pope, the one they obviously want, the one Cooper will obviously want. She's one of the great women of contemporary American history, having stood up to the forces of autocracy in her own party, both in public and in the court, who paid by being excluded and ostracized from the only world she had ever known, Republicanism. She would bring in millions of disaffected Republicans who could swing key states.

There's another question they have to ask all these candidates: how much are they willing to risk their lives? Cooper started this campaign knowing that he was going to face death threats, knowing that the possibility of violence is real. He had no idea how many death threats. He had no idea how real the violence would be.

The VP options will know what dangers they would face. In the last week, a still-at-large gunman fired a .50-caliber rifle into the offices of the Democratic National Committee. A Democratic county official in charge of administering elections in Idaho had his ranch shot up by right-wing insurgents. It was Idaho, but still . . .

Mikey's phone rings just as they turn to the section on Liz Pope's dubious real estate deals in Montana.

3:19 p.m., Brooklyn Bridge, Brooklyn, NY
By the time Martha has walked all the way to the Brooklyn Bridge, and cried for ten minutes, she's calm. Her heart is empty. The view of the Manhattan skyline is like a view of the mountains or the ocean. The smallness of your problems is self-evident. The city is sublime.

She still hasn't sent the audio of the senior leadership planning to end the Bill of Rights. She is prevaricating. One day, she decides she won't do it. The next, she decides she will but not yet.

The source of Martha's hesitation is unclear to her. For one thing, she might be fired from the *Times*. If she were fired from the *Times*, she would lose her income and her benefits. Without her income and her benefits, Martha and Zayn wouldn't be able to afford IVF. If she's fired, she might not be able to have a kid.

Then there's her physical safety. She has been threatened by the source.

Under these fears lies doubt. Malcolm Tanager is a very serious man. He's the editor in chief of the *New York Times*. His opinions on most things are probably correct. She is so sure he is wrong. But why does she think she knows best? She is bitter. Bitterness can make you stupid.

On the other hand, Tanager is the representative of a system, a system that has to be considered, by any sensible standard, a massive failure. How smart can he be?

When you're standing on the Brooklyn Bridge, the thought can strike: *Somebody did that. Somebody made that happen.* Americans did that. Americans made that happen. That's why New York is New York. It shows you what's possible. It dares you.

Martha drinks in the bridge, then thinks, *Fuck it*, and calls Mikey.

"What would you do with it?" she asks before he knows who's speaking.

"Hold on," Mikey says.

Martha hears him take some steps and shut a door. A fan turns on. It sounds like he's in a plane. But he can't be on a plane because he's on a phone.

"What would I do with *what*?"

"With the audio?"

He answers instantly: "I'd leak it."

"How?"

"I'm never going to tell you that or anybody else. Leaking requires secrecy. I wouldn't tell anyone about you either."

"Why would you leak it? Why would that serve your interests?"

"Now you're asking the right question. For us, it makes our point for us. Both parties aren't serving the American people. Both are dangerous. I mean, 'Only we can solve.' It's going to make everyone in the country think about voting Maverick. But that's not the point. The point is that you're an American and you believe in democracy, and you're a journalist, and you have materials that ordinary people don't know about that point to the end of democracy in America. So this is your job. This is your duty."

Martha snorts. "That's an old-fashioned word."

"Well, maybe duty falling out of fashion is why the world keeps getting worse."

"Funny how me doing my duty helps you win."

"Everybody, including me, will lose when those clips come out. But let's not pretend. Blood is going to flow when we leak that audio. And this conversation doesn't matter, Martha, because you've already decided to give me the audio, because you don't have much of a choice."

"I'll come and meet you at the convention in Philadelphia," Martha says. "I'm going to come because you're going to give me dirt. You're going to be my source. So we have protection. Do you understand?"

"I understand. I'll be your source. Under protection of deep background."

This is the deal they're going to make: If Mikey becomes a protected source, she can refuse to answer questions about their meetings, to her bosses and the police. Her cover for him will be his cover for her.

Once she hangs up, her despair is over. She's going to the convention in Philadelphia. Before every great story comes to exist, the writer lurches. If you don't articulate the story, it might not exist. You can cause events never to have been. She just needed to lurch. She thanks the Brooklyn Bridge for the gift of its ambition and heads home.

11:11 p.m., Lamplit Inn, 37470 Route 7, Sardis, OH
Balfour rouses from a nightmare: he was building his own

funeral pyre, standing on top of a collection of logs and dry leaves, arranging them so they would burn better, and then he started tying himself to a stake. He woke up when he sparked a match to find himself sitting in the hotel chair with a bucket of melted ice and a quarter of a bottle of Jack Daniel's at his feet.

On television, the Astros are shellacking the Angels 15-2 in the sixth inning. There are two more texts from Sevre:

> *The truth is that we are about to enter a new civilization. America has already become very different from other advanced economies. The Europeans no longer recognize us. Never mind China. We are the nation of innovation. We suffer more. We are freer. We are willing to pay the price for the future. We alone deserve the future because we are willing to shred the past.*

> *The point of America is that the future belongs to the people who build the future.*

Balfour knows enough not to write back, but he almost should. The future Sevre is dreaming isn't that different from the past, a country where everybody could grab whatever they wanted, the America of adventure serials, a country built by pirates and robber barons and machine politicians, who covered over the sources of their fortunes with whatever ideals they could cobble together on the fly.

The future would be the same. On Mars, you can take whatever you can find. The eternal dream of the final frontier. What you see belongs to you.

At any rate, Sevre doesn't seem aware that the future they're building is much worse than the past they're leaving behind. This doesn't matter to Balfour. He's going to own a piece of that lousier future if they win. At some point during this election season, he stopped fighting for a president. He knows what he's fighting for now. He's fighting for a presidential pardon.

Sevre explicitly asked not to be told about Balfour's work, and Balfour was happy to oblige. They don't need to communicate because their plan is simple. The plan is chaos. Chaos is simple. All it takes is will and machinery, like being a wrecking-ball operator. Sevre has the will. Balfour is building the machinery.

Chaos is both means and end. Chaos will lead to the destruction of the system. The destruction of the system will lead to chaos. In chaos, the strong and clever can do what they like.

They must win. Balfour must win. Winning means that the sewer he's crawling through now makes sense. His degradation has a purpose. *It was as easy to cross over as to go back.* Where is that line from? He tries to remember as he slumps back into the uneasy dreams he knows are coming.

August 24

THE UNCONVENTION

(149 days until)

The darkness is cloudy in the vestibule as Martha hides her phone in the slot on the side table where she and Zayn usually keep their scarves and gloves in winter. She can't, for a moment, understand how she's going to leave it behind.

She reminds herself that she's a journalist. She's supposed to go out into the world. That's the job. You go out into the world and you look at it. It's not supposed to be sitting at a desk, sieving the Internet for outrage.

She's told Zayn active lies, not just lies of omission. She's told him that her phone needs to be repaired, so she'll be out of contact. She planned a trip to the Catskills with friends then canceled at the last minute, so only Zayn went.

She feels guilty leaving the SecureDrop server, like a dairy farmer must feel when they leave their cows. But abandoning her phone—there it sits on the side table, and she must go on without it—that is like leaving the fingers of her left hand home. Leaving her phone behind is truly crossing over.

If she dies on the street, the police will have to figure out who she is. A woman without her phone is not the same animal as a woman with her phone. She is capable of things the other isn't capable of.

But she must go. She must go and she must not be traceable. She will go to Philadelphia for the convention, drop off the USB key she's loaded with the audio clips, and come home. She can do this. She has to.

Walking to the elevator, she itches for the place where her

phone should be. The USB key with the audio clips in her pocket is like a ring out of a fable leading her into dangerous territory, a quest. Today, at least, she is a woman with a destiny.

Things could not be going any better.

10:23 a.m., Philadelphia Convention Center,
1101 Arch Street, Philadelphia, PA

They call it the Unconvention, which is cute, and they want it to be somewhere in between a political convention and Coachella. Half the attendees seem to be in an altered state of consciousness, so they've succeeded.

The beautiful thing about a third-party convention is that it doesn't have to bother with the procedural nonsense of the other conventions, the dreary traditions like pledge allocations and the reading of the rolls. Rather, it is pure political spectacle and an actual good time.

Cooper has cashed in all his celebrity trading tokens, and the green room looks like a combination of the world's greatest cocktail party in a bunker and a wax museum with displays that have all magically come alive. Arnold Schwarzenegger is hanging around after giving the keynote address in the morning. That evening, the Rock is giving his speech. A steady stream of celebrities have filled the suite underground: Aaron Rodgers is talking to Rachel Siegel about crypto. Chris Rock and Shane Gillis are comparing notes on jokes. Kim Kardashian is offering advice to Matthew McConaughey about his gun-responsibility social media strategy. Finally, Chamath Palihapitiya and Elon Musk are arguing over artificial general intelligence. Anna Sanchez sits among them with a goofy grin on her face, but in her full Air Force uniform she projects gravitas. She will speak just before the Rock, in her first appearance as their vice-presidential candidate. *It's not all mushrooms and crypto,* her presence announces.

Real adults are in the room. Christina Aguilera is performing upstairs.

The Unconvention is a trip, on a number of levels. There are the drugs. There is the utopian political vision of America restored to technologically enabled mass prosperity. Cooper Sherman's policies, which neither of the other parties even consider, resonate as both common sense and radical innovation. A universal basic income is the only way to prevent the spiking inequality from turning the United States into nothing but the tech lords and the people who give them massages. There has to be a better way to deal with drugs than jailing everyone who's just unfortunate enough to be caught doing what everybody else is doing. Only the Maverick Party has figured out these obvious realities. Only the Maverick Party is dealing with them.

And that frankness and mood of cool they've managed to cultivate has brought in the celebrities. The dreamworkers, the conjurers and navigators of the mass entertainments, have overwhelmed the American mind. No one in the United States can resist celebrity. Mikey is no less susceptible than anybody else. When he saw Kim Kardashian in the green room air-kissing Matthew McConaughey, his heart beat faster. He felt himself lifted out of reality, apart from the scene, watching himself watching Kim Kardashian and Matthew McConaughey. Ridiculous as it is, he knows the scene will remain branded in his memory forever.

Mikey doesn't want to leave, but he heads up to the backstage entrance, where Nadav is removing weapons from members of Travis Scott's entourage.

Nadav usually says nothing, tries not to be there. When security professionals deal with even the insane, they rarely use their hands. They angle their bodies, filter the threat to the edges. Nadav is important. Nadav did not approve of the Unconvention. But nobody listened to Nadav. Now he is dealing with hundreds of targets to protect, dozens of interlocking security details. Mikey is embarrassed to be bothering him.

"Yes?" Nadav says.

"It's important," Mikey insists. "There's a woman named Martha Kass coming. Her name is not on the list. There's a reason her name is not on the list."

"Who's she with?" Nadav asks, writing down the name on a yellow legal pad on a fold-out table. Mikey rips the paper off the pad and scrunches it up in his fist. Nadav looks up. He realizes Mikey means it.

"She isn't a celebrity or part of an entourage, but she matters more than they do. Text me when she arrives. Text her name. Be sure to do it."

"What does she look like?"

"She looks like a real person. Remember what they look like?"

"Only by looking at you."

Nadav is maintaining his composure but Mikey can see he's in battle mode. At the Republican convention in Milwaukee, anarchists threw Molotov cocktails into a group of attendees, burning alive an insurance adjuster from New Mexico. The Proud Boys opened fire in response. The subsequent riot, pacified by the National Guard, left three dead and seventeen wounded. The Democratic convention in Chicago happened under a daze of tear gas used to clear protesters. Half the audience were rubbing their eyes during the final address by the Democratic candidate.

The candidates of both parties had very different reactions. The Democrat gave a tearful address at the press conference afterward, shouting, "What's this country coming to?" with upraised hands. The Republican declared, in a calm undertone, "When we get into office, we are going to find out exactly who is responsible and they will feel the wrath of the truth of this republic." His mouth, in these moments, tends to smile in a vicious open-toothed way that always reminds Mikey of a werewolf in a black-and-white movie. The Republican compared the violence in Milwaukee to September 11, and promised, "The radical left have our attention; now we're going to erase them from the planet."

The Maverick campaign, and the Cooper candidacy, appear increasingly vital and rational in comparison.

10:33 a.m., Amtrak, New York to Philadelphia
Without her phone, Martha has only her thoughts. It must be so easy to kill journalists, she thinks. They have regular habits and go out into the dark corners of the world.

She must stay positive. The cult of positivity that loomed over the infertility club depresses and infuriates Martha. She hated, more than anything, being told to stay positive, all the women who'd already had kids telling her that the best way to get pregnant is to "just relax." The elders who assumed life would work out were the ones who let the world fall apart. They should have been less relaxed.

There's no better option than hope, though. That much she knows. Infertility causes stress, studies show, but the studies can't tell if stress causes infertility, if the cortisol rushing through her after each procedure prevents nature from taking its course.

The real danger of stress, Janet assured her, is causing patients to quit treatment.

On the train, Martha feels like she's part of a historical recreation. She had sort of imagined, alone in her apartment processing information, that the era of men and women taking trains from one place to another was over. It seems so pitifully twentieth century. She bought her ticket with cash and bought herself a physical newspaper with the change. She is part of the pantomime: reading a newspaper on a train and out of contact.

There is a man with white hair in a gray suit who looks too young for either the white hair or the gray suit. If she were to imagine what an assassin looks like, it would be him. He is also reading a physical newspaper. The train is full. She is safe. She must stick to the facts. Paranoia is a disease right up to the point that it's prevention.

12:23 p.m., Philadelphia Convention Center,
1101 Arch Street, Philadelphia, PA

The control booth in the Philadelphia Convention Center is in the basement, directly across from the green room. Ren watches the coverage on one bank of screens, and the action inside the venue on security footage.

In between the performances and speeches, the crowd tunes out and the media interviews the mushroom-addled supporters. The Maverick Party has found a particular aesthetic: post-hope hackers, the #toofar angry middle who hate the outraged fringes of both parties, and UFC libertarians.

Underneath the feel and the look of the Maverick Party, rising up, lifting them in a lot of American places they never expected to connect, is an appeal nobody foresaw: they have a plan. Neither of the other parties has a plan.

The Maverick Party has a plan for electoral reform which could, at least in theory, lead to real practical change. Get money out of politics and get rid of party primaries, replace them with races where everyone can vote for everyone via ranked-choice voting. Make democracy real. Listen to the people. The others want to drift the way they were already drifting, or just claim victories in a culture war with no end.

A Politico reporter had asked Cooper why anyone should

vote for the Maverick Party when they didn't even possess party infrastructure in over half of US counties. "At least we got a plan," Cooper answered, opening his eyes and spreading his hands like an old lady in an *SNL* skit. Somebody put the clip to the theme music from *Curb Your Enthusiasm* and it went viral. It's Cooper's gift, this ability to make viral moments. There are shirts saying *Do the Math*, and hats saying *Unfuck America*, and now *We Got a Plan* is being tattooed on people's biceps.

Unfuck America remains the most popular, though. *Unfuck America* is as big as MAGA was. People wear pins with *UA* on them, and everyone knows what the letters mean. It's nearly as big as the Drake sweater meme. But all of the *Unfuck America* merchandise had to be removed for the Unconvention. That was their promise to the networks. The FCC can fine a network up to $325,000 for each usage of a curse word. The Maverick Party set up an *Unfuck* catcher to run through the crowd finding people who slipped past the door check.

"How are we looking?" Mikey asks.

Ren points to the bank of security cameras. "The good news is that the FCC doesn't like images of drug consumption, so that prevents the networks from showing just what a collection of freaks we've managed to assemble."

"Haven't you heard that we have a plan?" Mikey says.

"I think Cooper's got a plan to hook up with a celebrity tonight."

"You can have more than one plan at the same time."

"America," Ren says, then turns up the volume on CNN.

It's John King reporting from the convention floor. He's interviewing Christina Aguilera. "You know, for many years you've supported Democratic candidates. You've sung at Hillary Clinton rallies. You've worked with Barack Obama. What made you switch to the Maverick Party?"

Christina Aguilera looks momentarily confused by this obvious question. "I mean, I met Cooper backstage at 'Build It and They Will Come' many years ago, and he was telling me about his plans with the prison system, and he's so smart."

"Would you say you were disappointed by the Democratic Party?"

"I love Hillary and Obama. I still do. I really do. But it's time for a change. It's time for new ideas in this country, because the path we're going down, like, we have to get off that path. And we have to start bringing people together."

"So you're afraid for America."

"Aren't you? I'm worried about America. I think everybody's worried about America. I'm like the worried mom of America. If you're not worried about America, you're not paying attention. But also, I think, look at this party. Look at this Unconvention. American politics can still be a good time."

Ren switches to Fox. It's Greg Gutfeld, doing his best overwhelmed-dad impression as he talks to Sean Hannity.

"What we're seeing here, Sean, is the Hollywood-industrial complex on full display. I have to say that I've never personally seen such a display of Orwellian groupthink. These celebrities are like geese heading south for the winter. The Maverick Party is cool and so they go with cool, Sean."

"They got big names, did they?"

"The biggest. Christina Aguilera just sang, and I must say, she's a good singer. They liked her songs. Also, Sean, we're not allowed to show drug use on television, but this room is high. High AF, if you know what I mean. The Maverick Party is riding high in a lot of ways. Hollywood will never stop telling us what to think."

Ren switches to MSNBC, where Katy Tur is reporting. Unlike the other stations, they're shooting from outside the convention hall. "It does look like the violence which disturbed the Democratic and Republican conventions is making its presence felt here, Rachel." The camera pans over the parking lot. It looks like a prepper convention, with bands of armed cadres in camouflage or black, wearing gas masks, holding black guns, and waving American flags and Gadsen flags and other flags of lesser, more violent factions. "The worst fears of the organizers are being realized. Inside is basically one big party, with Christina Aguilera and the Rock. But outside it's getting pretty serious. These are many of the same far-right and Antifa groups that are disrupting political events across the country."

"Who are the people taking up arms against the Maverick Party, Katy?" Rachel Maddow asks.

"You know, there are both sides here, just like there were in Milwaukee and Chicago, Rachel." Katy Tur steps back so the camera can see the riot troops who have arrayed themselves behind barbed gates leading to the backstage entrance.

"But what are they against?"

"Honestly, I'm not sure they know anymore. These crowds that are gathering, I'm not sure they're even thinking much about the Maverick Party. They hate each other, and I think they want to go where there's energy and an opportunity to send a message."

"Did we hire those?" Ren asks, pointing at the riot police on the screen.

"The city hired them," Mikey says. "By the way, I'm going to have to step away for a while."

"Something more important than this?"

"Yes."

"You're serious?" Ren says, then laughs. "It's a girl, isn't it?"

12:34 p.m., Philadelphia Convention Center,
1101 Arch Street, Philadelphia, PA

Martha's plan is to show up at the backstage entrance. Security will have her name on a list. Mikey will come down and meet her. The plan makes sense for a different country in a different time.

It's only just past noon, but the rage is already in full effect, a demonstration on the brim of a riot. Martha didn't think there would be horrific protests at the Maverick Party convention like there were at the Democratic and Republican conventions. It didn't make much sense to treat the Maverick Party as a power to rage against.

One look at the rioters shows her that making sense is not their business. Rage is their activity now. It's something they do for their sense of identity and purpose. Political violence gives structure to their weekends. In Real Life isn't that different from the SecureDrop, it turns out. The human movement is the same—faceless rage moving wheels within wheels of fracturing exploitation, with humanity chewed up in the gears. Martha is wandering the wasteland of the digital world made flesh.

Under their masks, somewhere around a quarter of the men have the dead-eyed murderousness of losing warrior prophets. Another half are in a state of angry glee, like frat boys on some dare who know their times of impunity are arriving.

The politics has become real simple here. Their calls to freedom have splintered into a few separate obsessions, but they are clear that nobody is going to take anything away from them anymore.

The insurgents—is that the right word for them? Is that what they are? If they aren't insurgents, what are they?—are masked and wearing black, helmeted. They are defined by their armbands, not that Martha knows what the armbands mean. The blue-and-yellow armband probably has something to do with Ukraine. Plain yellow with *Don't Tread on Me* is for Second Amendment absolutists, black-and-blue for Blue Lives Matter, red, white, and blue, a single star, so many others.

She starts to walk through, toward the security forces where the backstage entrance must be, but the crowd is dense and she rubs up against guns before she can even see the entrance. It curdles her skin, and a thin silver stream of lucid anxiety pours down her spine.

A man wearing a Viking hat like the January 6 shaman fires a machine gun into the air beside her, takes a swig of Red Bull, and shouts, "Freedom!" Martha is the only one startled. She backs away. The rest of the crowd is yelling. Tonight is going to be crazy. It's going to be intense. They're going to love it.

Martha loops around to see if the other side might work. The military, or the National Guard, or some governmental force, stands outside their Humvees behind the blast-proof gates they're patrolling, their hands on their M4s, fingers on their triggers. They seem to sense they could be killing their fellow citizens in a couple of hours.

Protesters on either side are growling at them. No one has thrown a stone yet, but a stone is going to be thrown. The US military may be the last institution anyone in America has any faith in, but that faith is fraying. The USB key in her pocket will break that final bond of trust.

The left-wing side appears to be half hippie, half anarchist. Some are in tie-dye. Some are in black. The ones in tie-dye have beards. The ones in black wear masks. The ones in tie-dye have drums. The ones in black have guns, mostly pistols but a few AR-15s. Martha pushes through a group who appear to be having a collective bad trip, with a woman in white linen curled in the fetal position and three men lying on their backs, their faces stuck in terror.

"Who are you with?" a man entirely in black with a black gas mask asks her. He is carrying an AK-47. By his eyes, he looks at most twenty.

"I'm with nobody," Martha says.

"Police? NSA? Press?" This last word is sneered.

"I'm supposed to attend the convention. I'm a guest of the Maverick Party."

"So you're a Maverick voter then?"

"Who are *you* with?" Martha asks.

"Go back," he answers. "We're not letting any fucking billionaire bitches into their fancy fucking party."

Martha considers a confrontation but she's barely at the beginning of the crowd. How many twenty-year-olds with guns will she have to confront if she presses forward?

She retreats into the streets of Philadelphia.

12:45 p.m., Philadelphia Convention Center,
1101 Arch Street, Philadelphia, PA

The sound of gunfire outside has driven all the celebrities to the green room. Their entourages are surreptitiously trying to gauge, from each other, if they can flee.

Kim Kardashian is talking anxiously to Matthew McConaughey, the Rock is fidgeting with his fingers while discussing the situation with Elon Musk. *Is this what it looked like in the Parisian salons during the French Revolution?* Mikey asks himself.

The only one among them who seems immune from terror is Anna Sanchez, who has been in combat before. She is on her phone, communicating with the security personnel on the periphery. She's asked for a blueprint of the building, and Nellie is desperately trying to find her one on a laptop.

1:56 p.m., Days Inn, 1227 Race Street, Philadelphia, PA
America has overwhelmed the lobby of the Days Inn. Both sides of the madness are represented. At the coffee station, a man in camo with an AK-47 strapped around his shoulder politely offers milk to a man wearing a *God Hates Priests* shirt.

The concierge has let Martha use the phone four times, but Mikey isn't answering. The concierge is a sweet, plump man used to dealing with business travelers stranded by canceled flights, not the onset of anarchy in the United States. He must be wondering, as so many must be wondering, whether the violence he's read about, the violence he's seen on the news, is about to come for him.

"Do you have a business center?" Martha asks. Maybe she could write an email. Maybe Mikey would respond to it. She would have to send it by her Hotmail account because both her work and Gmail accounts require two-factor authentication. It might go to spam. Her hope is that since she used that Hotmail account back in college when they were friends, it might go through.

"We do," the concierge says. "But I'm afraid it requires a room number to access."

"Do you have any availabilities?"

"Um . . ." He looks at his screen. "You know what? We just had a cancellation."

"Somebody get arrested?" Martha says.

The concierge grants her joke a soft snort—he's trying to suppress his terror at what's taking over the lobby—as she fishes in her purse for her Visa. She didn't bring enough cash. So much for being off the grid.

3:45 p.m., Philadelphia Convention Center,
1101 Arch Street, Philadelphia, PA
The show must go on. Every now and then, during the speeches

and performances, there's a faint clatter of gunfire. Cooper has told his celebrity pals that it's firecrackers, but they're watching the gathering mobs on Twitter, and they know. An email from Martha comes in:

Hi Mikey,
So I couldn't manage to get into the convention center because of men with guns. I've checked into room 601 at the Days Inn on Race Street for now. Tell me what you want me to do.
All best,
M

Mikey doesn't tell anyone he's leaving. They wouldn't let him go if he told them where he's going.

4:15 p.m., Days Inn, 1227 Race Street, Philadelphia, PA Mikey shows up at her door, and she immediately wants to throw herself at him. In the spreading ocean of insanity, Mikey is a piece of floating wreckage she might cling to. Her room has a view of the parking lot outside the convention center.

Somebody on the right-wing side has started shooting regular red flares up. Machine guns are firing into the air. Ambulances circled the scene for a while but they have stopped circling. The military have held their line but they can't do more.

"I didn't think it would be so difficult," Mikey says. "I didn't think it would be so dangerous. It's good to see you. Come with me."

"Come with you where?"

"To the convention. We have security there. Ex-Blackwater. Linemen who've killed people."

"Mikey, there's no way to get there. Look at the streets."

Out the window, the chaos is panoramic. Men in black are

running in groups or alone to and from other men in black alone or in groups. It's like an anthill after the queen has died: pheromonic hysteria driven by a sudden lack of purpose.

"I just came from there, Martha. Nobody even noticed me. I'm with the party. They'll have to let me in."

Martha wants to believe Mikey. He's from the past. He's from the sensible and humane past. Everyone must cling to something.

In the elevator, two men with AR-15s and full tactical gear are chatting in between sips of Red Bull and vodka in red plastic cups.

"Expect a kettle," says one of the men.

"You think they'll try that after Milwaukee?" responds the other.

"I think the cops are so fucking dumb they wouldn't know tactical engagement from a Tic Tac. And besides, you remember when all our strategies kept changing in Afghanistan?"

"Not really."

"That's exactly my point. No one knows how to fight an insurgency."

Mikey feels Martha's arm slip into his. He tries to force a smile onto his face. With the right pose, they might look like a couple of Canadian tourists who have taken a wrong turn.

The hotel is like the backstage area of a theatrical performance of civil war. Groups of young men in armor put on gas masks and check their weapons. The Days Inn has attracted the right wing more than the left, but still, a party of anarchists wearing riot helmets and truncheons with shields heads out the front door unmolested. Some unstated rule, still alive despite the lunacy, holds the two sides back from violence inside the building.

"Mikey, I tried," Martha says. "I couldn't get through."

"We'll go through the hippie side," Mikey says.

The streets around the Days Inn are largely empty. Only the partisans are drifting along them. The police, or some other authority, must have blocked traffic. Martha has not taken her arm from Mikey's. They're in some movie about the end of the world, walking along a broken, empty city filled with rageful zombies, going somewhere they don't understand because at least it's going somewhere.

Mikey calls Ren. "Where the fuck are you?" she barks.

"I'm trying to get back in the building. I had to run an errand."

"Need to get some milk, did you? Or did you step out for a Subway sandwich?"

"Just tell me how I can get back in, will you?"

A big boom from the convention center. A blossom of rust. A rising black cloud. Mikey's phone goes dead. Martha is clutching his arm. They both hear staccato gunfire.

A crowd panicking doesn't move in a burst. It's like a car starting in a drag race. The acceleration, at first, appears calm, manageable. A few scared faces, fleeing, looking back. Then the gunfire doesn't stop and there are small groups running flat out, past Mikey and Martha, and then there are armed men turning around and firing into the crowd. And then Martha and Mikey run back toward the Days Inn, holding hands so they will not separate.

The hotel lobby has an aura of disappointment and confusion. The mob came all the way for revolution and missed it. They are hurrying their preparations, clicking off safeties and rushing away for a piece of the action.

The elevator up to the room is empty. It's only when they arrive in the room that Martha and Mikey realize they're still holding hands, and let go. They're panting. They say nothing, each as coiled and tense as an animal backed into a corner.

Beside the bed, she grabs his neck and pulls him close for a death-resistant kiss.

Sex comes on like a crowd panicking, almost imperceptible movement, then a rush outward, everywhere, all at once. She takes off her blouse as if it were wet. He undresses like a kid about to jump in a summer lake. This business isn't personal. They need skin on skin the way a smoker needs a cigarette.

Mikey pulls the curtain across the window. He doesn't want to look out anymore. As Martha straddles him over the shitty hotel chair, the action is somewhere between a massage and stress-relieving exercise, like cutting wood on a cold day to warm yourself. Each is throwing themselves, through the body of the other, against the encroaching darkness, the senselessness, the alienation and dissolution of their lives and their country and everything they have ever believed about their future. It is contact, necessary but insufficient.

They lie in the bed after, looking at the drawn curtain. There's a roar on the other side. How long can they lie there before pulling it back? How long can they pretend the world isn't there?

"You remember *Air Force One?*" Mikey asks.

"That old movie with Harrison Ford?" Martha says.

"Yeah."

"I remember it. What made you think of it?"

"That was, like, twenty-five years ago."

"So?"

"The president, in that movie, is like the most important human being in the world," Mikey says. "The president then was like a god among men. Invulnerable. He has the best people around him and he speaks for the American people. He wants to do right in the world, like the American people want to do right in the world. You know?"

"There were a bunch of those movies, weren't there?"

"*Clear and Present Danger.*"

"*Clear and Present Danger. The American President. Dave.* Fuck, *The West Wing.* Remember *The West Wing?*"

"*Clear and Present Danger* happens before Ford becomes president, but same thing."

"Would it be rude if I asked you what your point is?" Martha asks.

"Did people really believe that?" Mikey answers. "They seemed to. You got Glenn Close saying whatever the president needs. You got 'Get off my plane!' The president, not that long ago, was the good guy. Not just *a* good guy. *The* good guy. Do you see what I mean? That was only twenty-five years ago."

"Where have you gone, Harrison Ford?"

They can hear, past the curtain, another rattle of distant gunfire. Then there's a closer sound, like crystal shattering.

Martha is now in possession, fully, of a secret life. It's interesting. The only person who understands her, the only human being who recognizes the nature of her choices, is a string of numbers on a secure network. The only eyes to see her, to see her for real, are those of the surveillance state. She won't even tell Ross.

Mikey knows that this isn't what he wanted. He needed touch. He touched wrong. He needed wrong. "I guess it's over," he says.

"What's over?"

He gestures to the window. "This. American democracy." He stands up and draws the curtain open. The streets are a war zone, a battle for nothing, for the sake of battle. On the window, Mikey notices, there's a small hole in the top right corner, haloed by spiderweb cracks. He looks up. There's a bullet hole in the ceiling.

Mikey pulls the curtain back so that Martha won't notice.

October 10

THE DEBATE

(102 days until)

THE LAST MORNING IN AMERICA

The words are printed on a landscape: Andy Ponds overlooks the stunning autumnal forests of the Appalachian Mountains. The orange of dawn rises through the navy-blue sky.

The crisp air reveals his breath, as Ponds, crouching on a patch of moss between two boulders, looks wistfully over the region. "This is the morning America ends," he says. "This is the morning we all realize that the powers that be don't want America anymore. They want to take away the right to protest. They want to take away the right to carry guns. They want to take away the right to say what you want. They want to remove from the American people the ability to express themselves politically. To put it as simply as possible, they think we're not worthy of our freedom, and they want to put our freedom in the teacher's desk until we're grown up enough to deal with it like responsible adults."

Ponds holds up a USB key with stars and stripes decaled around it. "Somebody leaked this recording to me. Somebody who is a patriot. Somebody who understands what is at stake now, in this election, and we should all be grateful." He plays three clips while staring angrily into the camera.

"The first rule is: don't call it a coup. The American military will have to decide. Sooner or later. The voters are too crazed

with hatred. They want a civil war and they'll have one if we let them. You know, I don't think the voters want to decide anymore. They want us to take over. And let's be honest, real honest here, the US military is the only institution left in the United States that isn't overrun by careerist frauds. We're the only ones the people trust. It's natural that we decide the presidency. We may have to suspend the Constitution."

"It seems to me that if we learned anything from the past seventy years of spilling our blood and wasting our treasure on civil wars in the rest of the world, we can learn one goddamn lesson of our own. Stop this shit before it starts. Break these assholes. I want to round up the Oath Keepers now. I want them all in black sites now. And I want to crush Black Lives Matter too."

"I am increasingly uninterested in the sordid details of what you call the constitutional requirements. The public's faith is already broken. How can you fuck up something that's already gone? If the Constitution worked, we wouldn't be having this conversation. I swore an oath to the Constitution, but what did I swear to? Remember Iraq? Remember Afghanistan? The only way to win at counterinsurgency is not to play."

"At the very least, we're going to need plans to control the country in January and possibly afterward, and possibly for an indeterminate amount of time."

"You hear what they're saying? You hear it? I don't have the answer to this one, folks. Here, I guess, is the question you have to ask yourself: do you deserve rights? And if the answer is yes, if you *do* deserve rights, what are you willing to do to make sure you have rights? I mean, maybe it's time to vote for Cooper

Sherman, because I'll say this, he is the one guy the powers that be aren't talking to. I mean, I don't know where we all come out on this, but I for one am not going to vote for anybody who wants to end the Constitution. Here, I'll play them again."

As the clips repeat, Ponds bends and picks up an old Revolutionary-era rifle from the ground and begins cleaning it with an oilcloth.

"It was a beautiful country while it lasted," Ponds says at the end. Then he slowly pans his phone across the Appalachian hills, just as the sun crests, spilling sunlight over the mountain lip, blinding the camera.

This short video, slightly under three minutes, goes mega-viral. Politico picks it up first, but it's carried everywhere. It accumulates thirty-seven million views in its first three hours.

9:30 a.m., Embassy Suites by Hilton South Bend
at Notre Dame, 1140 E. Angela Boulevard, South Bend, IN

The training center, which is the top floor of the hotel, smells of stale testosterone. The Maverick debate team has been there for almost three weeks, prepping. They can see the small park beside the Joyce Center at the University of Notre Dame and the stadium and parking lot.

The entire point of the campaign—all the lunches with bundlers in fancy apartments, all the rallies in middle America, all the desperate begging for cash, all the legal filing from $800-an-hour lawyers to fulfill arcane jurisdictional requirements—all of it is to arrive here. Somewhere around a hundred million Americans will see their candidate at the debate or in the clips afterward, and he will be younger and smarter and cooler and more competent and funnier and more human than the other candidates. Tonight is their chance to show the world that they can win.

In most elections, debates don't matter. They move somewhere around 3 percent of the electorate. But this year, the debate is real. The Democrat stands nationally at 39 percent, the Republican at 35 percent, and the Maverick candidate at 26 percent.

Those numbers are less meaningful than the state battles. In Texas, the Maverick and the Republican are even at 39 percent of the polling. In Florida, all three candidates are hovering in the low thirties. The number of states the Mav is predicted to win is five.

Training for a debate is somewhere in between training for a prize fight and training for an appearance on *American Idol*. For the candidate, the shift from an atmosphere of love to an atmosphere of hate is abrupt. It's like going from a spa to a boot camp. Inside a campaign is, for the most part, a lovefest. You're with people who want to be around you. You're at the center of massive crowds there explicitly to worship you and what you represent. You hire a small army to hype you. That's what a campaign is: convincing other people to tell you how great you are.

At the debate, you face opponents who want to destroy you. You also have to face a small team of assassin-journalists who work literally for months to develop the nastiest questions they can ask you, questions tailored to your weaknesses and foibles, questions designed to discombobulate you.

For three weeks, six hours a day—three hours in the morning and three hours in the afternoon—Cooper Sherman and the team have been working out how *not* to answer the questions they will be asked. The first rule of a debate is to ignore the questions: you say what you have to say no matter what. Cooper will probably have forty minutes to speak. Each minute of those forty must be on his own ground. So when a candidate is asked, "What do you have to say about all those women you assaulted?" the candidate responds, "The problem in this country is political correctness." They ask, "What would you do about the price of gas?" and the candidate says, "America has always led the world in innovation."

Cooper has been working with two consultants for the three weeks of preparation. The first is the speech consultant, Terence, who has been honing Cooper's tone and manner. The second has worked out the answers together with Mikey and Cooper. They use the triangle system, a common debate technique. You aren't allowed to bring notes into a presidential debate, but the organizers give you five sheets of paper. On the top left of the first page, Cooper will write the acting advice: *Breathe, talk to a single person in the crowd, be calm, and smile.* The rest of the pages are for triangles on every issue he might face.

For each issue—economy, health care, abortion, electoral reform, etc.—they work out answers with three twenty-second components that can each be fed into the other. Thus, depending on the approach of the questioner, Cooper can begin an answer one of three ways while hitting all the points he wants to make. "What kind of judges would you appoint?" the questioner might ask. And Cooper will have a prepared triangle.

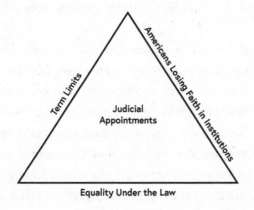

You simply move through the legs of your triangle, starting with the leg that is most relevant to the question. So in this case, Cooper would answer as follows: "I would look at judges on a case-by-case basis, but who any of us appoints doesn't matter nearly as much as how we would appoint them, and the terms of their appointment. I would select judges from either party who have shown true judicial independence. They would also need to agree to eighteen-year term limits. Seventy-two percent of Americans want this. The problem isn't the judges. The problem is that Americans are losing faith in their legal system because of the selection process. We know that our legal system has been held hostage by partisanship on both sides. It is time for institutions to listen to the American people, not the other way around. The legacy of this country is equality under the law. The other two parties have betrayed that trust. The Maverick Party will restore it and it will be my pleasure as president to deliver."

Cooper is also being instructed on an approach to each opponent. The Democrat radiates smugness. Cooper needs to wade into him, attacking on all points. The Republican is explosively angry. Cooper needs to laugh him off, make fun of his teeth and hair. Poke holes in one, and expose the other as impotent. Be confident without crossing over into asshole territory.

The substantive questions are easy enough. They aren't much harder than preparing for an exam. It's the screwball questions that can wreck a campaign. Like when they asked Governor Walker of Wisconsin whether Obama was a Christian, or Bobby Jindal if he would attend a gay wedding, or Palin which newspapers she read. So they have ended their afternoon sessions the same way, with the whole team ganging up on the candidate to ask the weirdest questions they can think up. "What's your favorite verse of the Koran?" "If you had to choose between fucking an octopus or a hole in a maple tree, which would you pick?" "If you were going to kill one of your opponents, which weapon would you choose?"

Today, they're supposed to be on a break. Before you run a marathon you train intensely and then you pause for a week so that your body can recover. Before a debate, you stop talking for a day or at least a number of hours. Cooper has been watching baseball, catching up on the play of the team he owns. But the Ponds video is an emergency. They need to build a new triangle. The whole team has gathered, in their utter exhaustion, to build another triangle.

Sarah Ren is flush, and the gloss on her hair makes her look like a racehorse on a track. She's a woman built for emergencies, built for the roadie life of campaigning. The others have aged ahead of their time.

Dominic's face has taken on a permanently appalled look, as though he just can't believe what he's seen. The stupidity is wearing on him. A rational approach to inherent irrationality is unsustainable for men with engineering souls. You can only endure so much institutional insanity before your soul starts to crack.

Nellie has taken on the look of a mother with a terminally ill child. This is what a successful campaign does to people. People on failing campaigns are much more relaxed.

"It's great for us," Ren says, not looking up from her phone. "Great for us! Fucking great!"

Dominic smooths the papers on his lap. "You think it's good for us that this country's about to descend into martial law?"

"Good for this campaign," Ren says. "We're the resistance. We're fucking Luke Skywalker and they're the Evil Empire and the Imperial Senate."

"Should we put that in a triangle?" Dominic says.

"I think this is an opportunity for us to show that we are more than a game," Nellie says. "This matters more than personal feelings. It is about the survival of the country. It is about the breakdown of the structure of government. And we are the only ones who can do anything about it."

"Sincerity," Mikey chimes in.

"If we're not going to be sincere now, for this, when are we ever going to be sincere about anything?" Nellie says. She seems sincere herself.

Cooper strolls in while putting on a shirt. "I think I got it," he says. "Gimme a piece of paper."

Dom hands him a yellow legal pad.

Cooper writes, *Leg 1: Protect. Leg 2: I am the only one. Leg 3: Reform.* "Go," he says.

"Mr. Sherman," Mikey says, doing his best Kristen Welker impersonation, "what do you think about the military's plan to clamp down on political violence and hate speech?"

"I'm glad you asked, Kristen. I'm going to start with the obvious. We need wholesale reform of our electoral systems. Everybody knows that our political order is on its last legs. Reform is coming. The Maverick Party is the party of reform. But let me make one thing perfectly clear. The American people are not going to reform into a people with fewer rights. What we need, first and always, is to protect the rights we already have. These tapes could not be clearer. Large forces within the established power structure are worried that the way things have always been done are changing. I am the only one not in the pocket of the powers that want to take away your capacity for self-government. Don't let them do it. Don't let them do it. I won't let them do it. *We* won't let them do it."

"Perfect," Ren says. "I can hear the applause."

"Couldn't be better," Mikey says.

Cooper finishes buttoning his shirt. He needs to talk as little as possible this afternoon, to save himself for the contest that's coming. He goes back to the dark room where the baseball game is playing on an enormous screen and a platter filled with exotic fruits takes up a large coffee table.

"What do you think?" Ren asks, once he's gone.

"It's shit, but it will have to do," Mikey says. "It's debate night."

10:01 a.m., 360 Clinton Avenue, Brooklyn, NY

LEAK UPENDS DEBATE

That's the headline on the *Times*'s home page. Martha is sitting in her apartment waiting to be fired. She watched the Ponds video once, but no more. Ponds did a good job. The clips playing over the calm mountain scene are jarring, conflicting. The virality was inevitable, constructed, achieved. The *Times* wouldn't have reached more people. It couldn't have.

Because she knows she's going to be fired, Martha is scrupulous at her job this morning. The tip line has lit up after the Ponds video. It's chum to the conspiracy sharks. New theories, with new bits of manufactured evidence, arrive several times a minute. Martha just deletes them as they arrive. If they were true, the paper wouldn't publish them anyway.

Instead of Malcolm Tanager calling to fire her, Ross calls.

"I'm starting to get the appeal of ignorance," she announces before he can even say hello.

"There's always a dark cloud when the story ends," Ross responds. "It's always depressing even when it works out for the best."

"You know of any waitressing jobs up there?" Martha regrets the remark instantly. She is speaking to Ross like he's a dead man. He isn't dead. He just can't tell stories anymore.

"It's not so bad," he says. "You know what the best part of a quiet life is?"

"What's that?"

"The quiet."

She wants hope but she cannot draw it from this well. Everybody's hope well is running dry. "When they assassinate me, at least I won't leave behind anyone but Zayn."

"Stop it," Ross says. "No pity parties here. There's no mercy for hunters. Think of yourself as a historical figure, which you now are. You are the anonymous source who leaked those tapes. That's the role you were given. You didn't seek it out. You played the role you were given as well as you could."

"What role do *you* play?" she asks.

"Intellectual in exile. That's obvious. Now, you know what you should do with the rest of today?"

"What's that?"

"Go spend the afternoon in bed with your husband."

"What would the point be?"

"To spend the afternoon in bed with your husband."

After the call, Martha checks the tip line again, and deletes the several dozen messages that have accumulated. She tells herself that the information is now out there, that she has done her job. But what kind of job is it where the end result is some fucking blogger sitting on a mountain playing the clips you gathered?

Nobody ever likes how a true story turns out—not the writer, not the subject. Nobody ever recognizes themselves in the mirror you hold up. But there is a relief Martha cannot help feeling as well, that even though it didn't go her way, she's done with it. There is nothing more for her to do. She bears no more responsibility. Martha is delivered of this story, and it's no longer hers.

1:15 p.m., Embassy Suites by Hilton South Bend at Notre Dame, 1140 E. Angela Boulevard, South Bend, IN

Ren and Mikey tuck Cooper into bed for a pre-debate nap. The hotel room is dark and soundproofed. Cooper must rest now. He is, after all, not a young man. He is to emanate energy for several hours to a global audience. He's sixty-four.

He's not quite as old as the other two candidates, but American politics is in a state of advanced decrepitude, a gerontocracy. Cooper puts on an amazing front. Nobody ever sees how vulnerable he is, with the plastic surgery, the workout routine, the teeth whitening, the hair dye.

But a sixty-four-year-old man aches at the best of times. A political campaign is like having two jobs and a dozen kids. It's like grabbing a live wire. It's so exhausting you don't have the energy to recognize the exhaustion. Every now and then, Cooper cannot help but allow himself to be seen. He is careful that it is only Mikey and Ren. The exposure of his vulnerability is strictly for the innermost of the inner team.

Ren and Mikey grip Cooper's liver-spotted arms as he guides his thin legs onto the bed. Mikey is talking to him like he would to a child: "One more push over the hill, buddy. Have a little rest and then you'll be ready to go, champ. You're going to sleep deeply and wake up like a refreshed giant."

"A refreshed giant?" Cooper mumbles.

"A giant refreshed."

From the bed, Cooper grips Mikey's hand in his. "Mikey, thanks for everything."

Mikey loves Cooper. He must love him. He's devoted the

key years of his life to the man, and it's not just the work. Cooper convinced him long ago that together they could save the republic. They've crossed the country two dozen times in each other's company. Mikey has raised Cooper, taught him how to be the person he now is. Cooper has raised Mikey, shown him the world. Ren beams down. They are like some perverse family, a mommy and a daddy and their sixty-four-year-old celebrity infant. Mikey and Ren tiptoe out and close the door behind them.

Ren takes Mikey by the hand and leads him down a long hallway. "Come with me," she says. "I've got to show you something." She leads him away from their hotel rooms, down the long, anonymous hallway with its chessboard-patterned carpet.

"Where are we going?"

"You'll see."

They go down three floors to a large emergency exit. Ren pushes it open and guides him through. They're outdoors. Across from the hotel, they can see the stadium parking lot, which is starting to fill with the partisan mobs screaming at each other, their red flares like small suns setting over the surging foam of placards. The military has prepared for violence, for the damage that the conventions witnessed. But the Ponds video is starting to reverberate already. A fresh batch of rage is starting to bloom.

"What are we doing out here?"

"Give me your phone so I can show you something."

He hands over his phone.

"You're fired." Ren says it the way a butcher might say that he's out of prime rib.

"What?"

"I'm firing you."

He's too stunned to say anything for a moment.

"We know you fucked Katie Danjou," Ren says. "We know that you insisted she have an abortion. You paid for it anyway. Never pay for these things, Mikey."

The circuits of Mikey's brain churn with strategy, but it's pointless. He knows. He's up against Sarah Ren. "Listen, if they knew, they would have already unloaded the book. If you fire me, they might figure it out. You'll bring attention. You'll bring scandal."

Ren smiles. "It's debate time. All scandals have passed their due date. You know that. It was the old man."

"Katie's dad?"

"The old Midwestern fuckers. Don't mess with them when they're on the war path. They're the real Sicilians on this earth. He put it all together from Katie's phone. He said he wouldn't go to the press if we dealt with you."

"So you're dealing with me this way? You think that will satisfy him?"

"You're talking to *me*, Mikey. You know I've thought through every angle, right? Listen, you're going to be fine."

"You're not actually going to keep my phone, are you?"

"I'm afraid so."

"You should have confiscated my dick instead."

Ren shrugs. "You're better with your phone, to be honest."

3:41 p.m., 360 Clinton Avenue, Brooklyn, NY

Ross was right. An afternoon in bed with her husband at least distracts from the imminent phone call from her editor in chief. Sex reminds her she's a person and that Zayn's a person. It's easy to forget when you think of yourself as egg and sperm attached to a couple of bank accounts.

Sometimes she can almost see the baby they're going to have. She can sense the presence, a package of lovely wonder.

The vision is not so much a face as a small tender body, a new human, *their* human. And this vision of a daughter—it is invariably a daughter—is always so close. All Martha has to do is reach over to gather her up, but she can't or she won't.

And a terrible guilt floods her: she cannot bring her daughter the first thing her daughter needs. She has a mother's guilt before she's a mother. Along with the guilt comes the envy, a palpable existential envy. She hates every new mother she sees, the yoga-panted Karens sipping their lattes as they push their Bugaboo strollers through the park, the expensive hippies with their front-facing slings taking their Australian shepherd COVID dogs for a walk, the old friends on Facebook posting shots from the delivery room.

She hides her bitterness from everyone, even from Zayn, but in private other people's pregnancies make her angry: Why should they be so lucky and not her? What do they have that she doesn't?

"Ever think about getting out?" Zayn asks.

They are lying naked next to each other. A ripple of panic courses through her body. Getting out of the marriage? Getting out of the apartment?

Zayn runs his hand through his coal-black hair. "A couple of students of mine have gone all digital. They've moved to Portugal."

Relief: he's thinking about getting out of the country.

Then her phone is buzzing and she reaches for it.

I guess it's in the Times, her source has texted.

What should she write back? It would be so much easier if she was already fired. As it is, she's still part of the *Times*.

I need you to know that I tried my best, she texts back.

We're all doing our best out here and it's not enough.

I know. I couldn't make them run it.

No. We both did what we could. I wish I could have done more.

You gave me everything I could have asked for. You did your part.

I'm going to miss America. BTW, I'd listen to your husband. Portugal is beautiful this time of year.

> 4:23 p.m., Embassy Suites by Hilton South Bend
> at Notre Dame, 1140 E. Angela Boulevard, South Bend, IN

In the daze of his downfall, Mikey watches the crowds amassing outside the Joyce Center among the rather lovely trees beside the parking lot, each side screaming at the other a vague inchoate version of, "You're not going to take away our freedoms!"

Is he part of the machinery? At some point he must have been proud to enter politics. He loves America and he has no idea what to do with his love.

On a campaign, more than in any other work, you meet America. You smell grease in gun-loving Texas towns, and you eat dry bagels in New York penthouses. You hear JPEGMAFIA blazing from the speakers outside an Amazon center, and you shake hands with Black ministers in front of churches pockmarked with bullets, and Iowa farmers usher you into barns to talk with them about the situation in Ukraine. You walk the tent cities of Los Angeles, and you warm yourself in factories rolling steel, and you refresh yourself at watermelon farms, and you amuse yourself in 3D animation studios where they're planning AI interactive characters. You see the sheer weirdness of charged freedom. Mikey has seen it, and now he sees it reduced to gangs in black masks who see and hear and smell and taste nothing but loathing and hatred.

Somewhere out of Mikey's dark corners bubble up his memories of Katie Danjou. Mikey met her right after she dropped out of her poli-sci PhD at Northwestern to work on the campaign. She was a beautiful soul, fragile and sensitive, but even for Mikey she had bought into the campaign too much. She pleaded with people on the street, warning of great dangers to the republic. Not that she was wrong. Katie Danjou was sweet. She was—in a true sense—idealistic. In the natural way she wore her hair, he should have known she was out of step, that her uncut face was un-social-media-ready. She didn't even have an Instagram account. He should have known it would all end in catastrophe.

He needs to find an Apple store. He has no phone and so no way to find an Apple store.

And then Nellie is standing there, holding something out in front of her. It's a new iPhone.

Mikey can't hide his gratitude. "They think of everything," he says.

"No, this is just from me," she says.

He rips the box open greedily. "Nellie thinks of everything."

"I want you to know that I'm the one who found out about Katie Danjou."

"I always thought it would be Ren."

"I became friends with Katie's dad. Good guy."

"Yeah, really good guy."

Nellie cocks her head slightly to the side. "What are you going to do now?"

He nods in the direction of the angry mobs in front of the Joyce Center. "I'm going to sit on the sidelines and watch my country burn to the ground."

Nellie leans over and grabs the back of his head and pulls him in for a kiss on the cheek. "Enjoy it," she says. "Soon enough you'll have to get back in the fight." She walks away, that most American of things, the killer with a heart of gold, a winner who wants to win the right way.

7:23 p.m., Comfort Suites, 52939 Route 933, South Bend, IN
Balfour turns the volume up on the debates as the candidates make their way to the stage. He hasn't been drinking today. He wants a clear head to see what he's done.

He wanted to know if he was willing to go all the way. Now he knows. He is.

He texts Max Sevre, even though his calls have been made, the connections drawn, the plans put into action.

You still want me to do what I'm here to do?

Absolutely, the master texts back. *Now is the time when violence has the maximum leverage. Give them a little push down the hill, so they'll run the rest of the way on their own.*

It's done.

Wonderful. Returning to Darwinian precepts. Everyone will once again return to the real question of this species.

The crowd inside has been handpicked not to be angry. You can tell as the camera pans over them. It must have taken the producers weeks to find two hundred and fifty Americans who don't want to assassinate the leaders of the other parties.

Everyone already believed it would be a debacle, even before Balfour's contribution. Presidential debates are always just people talking past each other. But now, what does one side have to say that's even meaningful to the other?

How many times has he watched the theater of presidential debates? It's always seemed so pointless, the competitive lying, the journalistic grandstanding, the inane questions followed by nonanswers.

As they come onstage, the three old men who want to be president, they seem like the most useless of all the useless old men who have wanted to be president. He hates their useless suits. He hates their useless smiles. He hates the way they wave their useless hands. He hates the stage they're gathering on. He hates the podiums they stand behind, the bullshit of the red, white, and blue bunting, the bullshit of the eagle seal. But now all the bullshit possesses the grandeur of an antique ritual. Somewhere, hidden inside all the bullshit, lies the belief in talking through problems, an assumption that isn't bullshit, that the powers in this world, to be legitimate, must submit to being called to account.

Kristen Welker sits between the three men. After welcoming the candidates and explaining the debate protocol, she asks the first question: "We've seen some disturbing footage today claiming that members of the military and intelligence services are preparing to exert control over the country to deal with growing violence. Let's start with you, Mr. Sherman. How would you deal with the violence?"

Cooper looks at the camera and begins: "I'm glad you asked, Kristen. I'm going to start with the obvious. We need wholesale reform of our electoral systems. Everybody knows that our political order is on its last legs. The good news is that reform is coming. The Maverick Party is the party of reform. But let me make one thing perfectly clear. The American people are not going to reform into a people with fewer rights. What we need, first and always, is—"

A howl pierces the room. It's coming from offstage. Sherman looks across with shock in his eyes, and the words die in his throat. Then a mob streams through the Joyce Center firing—bright flashes of automatic weapons, screams, and the camera shuts off.

American debate is over.

November 5

THE ELECTION

(76 days until)

8:17 a.m., Equinox Hotel, 33 Hudson Yards, Manhattan, NY
Voter turnout for the last election in the United States is 51.2 percent, not quite as low as 1996 when less than half of eligible Americans showed up, but in 1996 voter turnout was low because American politics didn't seem to matter all that much. During the last election in American history, voter turnout is low because American politics matters *too* much.

After the raids at the debate in Notre Dame, which killed seventeen and injured fifty-four, the threat of violence keeps the public away. An early voting site in a largely Black district in Georgia is firebombed. The solicitor general of Oregon is assassinated at her doorstep when leaving for a morning run. A gunfight breaks out in a line of voters in Arizona, an open-carry state.

But every election is a miracle, including the last election in the United States. The premise is beautiful even when the results are ugly. People count in an election. Everyone has a say, even if they don't want a say. Modern democracy began in the eighteenth-century Enlightenment in the United States, but its roots can be traced to the religious ideal that every soul is equal in the eyes of God, and that this truth of our basic dignity should find political reflection on earth.

Every election, aside from being a miracle, is also a nightmare. As a piece of work, it is a vast, inchoate, nearly impossible act of communication. Everyone of voting age, on roughly the same day, ticks a box beside a secret name. These secret boxes with their secret names must somehow, at once, be collected and collated and verified and tallied.

The election is not the process of voting. The election is an information system. And as Stalin said, "Those who cast the votes decide nothing. Those who count the votes decide everything." An election is not over when the votes are cast. An election is over when the media decides how the votes have been counted. The political class calls this "media certification."

The results come in like a traffic accident: a burst of sharp shock, then a lot of officials trying to trace out the mayhem and reckon with the causes. The chaos is exactly the expected chaos, the intentional chaos. Every state is subject to challenges. Any win by a Democrat or the Maverick Party in a state with a Republican legislature is being challenged. The right-wing solicitors general are lining up. Schoolyard stuff works. You justify your theft by shouting, "He stole first!" American politics is a schoolyard without teachers. Some children believe in the rules and some don't.

Mikey is smart—he goes to sleep at a normal time. The media won't decide who is president for at least a couple of days.

In the afternoon of the second day, Nellie shows up at Mikey's hotel door, her hair wet with November rain. He looks at her and thinks, *Like in the movies.* Cooper, she tells him, is flying to Hawaii to recover. The sheer volume of death threats has convinced him he isn't safe in New York.

"It's the end," Nellie says.

"You'll have to be more specific. The end of what?"

"The end of our ability to do anything." She comes into the hotel room.

They sit together for sixteen hours, like junkies of story, narrative addicts snacking with the television on, unable to sleep and then passing out in shallow rest that rustles over them like chop until another wave wakes them and they reach for the television remote or each other's hand, before the next pseudo-announcement of a pseudo-result to a pseudo-election in a pseudo-democracy. They sit on the bed, holding hands for hours on end, watching in silence.

"CNN is about to call it," Anderson Cooper finally says, and Mikey's hand squeezes Nellie's. Politics happens to everyone alone, no matter who they're in the room with.

Ten minutes later, Anderson Cooper gives an update: "Our call is inconclusive. I know that's not what any of you who have been waiting up want to hear, but the election is too close to call, or, John, is that really even the word?"

John King looks burdened by the information he has to impart; his mahogany voice is permeated with considered sadness. "We are at the point, Anderson, where we know what we know and what we don't know."

"So what do we know?"

"We know that the Democratic candidate has taken 38 percent of the national popular vote, and the Republican has taken 32 percent, and the Maverick Party has 30 percent. That's what we know. But none of that will matter much because . . ."

Here a map is rolled out.

"My Lord," Anderson Cooper says, "that looks like a quilt or something."

"Let me talk you through it."

"Please."

Nellie leans into Mikey's body, preparing for horror. She has a small frame. Her skin is white like the flesh of a poplar when you pull back the bark. *Martha's skin was so soft,* Mikey remembers, before John King pulls him back to the screen.

"So the red states here are, you know, like in other elections, red states, and the blue states are the same. You have California and New York that went blue and you have Idaho and Montana and the other Midwestern states that went red."

"So those are the easy ones?" Anderson says.

"These are the states that voted Republican with Republican legislatures and will send Republican electors to the electoral college, and states that are Democratic with Democratic legislatures that will send Democratic electors to the electoral college."

"So what are these green-and-red and green-and-blue ones?"

"So those are states that Cooper Sherman took."

"And why are they divided between red stripes and blue stripes?"

"Some of those states have Democratic legislatures and some of them have Republican legislatures."

"And why does that matter?" Anderson Cooper asks.

"Because, technically, legally, it is the state legislatures that approve the electors for the electoral college," John King answers.

"And whether they send Sherman electors is up in the air?"

"Everything's up in the air, Anderson, because if we look at these final bits here . . ."

"The purple in red and the purple in blue?"

"The purple in red is states where CNN has called the election for a Republican but there are claims of fraud or intimidation or recounts."

"And the purple in blue is states we've called for Democrats but with disputes?"

"You got it."

"Those are like old-fashioned Florida-recount states."

"Yes. Well, Florida was a straight recount. Some of these, like Georgia, are too close to call. Others, like Florida, are reporting illegalities and fraud. So it's . . ."

"It's a mess."

"It's a mess, Anderson."

Anderson Cooper blinks his eyes. The exhaustion, though carefully suppressed, is starting to show in a few slower eye movements, a tiny hesitation now and then. "John, do you think this is what the Founding Fathers intended?"

John King inhales deeply as his eyes narrow. This is the question that he has wanted to answer but hasn't been asked. "You know, Anderson, I would say no, but it's also fair to say that there have been chaotic elections in American history before."

"Like 2000. Like 2020."

"Like 1824 and 1828."

"Turn it off," Nellie says.

Mikey mutes the screen. History is disappointing when it happens. There you are, in a quiet room, in a changed room, lying surrounded by empty bags of pretzels and peanuts, confounded, wondering. Mikey looks at Nellie's raincoat, which hangs where it was tossed over a chair. There's a small silver brooch, an antique, Mikey thinks. It bears the slogan, *Though she be little she be fierce.*

Nellie looks dazed, like she's been punched in the mouth. Her gift for anticipation is morphing into torture. She tries to figure out where the world is going so she can improve it. Mikey wants to hold her close. What will happen? What can she do about it? A wheel in her mind is spinning. She can no longer process the future. If she can't figure out what will happen, what can she do about it? Her mind is fluttering as desperately as a pinned butterfly. The question she asks is not the one Mikey is expecting.

"Do you think we messed it all up?"

Who is the "we" in that question? Mikey thinks but doesn't say.

She means the Maverick Party because of her blossoming sense of guilt, but her question is the one the future will ask of the whole country. When the history books of this moment are written, they'll ask how a single generation of Americans managed to mess it all up. They had America. They had the most beautiful, powerful country in the world. America was theirs. And they squandered it—in the name of what? What did they sacrifice their country for? That part is unclear right now, a mystery for historians.

Mikey taps Nellie's back. "No," he eventually says. "It was already messed up."

"That map," Nellie says. "That map wouldn't look like it does without us. Without what we did."

"You mean the campaign?"

"What else?"

Mikey is unfocused. He needs proper sleep. He needs proper everything. He needs a proper meal. He needs a proper shower. He needs to call his mom. He needs something more than this shiny hotel room blued with flashes of talking heads. He doesn't know much at this point, but he knows he wants Nellie to stay. He knows that the moment she leaves the room, he will be utterly lost. She's going to leave, and soon, and it panics him.

"It was already messed up, Nellie. We fought against this. We fought against the absurdity of the system, we fought to *recognize* that the system is absurd. We lost but we fought. Besides, without us there'd just be two sides fighting over who won, not three."

Nellie sits up straight and pulls herself away from him.

Mikey is afraid to move.

Nellie turns and faces him like a warrior, firm in her movements, deliberate. "I want to live in a democracy," she says, staring at him. "I want to live in an American democracy. I'm *going to* live in an American democracy."

Mikey realizes that she is perhaps his favorite person in the world. It is bizarre but utterly natural that they have spent hours alone holding hands. He is falling in love at first sight with a woman he's known forever. "Yes, you will. We both will."

CNN is playing scenes of open violence now, street battles between masked gangs in black and masked gangs in camo. The closed captioning describes it as a street battle in Seattle, but Seattle merely provides the best footage. There are similar struggles in every major American city. The death toll is mounting. A member of the America First group mowed down five Black people in line while they were waiting to enter their church for a meeting. The Wilshire Boulevard Temple in Los Angeles was fortunately empty when it was bombed.

If there is to be no America, can there not, at the least, be Mikey and Nellie? Yet he also knows he could easily lose her. Is the threat of loss the source of love? Can we act *before* we lose everything rather than after?

Nellie doesn't look at him as she grabs her coat and slides into her shoes and walks out of his suite like an agent on a mission.

11:08 a.m., Wyndham French Quarter,
124 Royal Street, New Orleans, LA

The sex worker Balfour hired is from Laos or Cambodia or somewhere around there. He hasn't asked. The violence of the rioting on television doesn't seem to bother her. She is in the bathroom cleaning up.

Maybe she's used to political violence wherever she's from. Or maybe it's just part of life as a New Orleans hooker.

Gangs in black hoodies against gangs in camo—for the rest of the world, that's normal. That's the way things have always been, violence as a basic condition of human existence. Balfour is excited. The shit is finally going down.

"Did you ever go to rehab?" Balfour shouts to the bathroom.

"What?" the sex worker calls back.

"Rehab. Did you ever go to it?"

The young woman does not respond. He hears only the sound of running water. When she comes back, she is fully dressed in what he picked her up in: a short neon-pink skirt, a black leather jacket, hoop earrings. She can't be more than five feet, he figures. She has already taken the money from the dresser. She sits down beside him on the bed, watching the scenes of the riots in Chicago on Fox with cool indifference.

"In rehab, they tell you that there are low-bottom drunks and high-bottom drunks," Balfour says, "and it's basically a matter of taste, of character. It's not really high-functioning or low-functioning alcoholics. It's more a question of how much degradation you can take."

The woman whose time he has purchased does not acknowledge him, but there is a way she turns her body toward him that implies that she is listening.

"A high-bottom drunk realizes when they drive drunk the first time that they have a problem and have to fix it. A low-bottom drunk has to wake up naked and robbed in an alley to stop drinking, and sometimes not even then."

Balfour sits up in bed, splintering the back of his neck into a vast world-consuming headache, and looks around the floor for a place to throw up. There isn't a place so he doesn't throw up. He drank everything last night. The sex worker ups the volume on Sean Hannity.

". . . One thing for sure is that this election is far from over.

Far, far from over. And, you know, people on the left, sneering liberals, you know they are going to say: 'Well, the Republican candidate, he didn't win the popular vote.'" Hannity slaps the desk in front of him. He looks like he might explode. He shouts, "That's not how this works! We have never been a democracy. Mob rule was not the vision the founders had for this country. We are a constitutional republic. And if that means that some people's votes count for more than other people's votes, then suck it up, that's the way it is. There are reasons for that.

"We have become the greatest country in the world not because we are a democracy, but because we are a republic. So remember that in the struggle ahead, when liberals tell you about how many votes their guy got, or how many votes Cooper Sherman got, it doesn't matter. We are America. You and I are America."

Fox cuts to an ad for Carl's Jr., erotically fatty hamburgers filmed in the highest possible definition.

"Which are you?" the sex worker asks.

"Which what?"

"Which kind of drunk, low-bottom or high-bottom?"

Balfour considers his worst moments. The car crash in that mall in Dallas. Punching his father in the face. That time he woke up in a park in Tulsa. He lost women and friends, but they had been women and friends worth losing. He has always been grateful to booze for giving him the strength to punch his father in the face. Balfour has mostly hurt others rather than himself.

"I'm a lucky drunk," he says. "Blessed by God. Like America. Things always work out for me. Things always work out for America. Don't know why."

The sex worker switches the television over to BBC. Rory

Stewart, with his goofy British face, all concern and ears, is speaking on Zoom. He has the calming distance of a civics teacher explaining the basics of the democratic system. "The American system doesn't properly possess a mechanism for redoing a presidential election. So I'm afraid that on January 3 a new Congress will be sworn in. On January 6, they will have to certify the election if at all possible, and on January 20 they will inaugurate a new president."

Reeta Chakrabarti looks down at a page of notes. These are not ordinary political questions she is asking. "And what does that certification process look like, Rory?"

"That's hard to say, Reeta, when so many factors are in play. There are so many competing claims of illegitimacy in individual cases and nobody knows how that sense of illegitimacy will spread. If a Republican state legislature decides not to count a Democrat's electoral votes, does a Democratic state legislature do the same in retaliation? How many of these recounts and legal cases will even be completed by January 6?"

"I mean, I don't mean to push, Rory, but I actually need answers to those questions," Chakrabarti says.

"I just don't want to speak about what we don't know, Reeta. One thing we know is this: the Republicans will have a slim House majority, so they will set the terms of the certification. I also know that the Twentieth Amendment spells out the line of succession relatively clearly, so that if, God forbid, they can't certify on January 6, which they have to do, the Speaker of the House will have the nuclear codes."

"We're hearing, Rory, about the possibility of a contingent election."

"Ah yes, a contingent election. I'm afraid I know very little about that, and I say that because *nobody* knows much about contingent elections. The last one was in 1824."

"How did that end?"

"Well, I will say that the man who won the popular vote didn't become the president. That was Andrew Jackson. But it does look increasingly possible."

"Uncharted waters."

"Uncharted waters at night," Rory Stewart says.

The sex worker turns off the BBC and smiles at Balfour, the smile of a busboy cleaning off a table.

"Hold on." Balfour fishes out another hundred-dollar bill, which she accepts with a look of skepticism. "Go," he says. "I'm feeling lucky."

3:48 p.m., 360 Clinton Avenue, Brooklyn, NY

Martha hangs up the phone. She half staggers into the kitchen, where Zayn is doom-scrolling. He hasn't even turned on the kitchen light. Martha is vibrating. Her soul is crackling. She is a traitor, the traitor who got away with it. She has what she has always wanted and it couldn't be worse.

"They fired you," Zayn says, sensing her discomposure.

"They promoted me."

He laughs. "The *New York Times* gets it right!"

"They're putting me on democracy watch."

His brow furrows. "What democracy is there left to watch?"

"It's Enterprise," she says. "Big stories. I think Malcolm has decided that we're going to chronicle the end of American democracy."

"But this is a promotion? More money?"

"No, but I'm not going to be on SecureDrop duty anymore. No more tip line. They're going to bring the hardware back to the office. I'll be a reporter again, you know, like out in the world."

Zayn nods but doesn't move from his phone. Martha goes

into the bedroom and turns on MSNBC. She can't keep track of how many secrets are in her possession, who she is keeping them for, on whose behalf, and why. It is hard to keep track of things collapsing. Somehow she's won. She doesn't know how she's won but she's won. The idea that she won, that this, today, this is what she had craved, is so ludicrous she laughs.

Rachel Maddow has her head in her hands. She has a stack of law books beside her, like props. Laurence Tribe is suffering with her. He looks like a man whose house just burned down.

"Talk me through this one more time, Laurence."

"Okay, so, there is a provision in the Constitution for exactly this scenario, the Twelfth Amendment, for when nobody has taken the electoral college, when nobody has the 270."

"Okay, and we're pretty sure nobody's going to get there."

"And at this point, because the Republicans control the House, they will control certification, and they will probably propose a contingent election. So, even if, somehow, Cooper Sherman decides to throw his votes to the Democrats, or if he threw his electoral college votes to the Republicans, it might work, because the House would possibly vote to certify. But I don't think they will. I think they'll insist on a contingent election. It will look fairer."

"Fairer?" Maddow throws her hands up in desperation. "What's *fairer* got to do with this?"

"It will look fairer, Rachel, because it corresponds to the actual words of the Twelfth Amendment. Nobody has the numbers, so it would be unfair to Maverick Party voters. So—"

"Okay, okay, okay. I think I understand this. I think I'm okay to that point. So tell me about the contingent election."

Laurence Tribe takes a deep breath. He's embarrassed for the legal system he has spent his life studying. "Okay, there hasn't been a contingent election in two hundred years, but the rules are still in place. There are two elections—one for the president in the House, and one for the vice president in the Senate. In the House, they take the top three winners in the electoral college and then it's a vote by state."

"And each state has to call its electoral college roll?"

"No, Rachel, this is really crucial: each state delegation gets one single vote."

Maddow's eyes widen in horror. "So . . ."

"That's right. Wyoming has as much say as California."

Maddow quickly grabs a map. "So it will be a Republican landslide on those terms."

"Unless you can convince Republican legislators to vote against the Republican candidate."

"Which you can't." Rachel Maddow looks straight into the camera. "So, America, that is how you get a president who didn't win the popular vote and who didn't even win the electoral college."

Martha turns off the screen. She finds herself thinking that it's going to be a good year to be a scholar of the election of 1824. She wonders if any of them are television-ready.

Zayn in the next room shouts: "You read this about a contingent election?"

What a job I have, Martha thinks. Americans need democracy explained to them like toddlers or Alzheimer patients: *This is your country. This is how it works.* Illusions are dying. And she is one of the explainers. She's late.

She shouts back: "Am I a bad person?"

January 6

THE CONTINGENT ELECTION

(14 days until)

T he Battle of Portland is still raging, even though the National Guard has stepped in to restore order. Police forces and employees from the Department of Corrections and even bands of veterans have joined forces. Often it is unclear which side is which, or if there are any sides. It's less a battle for control over the city than a prolonged urban riot. The suburbs have emptied into the country.

Portland is only one flashpoint. There are street battles everywhere in America. As Frank Bruni puts it in the *New York Times*, "The mass shootings are linking up." An official number of deaths from political violence since the election doesn't exist, but the *Times*'s best estimate—a running tally on its home page—is 857. If the violence continues at this rate, America will pass the technical threshold for a civil war—a thousand deaths a year—by the time of the inauguration.

Chinese jets are testing Taiwanese airspace, and huge naval forces are amassing on their manmade islands in the South China Sea. The president shipped out fifteen hundred RQ-11 Raven drones in the last gasp of his lame-duck presidency, but China knows, everybody knows, that the world is about to be lonely.

Meanwhile, the Republicans will soon complete their entirely legal, entirely constitutional takeover of the US government, without a popular mandate or an electoral college victory. Ordinarily, today would be the date of the certification. It's not. It's a rare but not unique moment in American history. It's a contingent election.

Mikey finds himself, as everyone who ever enters politics eventually does, lying on a random bed in a random hotel, utterly powerless, watching history unfold without the ability to alter its unfolding by a fingernail. He decided, for reasons even he doesn't understand, to be in Washington for the end of American democracy, though like everybody else in the world, he's watching the decline and fall on television. Politics in the twenty-first century is something that happens to you when you're in front of a screen, alone, in a room.

Still, Mikey's glad the room he's in is in Washington. The destruction of everything he's ever loved is making him sentimental. The fall of the republic brings out strange schoolhouse dreams and his awareness of his own failure to live up to those dreams. All the men who died in World War II—the Americans of Mikey's generation have failed to live up to that sacrifice. Lincoln at the graves of the Union dead, preaching that government of the people, by the people, for the people, should not perish from the earth—Mikey's generation has failed them. As Benjamin Franklin left the Philadelphia Constitutional Convention in 1787, he is said to have met a lady in the street who asked him, "What kind of government do we have, a republic or a monarchy?" and he answered, "A republic, if you can keep it." The Americans of Mikey's generation haven't kept it. The wound is real.

He has the phone Nellie bought him, but she won't take his calls. He's worried. There's a mass democratic resistance forming, filling up with educated idealists, educated idealists like Nellie. The offices of Palantir, two days after they announced the sale of general-surveillance artificial intelligence software to the Department of Justice, had a bomb set off in their lobby. Two employees were killed and three were wounded. Mikey's first thought was of Nellie and Dom. He couldn't shake the suspicion that they were involved.

        12:15 p.m., 360 Clinton Avenue, Brooklyn, NY
Martha steels herself to make the call. It's her job. She must be professional. Like any salesperson, working up to the call *is* the work of the call.

Zayn's in the kitchen, so she's making the call from the bedroom. In the background, Fox News plays the breakdown. To procrastinate a little further, Martha turns to C-SPAN. She can't bear to listen to the news anymore, but she can't stop watching it either, so she turns the volume off and leaves the screen on. The cameras are outside the House of Representatives. They are filming the stream of happy Republicans entering the chamber. Mitch McConnell is smiling and talking. The closed captioning reads: *Well, this has happened before, and Andrew Jackson conceded gracefully, so we should take a lesson from our ancestor on this one.*

The end of democracy became normal quickly. Its possibility, and then its inevitability, seeped into the fabric of life with little to slow it down. The moment it became clear that the election would never be resolved, and the will of the people would not determine the leadership of the country, the justifications kicked in.

The contingent election has at least a patina of legitimacy. Nobody believes that it is fair. Nobody believes that it is democratic to select your leader from the votes of individual states' congressional delegations. Everybody understands that the process of the contingent election is an absurd holdover from a rural eighteenth-century society that should have no bearing on twenty-first-century urban society, but at least it's a system. And nobody has a better system to suggest.

As long as there is a system, if you don't think about it too much—if you keep your eyes firmly half-shut, if you forget that your vote doesn't count, that your rights are evaporating, that your control over the people who control you has vanished—you can accept almost any outcome. In a state of lulled half forgetting, a suspicion ripens: that democracy isn't working anyway, that all politicians are filth, that maybe, in the end, given the circumstances, it's better this way.

And so the soul heals around the scar as the wound bites.

But to see it happening, to see it taken away in front of your eyes, is another matter.

On C-SPAN, the reporter, whose face is off-camera, asks a question about the lone Republican who opposed the contingent election, Beth Link. She was assassinated two days ago by professionals outside her home in Georgetown.

"It is a tragedy, part of all this liberal chaos that has overwhelmed the country" McConnell says. "And the first thing that this new administration will do is restore order."

The phone call is less grotesque than the news, so she makes it.

Mikey answers: "Nellie?"

"No, it's Martha."

"Oh, sorry. It said *Unknown Caller*." He sounds sad at the other end of the line.

"New phone," she says, and she's not lying. The Enterprise section has given her a new phone with better security settings. They are operating under the assumption of government surveillance now. "Who's Nellie?"

There's a sigh on the other end of the line. "She's a friend of mine and I'm trying to get in touch with her. What's up?"

Martha needs to warm him up: "I was hoping you could explain all this to me."

"End of the republic," he says. "Obvious to everyone."

"No, but this contingent election. What do you think is going to happen?"

"We'll never know. That's the brilliance of it. The House's jurisdiction committee has set the terms. It's a cakewalk now. They'll just walk in the votes state by state."

"Why can't we see it?"

"The jurisdiction committee set the rules. They've decided that the media is the enemy, in agreement with the bulk of the American people. So they set two rules. The first is that the contingent election will be held behind closed doors, and the second is that the vote will be confidential. So there will be no record of what happens in that room. That's by design."

"Democracy dies in darkness," Martha says.

"That's your competitor," Mikey reminds her.

"So why are the Democrats going along with it?"

"What can they do?"

"Well, one thing I heard"—she tries to render this as casually as possible—"is that Cooper could shift his electoral college votes to the Democrats in exchange for, I don't know, secretary of state or something."

"He couldn't do that, and besides, the Republicans are setting the rules of the game, so it doesn't matter. There is no electoral college anymore. As stupid as that system was, it reflected some kind of popular will. Now it will be the state delegations who decide. But that's not why you called, is it?"

"Sorry?" She tries to act confused.

"You called to see if I still know anybody on Cooper's staff and if I know anything about the backroom machinery."

She thinks about denying it, then says, "Yeah, that's why I'm calling." It's *one* of the reasons she's calling.

"The Democrats aren't putting up a fight. Their only

chance to make a rush for power was not to appear, so there wouldn't be a quorum. But look, you're watching C-SPAN, right?"

"I am." On the screen, Chuck Schumer arrives with his bodyguards. He is surrendering his phone outside the doors of the Senate. "Why is he going along with it all?"

Mikey laughs chokingly. "To preserve the value of the institutions. Sorry, no info here on any last-minute backroom deal. I'm sorry to be rude. Everything I love is dying today." He hangs up.

Martha watches the screen. There is in her, against all reason, a measure of hope. It's like when a ship goes down and as you're drowning, you must think that some miracle is coming on the horizon.

On her new phone, a text arrives from someone she thought she would never hear from again. It's her source: *I tried to tell you.*

1:33 p.m., 1029 Vermont Avenue NW, Washington, DC
Balfour is back at Stan's. Stan's is different. Balfour is different. America is different. The world is different.

Washington is in lockdown, and negotiating the streets requires tact and courage. It's unlikely that an American soldier would shoot him, but the troops are keeping their badges covered. They let him move around, though. In his rumpled suit, left on a bunch of floors over the past few days, and his briefcase, he looks the full Washingtonian: part bureaucrat on the way up and part politician on the way down.

The bar at this hour is confirmed drinkers only, he and two Black men, one older, one younger, both in suits as rumpled as his own. They're watching the locked door of Congress on a screen over the bar playing CNN with the volume off.

Behind that door, Balfour's side is winning. He sips his brandy and coffee. He's a winner. He doesn't yet feel he's a winner, but it's the only word that suits him. He's a winner. He's winning. Soon the leaders of the free world will come out and tell him he's won.

Meanwhile, a string of texts from Max Sevre arrives:

I need you to come to Washington.

Come when I call, for the rewards are at hand.

We've won and the Emperor will require ninjas as well as samurai.

It seems ridiculous to watch a closed door, though it would be ridiculous to watch a meteor hitting the earth too.

"I'm glad they're doing it like that," the older Black man says to the younger. "It's like a slaughterhouse. I don't want to know where my fucking sausage comes from."

"We gotta know, don't we? We've got to know what our government is made up of, what's done in our name."

"It's not done in my name."

"Still, I want to know *how* they're ripping me off."

"You'll never know. Not you and a dozen like you. You think they let the likes of you and me know they're ripping you off, or how, or why?"

"I suppose that's right."

They drink their drinks. They aren't hiding. They're having gin and tonics. Balfour orders a Dewar's and soda. Why not? Why ever not?

"Can I ask you?" the younger man says. "Was it always this shitty, or is this normal? As an older man to a younger man, tell me. Give me the measure of your wisdom."

The older man clears a space at the bar in front of him. He points down as he makes his argument. "You read how much more a white vote counts than a Black vote in this whole contingent-election scheme?"

"I didn't," the younger responds.

"1.7 times. A white vote counts 1.7 times more than a Black vote, and the president isn't the president the people of the United States chose."

"Three-fifths clause."

"Worse. They made it worse, man."

"Point?"

"If it ever changes, they just change it back."

The younger man receives a notification on his phone. He reaches over the bar to the remote control and raises the volume on the television.

"So it's the decision we all expected," Wolf Blitzer is saying. "The Republican delegates have selected the Republican nominee as president and he will be inaugurated on January 20."

The two Black men look at each other with nothing to say, then peer down at their drinks.

A small jolt passes through Balfour. It is the winning rising up in him. The power and the glory are his. He fishes in his pocket for a hundred-dollar bill, which he slams on the bar. He needs to go outside even more than he needs that Dewar's and soda.

To the frosty Washington air, he opens his chest, he opens his throat, he opens his mouth, he releases a howling war whoop. The sound reverberates into a silent, terrified city that is his.

January 20

THE INAUGURATION

(the day)

The modern inauguration ceremony is not a requirement of the Constitution. The Democrats do not need to be filtering onto the stage outside the Capitol building. They are, though. They still believe, to the point of their permanent irrelevance, in the rituals of American public life.

Washington is still in lockdown, as it has been since the contingent election. The police and the military have asked for people to stay home, but the man who is about to be president went on Twitter the night before and, under a picture of the Capitol, declared, "It's time to celebrate America becoming great again. Patriots, come join me! Tell them I sent ya!"

Martha has been crying, off and on, since the contingent election. How is she supposed to live in this country with all that she's done, with all that she's carrying? She watches the pre-inauguration on Fox, which is in effect a state broadcaster at this point. Since the certification, it has been the only reliable source of information on the inner workings of the Republican Party. They are the only press the Republicans will speak to. The Republicans are the only ones in Washington who matter.

Ainsley Earhardt is smiling on the screen as she describes the expected arrival of the president-elect. Sean Hannity pops up and Martha raises the volume. Hannity looks almost nervous. On his alabaster block of a face, there's a look of, if not shock, then *How did it come to this?* He is making an attempt at beaming, like he's happy, but one of the reasons he's so good on television is that he can't hide his emotions, even though he tries to.

"So I hear you've seen an early draft of the president-elect's speech?" Earhardt says cheerfully.

"I have, and I have to say, Ainsley, that this is not a speech that is going to please our liberal countrymen, and I emphasize that they *are* our countrymen, because now is the time for everyone to acknowledge that we are one country and we have one president, as a constitutional republic, even if you don't like the way he became president."

"So what's in the president's speech?"

"It is a call for unity, but it's also a plan for strength, Ainsley. The president has recognized that strength is what we need in order to oppose these liberal gangsters and their enablers in the Democratic Party, who are against the rule of law, and who are ripping this country apart. This country has decided that it's a constitutional republic, not a multicultural democracy, and that question, if you listen to the speech carefully, has been answered for good."

"For good?"

Hannity nods gravely. "The time has come for peace at any price. That's in the speech. Peace at any price."

Ainsley flashes a fake smile. "Well, peace sounds good."

10:59 p.m., 1029 Vermont Avenue NW, Washington, DC
The Mall is lined with military checkpoints, but all of Washington is broken up by blast-proof gates. The US Marines are in control of the city, though under whose command is unclear.

Balfour has two all-access tickets. A twenty-three-year-old blonde is with him, but he holds her pass. If it was around her neck, she might walk away into the small milling crowd. The only people allowed on the Mall for the inauguration have passes. The RNC has been selling them on its website, but the president-elect has been selling them on his website too. The technical distinctions between the RNC and the president-elect's businesses are no longer relevant. The lines between his persona and his businesses and the Republican Party and the US government are blurring further with every passing hour.

Balfour didn't buy his tickets. They are political gifts—that's why they're red. The president has asked that everyone wear red. Balfour's been drinking Coors Light with lime, and with Coors Light with lime you don't count how many beers you've had but how many times you've had to piss, and he's had to piss three times. The young woman at his side is a student at George Washington University Law School. She might do well in the administration, depending.

"You want to get inside the halls of power, don't you?" He puts his unwelcome arm around her waist as they lean over to have their badges scanned.

"I've always wanted to attend an inauguration."

"Come with me, come with me." Balfour half dances around the men with guns, into the addled empty space of the Mall. There are usually so many people at inaugurations, but now only a thousand or so are crammed near the stage.

Balfour whispers something into the woman's ear.

"That's gross, and besides, you're too drunk."

"I may be drunk, madam, but I'm integrated into this administration," he says. "And in the morning I shall be at least somewhat sober."

"Can you really get inside the Capitol?" she asks.

"All the offices are empty. It will be cool. We'll have a story. What we were doing on the day America was restored to strength."

He giddily drags her through the crowd by the hand. Her reluctance is only partial. She seems to understand that in the new system, if you want to go where the guy with the pass is going, you play along.

The Democrats shift in their chairs. They agreed to attend the inauguration "for the good of the country," and in the hopes that the ceremony might lead to a decline in the violence that is wracking the nation.

The street violence is still widespread. No city is untouched. The riots in Chicago grow every day. Small groups have taken to raiding small towns in Illinois. A white power group organized a "Triumph of European Civilization" rally in Austin, in which a convoy of trucks drove into the heart of the city. Protesters met the convoy with machine guns and Molotov cocktails. Eight people were killed.

The military has been ordered to barracks in Texas and California. Nobody can say who is in control of either the police or the military, and many of them have disengaged. They've been sent to secure certain public sites, but the crowds are too big.

The physical violence is only a portion of the disorder. A digital underground, DUX, has already formed. Images of ducks are now symbols of resistance. "They have the guns and the electoral college," their only communiqué states, "but we have the machines." The RNC website never stays up longer than a few hours. DUX attacks businesses that are pro-Republican. Publix has had its entire logistical chain annihilated. Seniors in Florida have started shoplifting from food depots. The governor of Kentucky takes to publicly begging for the restoration of their water-processing plant. A number of Democratic members of Congress have declared themselves part of the resistance and have gone underground, appearing primarily in darkened social media videos.

The promise of a return to order is faint.

The president-elect has already announced through Fox that he plans to make his daughter-in-law attorney general.

The Democrats onstage had imagined that their presence at the inauguration might lower the temperature. It hasn't. The crowd has one last chance to own the libs, and the thousand or so partisans allowed near the stage are shouting, "Lock 'em up!" at the Democrats who have decided to go down with the ship of US institutions. The crowd keeps chanting even though they've already won. They have nostalgia too. They will miss the institutions they are destroying, and part of them realizes this.

12:01 p.m., Hilton Garden Inn,
2020 Richmond Highway, Arlington, VA

In a hotel by the airport, Mikey prepares himself a massive drink and watches CNN. Jake Tapper is speaking: "The day of an inauguration is always a solemn day. But this inauguration is more solemn than most. The tradition of the peaceful transition of power has united Americans for centuries, yet now it seems that even this has been consumed in the partisan fires. Oh, and here, here is the president-elect, who is . . ."

Mikey mutes the television. He cannot stand sound with the sight of the president. It's either one or the other.

On his phone, a message from Cooper: *Fuck.*

He texts back: *Fuck.*

Cooper is in Hawaii with Ren, broken by the loss. Candidates, in defeat, are destroyed in a way that few people are ever destroyed. At a minimum, he won't be able to get out of bed for three weeks. Ren can only help so much. Eventually Cooper will find something else to do. That's money. If there is no US anymore, Cooper's situation won't change much.

There the new president stands, shaking hands with the last elected American president. The face of the incoming president has changed since the election. The etched fury that had stamped its presence across a couple billion dollars' worth of advertising is resting now in self-satisfied assurance. The man now has, Mikey thinks, the same face of the dictators and pseudo-dictators of this world, the Putins, the Erdoğans, the Kims—oddly relaxed, saturated with entitlement, complete in the knowledge that only *his* desires register. These men have placeholders for faces. Now the world is seeing the American version. There is the old order shaking hands with the new regime, the republic welcoming in a king. The new president is America's abusive father, and like so many abused children, Americans have rallied to their abuser. Maybe America was always a dysfunctional family, ever since Thomas Jefferson and his kids. Jefferson looked at his own offspring and submitted them to be property.

The president is the lord commander now. His family is beside him, gleeful, weighing up all the goodies they'll be able to enjoy. The new president has changed the meaning of the past as well as the future: the people driven to the new world, wretched and rich alike, had come for the chance at free land on which you could do what you like. The new president represents impunity. That is what liberty has come to mean to its loudest defenders—the ability to do what you want to other people without consequences. That's what America means now.

Two hundred and fifty years isn't bad, Mikey texts Martha. The scene reminds him of their time together. The best years of his life are over. He doesn't have a job. He's not married. He doesn't have children.

We should talk, she texts back.

We are talking. How's your end of the country going?

Don't joke, Martha writes.

A part of me is relieved. Nothing to fight for anymore. Hope was misplaced.

That was always your problem. You were always too proud for hope.

Mikey watches the old ritual eviscerating itself. The Supreme Court justice holds out a holy book. The leader of the free world puts his left hand on it and raises his right. The crowd behind him is trying to smile. Everyone must smile to please the new president now. The old words come out rustily, ridiculously. The man whose word means nothing is swearing an oath to end the stretch of American history when oaths meant something. "So help me God"—will anyone ever hear those words again?

Mikey looks down at a new text from Martha: *I'm pregnant with your child.*

Life goes on, inconveniently.

The last elected president of the United States steps to the podium. "My fellow citizens, our long national nightmare is over. The time has come for strength and unity."

Andrew's Acknowledgments

Thank you to my partner in writing this book, Stephen Marche, for being an awesome storyteller and visionary.

To Zach Graumann, my campaign manager on the presidential race, whose stories and recollections form the backbone of this book. If you want the scoop on the real campaign, his book *Longshot* is a must-read.

To Johnny Temple and Akashic Books, for being such a collaborative publishing partner. You all are a pleasure to work with for any author. To my agent, David Larabell, who believed in this book from the first time I raised the idea, and the rest of the team at CAA.

To everyone who supported my presidential campaign—I treasure our time together and am still trying to make our hopes for the world come true. And to everyone who believes in and supports the Forward Party—you are the real-life Mavericks, only more wholesome and clean-cut.

Thank you to my wife Evelyn and my boys, Christopher and Damian, for believing in me and motivating me to do more. Dad loves you.

Stephen's Acknowledgments

Thank you to Andrew, for being the best possible collaborator, and for his courage and decency and his willingness to face reality when so many won't. To Zach Graumann, for always being willing to pick up the phone. To Naben Ruthnum, for his writing advice. To Johnny Temple and everyone at Akashic Books, for their hard work and dedication to this project. To PJ Mark, for his strategy. To my wife, for putting up with me while we wrote this.

I am particularly grateful to all the sources who helped me understand the mechanisms of the world but who desire to remain anonymous. Thank you.

...as we trudge...

...as we trudge...

clint boshears

Cannon Gate Publishers, Inc.
LITTLE ROCK

Printed in the United States of America
10 9 8 7 6 5 4 3 2 1

This is a work of fiction. All the characters and events
portrayed in this book are fictional, and any similarity
to real people or incidents is strictly coincidental.

Project Editor: Jody McNeese Keene

The paper used in this publication meets the minimum
requirements of the American National Standard for Information Sciences—
Permanence of Paper for Printed Library Materials, ANSI Z39.48-1984.

To Cynthia, Bowden, Shannon, and Jessica, who nourished me with love and comfort; and the many friends who encouraged and helped me write this manuscript.

~1~

My name is Father Clayton James. I am a Roman Catholic priest commonly known as "Father Clay." At Calvary, a Catholic cemetery, I had just completed the final blessing and sprinkling of holy water on the casket of the deceased. Resting on the coffin was a small bronze crucifix. Along with me, two gravediggers, draped in brown camouflaged ponchos against the rain, were the only people present. One was seated on the backhoe, and the other leaned on his shovel handle. They were waiting for me to depart so they could lower the casket and close the grave.

A mesmerizing drone of rain splattered on the tent canopy covering the open grave. A plain wooden coffin covered in light gray cloth sat atop the casket's lowering device. The mound of dirt that had been dug from the grave was covered with an artificial grass mat, and there were two rows of empty metal folding chairs. This comprised the mortuary's "setup." Only a chill from the January shower broke the trance.

As I was walking away from the gravesite and almost beyond earshot, I turned my head and overheard one of the cemetery workers ask, "Who was this guy, anyway?"

The other replied, "There were no mourners, even family, so I reckon that he was just some good-for-nothing who never amounted to anything. Good God! He's probably better off dead. After all, what's a man like that ever get out of life?"

My eyes drifted to a gray granite tombstone close by and I noticed the blank space after the birth date where the person's mate had not yet died, confirming the nothingness, the emptiness in that space which morbidly seemed to agree with the cemetery workers' appraisal of a meaningless life.

The cemetery was about twenty acres large and had been started soon after the Civil War. By this time of year, the many giant oaks had lost all their leaves. They reminded me of the loneliness and nakedness of mankind in the Garden of Eden. The setting made me more aware of the depression and anxiety that came with the dawn of my day and lasted until I passed out somewhere in the cobwebs of my mind.

The dead man had been with a traveling circus in town when he died suddenly. The show was departing that day, and the management had left the body along with a sufficient donation to the Bishop's burse. They had requested that the deceased receive a Catholic burial, so the Catholic cemetery got the call, and they, in turn, passed it to the Bishop's office. The Bishop called the rectory and left instructions that I was to perform the graveside burial.

In the beginning of my priestly career I had looked forward to funerals early in the day. They gave me an excuse to drink "before the sun was over the yardarm." Now an alibi was no longer necessary.

As a result of my indiscriminate past with the bottle, I had been assigned by the Bishop to live at the cathedral rectory. My immediate superiors were to be the rector and a semi-retired monsignor who would substitute at mass when needed. Unlike these two brother priests at the rectory, I was not in very good standing with my bishop. In the old country, my malady would be called "the failing." In this country, I am called an alcoholic.

Once, I had been advised by a lay person I met at an AA meeting to use grape juice instead of wine for consecration. Rome had approved this for alcoholic priests. But, being of Irish descent, redheaded, and somewhat stubborn, the idea of using grape juice for the Blood of Christ was not only unthinkable but also unholy.

Just three weeks previously, I had returned from an imposed six-month leave of absence at a recovery center for alcoholic priests. I had received my primary detoxification from alcohol followed by an intensive secondary instructional treatment. Now forty-one years old, I had experienced this humiliating process twice. The Bishop's rule was that, after two attempts at sobriety in treatment centers, if a priest started drinking again, he would be sent to a monastery for an extended period of mandatory sobriety. Failure in the face of this remedy would bring on forced retirement from the priesthood.

So I had agreed to the treatment and participated in the rigors of rehabilitation at the center. This included two AA meetings a week in town with the lay people. The meetings came at the end of long days which began at five A.M. The endless days of meetings and lectures and draining sessions made staying awake and being alert at the evening meetings extremely difficult. With only one hour of quiet time daily and Sundays free, inattention and depression had begun to overtake me.

In this state, I had become filled with contempt for the lay people who had gotten sober around me. They cussed, smiled, and laughed a lot. But what was really hard on my hammered ego was when they commented about my condition and made suggestions about my life being "powerless, unmanageable, insane, and without spirituality."

They had this ridiculous acronym, HALT: Don't get too Hungry, Angry, Lonely, or Tired. Another was EGO: Easing God Out. They also had a dumb quote from the last paragraph of the Big Book that said, "We shall be with you in the Fellowship of the Spirit, and you will surely meet some of us as you trudge the Road of Happy Destiny."

This was not only inane but also insulting. None of that applied to me. After all, I was an ordained priest, and I knew that my station in the prestigious hierarchical pyramid was separate and above the common lay people.

Arriving at my parked car in the cemetery, I fumbled for the keys in my pocket. The cold rain continued at its steady pace. I had trouble closing my umbrella and was half drenched by the time I got inside and closed the door.

It was eleven in the morning as I began the drive back to the rectory. I was beginning to shiver in my wet clothes when I remembered the half bottle of wine used in the consecration at mass. It was in the briefcase beside me on the front seat. The chill from the cold rain had soaked bone deep through my wet clothes. I surely wasn't going to stop and buy a bottle of vodka, as I would have done in the past. That would be foolish. But just one drink of altar wine to prevent a chill wouldn't be. Besides, this was medicinal.

–2–

Pounding pressure gripped my head as my eyes watered and blinked at the early morning sun. I was in my car. I recognized the back of the rectory as I pulled myself up. "My God!" I thought with familiar despair. "Where have I been since the funeral?"

My head was about to split. Cold sweat covered my forehead. A knot clutched my gut, and all I could think of was the ice-cold beer in the rectory refrigerator. I knew that would slake my parched mouth. I could feel the cool liquid as it filled my mind. I could sense the comfort and ease that would fill my body and mind.

With trembling hands I opened the car door and swayed toward the rectory. The six-pack of cold beer was right where I knew it would be. My hands shook severely as I pulled two beers out of the pack. I noticed a tinge of blood on the tip of my index finger. My fingernails, chewed down to the quick, made it difficult to open the tab on the can. With the snap of the tab I tilted the cold can straight up and sucked it dry. The carbonated, bitter bite soothed…calmed. Ahh, this was the answer. Now I could think.

As I was about to sit down at the kitchen table, the rector walked in and said that the Bishop wanted me in his office at eleven that morning. Immediately, I knew I was caught and couldn't lie my way out of this one. I asked the rector, "What happened?"

"You were supposed to officiate at the marriage of your niece last night at six o'clock."

Instantly, realizing I had forgotten the wedding, the feeling of impending doom that I had awakened with turned into stark terror. At the same time, pangs of remorse fell on me like a crushing waterfall. Attacked by the implosion of my own devices, I felt completely powerless. Without the aid or help of anyone, I had inflicted this terrible embarrassment on myself, one of the greatest sins a self-obsessed person can commit.

It was ten o'clock and my hand was beginning to tremble again as I attempted to shave. I needed a couple more beers but didn't dare drink as much as a drop. My hazel eyes looked as if they would hemorrhage any minute. I combed through my disheveled red hair. My once fair skin was beginning to have red splotches, and my face looked as if it were permanently blushing. My six-foot, one hundred and seventy-five pound frame seemed to be sagging from wear, tear, and the constant exhaustion I experienced.

It took me about fifteen minutes to complete the task of freshening my appearance. It generally took five. I drank a swig of mouthwash to conceal my beer breath. Then I popped a chlorophyll tablet in my mouth. A green tongue was better than booze on my breath.

I arrived at the chancery office—late, as usual—and broke out in a cold sweat waiting to see the Bishop. He opened his door and, without a greeting, motioned me into his conference room. After he closed the door, I genuflected and kissed his ring. He pointed to a chair for me at a large conference table that would seat about ten or twelve people. He sat down across from me at the table. I had an overwhelming feeling of being separate and alone. Rejection and insignificance seemed like bookends squeezing me in the middle. A prolonged stillness and silence absorbed me like water on a sponge.

The Bishop asked me in a stern voice, "Do you have anything to offer?"

After I shook my head almost in slow motion, he said, "I have called the Abbot at the monastery and he is expecting you there before vespers tonight. I need not explain the consequences of your actions if you drink. May God be with you."

I returned to the rectory to pack my belongings. My destination was ninety-five miles down the interstate. The location of St. George's was in a mountainous area that resembled the Swiss Alps. But, oh sweet Jesus! I hated to go there. Rising at four-thirty every morning, prayer with all the monks five times a day, and work the rest of the time except weekends.

My mind was lethargic and I was in a state of deep depression. I felt like an observer of what was happening, like I was having an out-of-body experience rather than participating. As I turned the key in the ignition of my car, the starter engaged with the dull, grinding sound of a starter with a low battery. I sluggishly turned the steering wheel as I left the rectory. My life had become unmanageable. It seemed as if I was strapped on a non-stop roller coaster and unable to get off.

After driving about thirty miles, I approached a liquor store with a crudely hand-painted sign that read "Last Chance." I mentally struggled to drive past, which I did successfully. After a few miles of rational accolades and self-praise, I was amazed to find myself turning the car around.

The thought of buying several bottles to stash in my room overcame all other thoughts. I purchased five fifths of bourbon and five quarts of vodka. A couple of drinks before evening vespers wouldn't hurt. Besides, if I drank vodka, nobody would be able to smell alcohol on my breath. The twofold meaning of the liquor store's sign had become prophetic as, with shaking hands, I stripped the red plastic wrapper from the neck of the vodka bottle, unscrewed the cap, and took a big swig to settle my nerves.

The last thing I remember is turning the keys of the diocese's car over to the Abbot at the monastery and catching a bus. I can't even remember where the bus was going.

Some time later I came to from a blackout. I was dressed in street clothes and muddy shoes. Alone at a table in the corner of a large room, I found a cup of cold black coffee in front of me. The room was filled with tables and chairs and adjoined a food-serving area. I had no earthly idea where I was or how I got there, and I was too confused and disoriented to have the nerve to ask anyone, let alone have someone think I was anything less than intellectually self-sufficient. As I looked around, I noticed many people were wearing cowboy boots, work shoes, blue jeans, corduroys, down jackets, and western hats. Still in a state of confusion, I looked out a window and saw horses with jockeys riding by. Oh sweet Jesus! Help!

As I sipped the cold coffee, a clean-cut man in his mid-sixties with salt and pepper hair walked up and sat at my table. He was about my height, but about twenty-five to thirty pounds heavier. His ruddy complexion and facial structure, including a slightly curved nose, reminded me of southern Italy, Rome or Naples maybe. It was easy to imagine he had been a striking man in his younger years. He still was quite handsome.

In a polite, matter-of-fact manner, the man said, "Hurry up with that coffee. We gotta get to the office for the license."

I froze in silence, thinking it would be better just to listen and follow the stranger's instructions. In my confused state of mind, I hurriedly downed the cold coffee, attempting to soothe my dry mouth, and said, "I'm ready."

Smiling, the man answered softly, "No, Red, I don't think you're ready, but if you'll get off your ass and come with me, maybe your mind will follow."

As we went outside, I noticed he had a slight limp in his left leg as he walked. Horses and people coming and going in every direction surrounded us. The clock over the exit had read eight o'clock in the morning. I was told, "This is the stable area, known as the backside."

It was a very busy place at this time of day. We fell in with the others and walked up the slightly inclined chute toward a gap in the rail that led onto the racetrack. The horses coming off the track on the down side of the ramp appeared docile and relaxed, their ears slightly drooped. Those being led up the ramp perked their ears at the sound of the thundering hooves running around the clubhouse turn. Up on the track, the hooves of the working horses on the rail pounded the dirt as they rounded the clubhouse turn, while others were walked, jogged, and galloped in the middle and along the outside.

From the up ramp, some of the newly arriving horses lunged, jumped, snorted, squealed, and strained to "run off." Rocky said, "The hot blood of thoroughbred racehorses pulses through their veins at the sight and sound of this excitement. The prospect of being able to join in 'the flight' is the reason for their birth. This is an experience for horse and man that touch the basic instinct of 'fight or flight.'"

We continued walking through the soft sandy loam of the track, and I remained completely quiet, trying to get a handle on my situation. Several people called to the man I accompanied, referring to him as "Rocky."

One said, "Hey, Rocky, is your barn going to run that gray filly in the opening day stake?"

He answered, "Hell yes," as we turned through a gate and went around the side of the grandstand to an office door. The sign over the door read "Racing Secretary's Office." We entered a large room filled with counter tops, aisles, and many men and women standing in lines and holding papers in their hands.

The man called Rocky turned to me and said, "Red, grab a hot walkers application off that counter top and get in that line for the Steward's office."

As I picked up the paper, Rocky handed me a pencil and said, "Fill out the app, Red, and I'll be back in a minute."

I looked at the paper and froze with fright. The first line commanded my full name. My mind raced wildly like a rabbit being chased by a pack of dogs. It seemed no one knew I was a priest, and

I figured I must have gone on a bender and somehow wound up at the track. I must keep them from realizing the truth. If I just played dumb, maybe I could fake it through. I needed a name...an alias. "Jesus, Mary, and Joseph" kept racing through my mind like lightning. Sometimes I used this term as a substitute for swearing or as a short prayer. I decided to use the initials "JMJ." Yes, that was it...Joseph M. James, hot walker.

— 3 —

Wearing my new hot walker's badge with my picture on it, I briskly followed Rocky as we retraced our route across the track to the barn. As we moved under the overhanging shed's two story roof that was at the corner of the concrete block building, I followed Rocky into the tack room—a medium-sized room that had saddles, bridles, and other equipment.

I was struck by the orderly activity of parading racehorses circling under the shed row, cooling out after being tracked. With few exceptions the horses were calm as cows chewing their cud. I followed Rocky across the shed row and down the aisle of stalls to the fourth door. Rocky stooped as he slid under the canvas webbing across the opening of the stall. He stood up and reached behind and between the horse's ears, and in one smooth motion, he lifted the bridle over the ears and allowed the bit to slip from the horse's mouth. Across the webbing, he handed me the bridle.

"Dunk the bit three times in that pail of warm water," Rocky ordered, nodding towards the rail immediately across the shed row, to the space under the roof between the stall and the edge of the barn. "Now, hang it here on the stall door." The door had been opened back on its hinges and fastened with a hook on the side of the wall. "Slide under the webbing," he said. "I'll show you how to put the halter on and weave the lead shank chain over the nose."

I moved to Rocky's side and watched him slide the halter onto the horse's nose, attaching the strap over and behind the ears. Then he showed me how to weave the brass chain, attached to a leather shank, through the halter, over the horse's nose, and snap it to the other side.

Rocky unhooked the webbing and, as it fell to one side, he led the horse out of the stall and fell in with the moving traffic of horses being led by their hot walkers. I followed them to the end of the shed row and out beyond the rail to the washing area.

The groom, Lucas, whose name was also on his badge, was big and husky like a bull. He showed me where to stand out from the horse and how to hold the shank while he gave it a bath and whisked off the water with the scraper, an aluminum blade about a foot long and an inch wide with a slight curve at one end that worked like a squeegee on the wet body of the horse.

He then pulled the blanket over the back of the horse, up the neck, and attached the loop at the front over the ears. He told me to keep the blanket straight on the horse's back so that it wouldn't slip and twist or allow him to step on it. I was to lead the horse counter-clockwise around the shed row and allow it no more than three sips of water after about every three rounds of the shed row from the bucket in front of its stall.

"If a horse drinks too much too soon while it's still hot," he told me, "it may cripple him in the hoof or give him colic." Colic is a giant stomachache that sometimes causes horses to die. The groom continued, "If a rider were sitting on the horse, his left side is called the near side. His right side is called the off side. Always stay close to the near shoulder of the horse whether he's standing or walking. When in this position, if the horse cow-kicks with its hind feet or strikes with its forefeet, it can't reach you."

After the first couple of rounds, my fear of this twelve hundred pound animal subsided because the horse had been worked hard and was as gentle as an old hound. I noticed that a few horses being walked had not been to the track. They would sometimes be a handful for the hot walker, and I could hear one of the walkers up in front occasionally shout, "Ho back!" Then all of the walkers were to echo the same warning, so they didn't get too close to the horse in front of them. When horses feel good, they like to kick.

I walked the horse for an hour keeping at its shoulder, letting it have the three small sips from its bucket every couple of rounds. About halfway through the routine, Lucas folded the blanket back from the neck, feeling to see whether it was dry. A few rounds later, he removed the blanket and hung it on the rail at the end of the shed row. I led the horse to the stall that stood a foot deep in loosely-tossed straw bedding. The fragrance that emanated from the rope bag of fresh hay suspended from the front corner of the stall contained a mixture of green clover, timothy, and alfalfa. Standing close to the hanging bag, I inhaled deeply, and it was so invigorating it almost reminded me of a high.

Rocky was in the tack room cleaning and soaping the saddles and bridles. He hollered to me, "Red, we have a meeting every morning at eleven in this room, and that's in ten minutes."

I still had not uttered a word to anyone other than to nod in understanding or to clarify an instruction. I leaned against the outer rail of the shed row and watched a groom rake the dirt and sand, then smooth it out from one end of the barn to the other. Rocky yelled, "Let's have a meeting!" I looked at my wristwatch. It was exactly eleven.

There were seven of us crowded in the tack room, sitting in a rude circle. All eyes were turned toward Rocky. He appeared to be in charge.

Rocky said, "Spot, you have a horse that has to be shod at noon, so you break out after thirty minutes and go to the kitchen for lunch." It was plain to see that the circular birthmark about the size of a quarter on the side of his neck gave Spot his nickname.

Rocky's next words stunned me. He bowed his head and recited, "God grant me the serenity to accept the things I cannot change, the courage to change the things I can, and the wisdom to know the difference. My name is Rocky, and I am a grateful alcoholic."

Everyone said, "Hi, Rocky."

He then recited the preamble that is read before each AA meeting. "Alcoholics Anonymous is a fellowship of men and women who share their experience, strength and hope with each other that they may solve their common problem and help others to recover from alcoholism. The only requirement for membership is a desire to stop drinking. There are no dues or fees for AA membership; we are self-supporting through our own contributions. AA is not allied with any sect, denomination, politics, organization or institution; does not wish to engage in any controversy, neither endorses nor opposes any causes. Our primary purpose is to stay sober and help other alcoholics to achieve sobriety."

Glancing towards me, Rocky said, "It's my pleasure to introduce a new candidate for the program today. This new hot walker here is Red. Now, Red's not smart enough to come to these meetings on his own, so's we're gonna give him a leg up and help him ride this fellowship 'til he gets his legs under him."

Everyone said in unison, "Hi, Red!"

I smiled rather weakly, as my frenzied mind yelled, "Jesus, Mary, and Joseph, how in the hell can I get out of here?" AA was the last place in the world I wanted to be.

Rocky said, "Matt, get Red a Big Book and I'll take it out of his pay. Today, we're gonna talk about not playing God. Now Red, it's pretty apparent you don't know God, so this morning you're gonna get your first lesson from this group."

I winced.

As Rocky leaned toward me, calmness appeared to move across his face. He said, "In the Big Book, at the bottom of page sixty-two, it says, 'This is the how and why of it. First of all, we had to quit playing God.' The next sentence is the wisdom of that statement. 'It didn't work.'"

Several of the men chuckled in agreement.

"One of the greatest lessons that can be learned about life and living," said Rocky, "is in the Adam and Eve story. Now I don't know if Adam and Eve represent two people, two cultures, or two civilizations; who they were is not all that important. What they did is the point of this discussion."

He continued, "After God created Adam and Eve, He told them they had everything they needed in life, but there was one thing they couldn't do. They couldn't eat the apple from the tree of knowledge of good and evil. Everything was AOK until the snake showed up and convinced Eve that if they ate an apple from the tree of knowledge of good and evil, they would be gods and could even judge the state of someone's soul. This sounded big-time, so Eve got Adam to eat the apple. God reappeared and asked Adam, 'Why'd you do it?' Adam said, 'She made me.'"

Rocky leaned back in his chair. "Now there, my friends, whoever wrote this is pointing out that from the very first story of human interaction, man does not want to be responsible and likes to blame others for his mistakes. The serpent maybe represents immortality. Back then they thought that since the snake shed its skin, it renewed itself and therefore lived forever, making it immortal. What that's saying to us is that the serpent represents temptation, and we are going to be faced with it forever."

Rocky asked, "What was the benefit Adam and Eve were going to receive from eating the apple? They were going to become gods. So it seems that God is trying to tell us that playing God just won't work, and that we will be tempted to take a bite of the apple many times in life. Disobeying God is not the real sin, trying to take God's place is.

"Now, I'm going to share a bit of my personal theology with you guys. I think the only thing God is powerless against is a towering ego, a person playing or thinking he's God. And by the way, fellows, that's the underlying theme throughout Jewish and Christian scripture. But the one thing for me that's certain is that the secret of living a good and meaningful life is not to try to be God, but to be God-like."

There was a prolonged silence, then Rocky said softly, "There is but one God, and today I am not Him!"

Everyone got an opportunity to share his feelings on the topic, then we stood, formed a circle, joined hands, and with a single voice recited the Lord's Prayer.

— 4 —

Later, after feeding the stock, Rocky approached me saying, "Let's go over to the kitchen. I'll buy lunch." I was still stinging from the remark about me not knowing God, but I was going to cool it for a while.

The kitchen was a cafeteria setup, with a steam table, service line, and a food preparation room behind, enclosed by a wall with a stainless steel pass-through for the food pans and special orders. Rocky proceeded to the stack of brown plastic trays. I followed, placing my tray on the slide that passed in front of the steam table where ladies served the food. On the back wall was a blackboard with the day's menu written in chalk. I could chose from three meats, receive three vegetables, and a biscuit, cornbread, or slice of light bread.

I chose fried chicken, mashed potatoes with brown gravy, green peas and the salad that was a substitute for one of the vegetables. The ladies who portioned the food were more than generous. They put enough on my plate to feed a field hand. My stomach was still in a knot, but I was regaining some appetite because I had not eaten all day. I thought to myself that I would never be able to eat even half of what was heaped on my plate. As I approached the cash register at the end of the line, I noticed bottled beers standing in ice up to their necks. I imagined how soothing the tingling amber liquid would be to my parched and cottony throat. Good sense overcame my desire and I got a large plastic glass full of iced tea with a lemon wedge.

Rocky paid for the food and said, "Follow me."

We walked into the next room, which was filled with tables and chairs. On the walls were horses' portraits, photographs of race finishes, racing silks, jockey boots, and an assortment of racetrack memorabilia. I followed Rocky to the far corner where nobody was near, and we sat down.

Rocky finished his meal without saying a word and took the first sip of his coffee. Looking at me he gently asked, "Red, do you remember how you got here?"

I shook my head.

Rocky began his story in low tones. He said, "I have this friend who is a policeman here in town. Last night, about midnight, my friend found you passed out on a bench in the bus station downtown. He woke you up and took you to his squad car. He told you he had a friend at the racetrack that had worked with many people like you and offered you a choice: possible sobriety with his friend or thirty days on cake and wine at the castle. You pleaded with him to not take you to jail."

Rocky smiled. "I am the friend the policeman was talking about. He brought you to me here at the track. I put you in a bunk upstairs at the barn. We woke you up at six and took you to the kitchen for coffee. You wouldn't eat breakfast. You smelled like an empty whiskey barrel. I told you to drink coffee until you got sober. Then I came back around eight, and we went to the office and got you OK'd by a track steward who happens to be a special friend too.

"If you're sick and tired of being sick and tired, you made the right decision. If not, at least you've had a cot and a couple of hots. It's your life, and if you're willing to do a one-eighty, you're welcome in our group. We'll guide your life and take care of you for the next month or so. If not, you can hit the road. But if you decide to stay, I have to ask you three questions. Although it is not necessary, do you believe in God? Are you willing to go to any lengths to change, and will you let the zyx club run your life for the next thirty days?"

I was trapped. I sure as hell didn't want to hang around Rocky and his bunch, but I didn't know what else to do. I had discovered long ago that if you answer a question with a question, it may give you enough time to think your way out of it.

I asked, "What is the zyx club?"

Rocky said, "If ABC is the beginning, then zyx is when you have gone to the end, the bottom, and start trying to get back to the top. It's like starting over again. Sort of a reprieve or second chance. And that's the name of our AA group at the barn."

I couldn't see a better way out of my present dilemma. I asked what he meant by being "willing to go to any length."

Rocky said, "Red, sometimes it takes every fiber in your body to do something or keep from doing it. The important thing here is not the action or inaction, but simply the willingness. I promise you that we will not ask you to do anything that we have not already done ourselves."

I just couldn't think quickly. Solutions weren't getting through to me. Maybe too much booze over the years had burned up too many brain cells. I had no place else to go. This was the bottom of the barrel, no more exits or escapes. Looking at Rocky, I said, "The answer is yes to number two and three." I paused and then affirmed that I did in fact believe in God.

"Good," Rocky said. "That's a mandatory part of rehabilitation and our suggested program."

— 5 —

I painfully and wearily climbed the steps to the bunk room and flopped on the cot without removing my clothes. A musty-smelling army blanket and pillow without a case were under me. I lay there silently, feeling restless, irritable, and discontent. I was forty-one, and my life was a shambles, unmanageable and out of control. I tried to collect my thoughts, starting with my earliest memories. Where had I gone wrong?

I had always been blessed with good beginnings: I had received an excellent formal education at Notre Dame and then Rome; ordination to the priesthood by the Holy Father himself; the blessings of skills, knowledge, and understanding throughout my schooling and adulthood. But somewhere the fabric of my life had come unraveled, despite my good family with its Christian background. I was living in the garbage can of existence and was seriously thinking of ending it all.

I meditated long and late into the night. Finally, I wept softly and made a simple prayer of petition from the deepest recesses of my heart, "If you're real, Father, help me, please."

Suddenly my entire person seemed to tremor and come alive as a stimulated spiritual understanding flushed throughout my being. The feeling was strangely wonderful yet unexplainable to me, triggered by the understanding that everything was going to be all right. This was a new experience, an inspired relaxation of peace permeating my mind and me. Maybe, just maybe I had opened my heart enough to let the "hound of heaven" get a foothold. For a long time my mind tingled with a sense of self-affirmation that seemed real and genuine. I knew positively that I had just experienced God's love, mercy, and forgiveness.

This truly was an encounter with God. This was wisdom, something never experienced even at the times when I had consecrated the bread and wine, when transubstantiation took place, that miraculous moment when the elements change to the Body and Blood of Christ while keeping the appearance of bread and wine.

My new awareness of God was paradoxical. I felt as if He could reach out and touch me, yet at the same instant I realized that I knew so little of God that I seemed a great distance away. At that moment I knew I would spend my life trying to bridge the chasm created by fueling my egoistic and prideful self-obsessive life. I realized I had only existed and not really lived. Now I clearly saw my ministry and mission. It was to show God's love, mercy, and forgiveness. This had been my moment of grace.

— 6 —

I don't remember falling asleep, but I slept hard. I awakened to Rocky shouting from the bottom of the stairwell, "Let's hear those feet—after you get up off your knees!"

Kneeling by the cot, a smile crossed my face as my mind interpreted Rocky's command. In the washroom, I put my head under the warm water from the spigot. I let it run over me for a full five minutes, through my hair, over my closed eyes, rubbing my face with it.

Drying myself with a towel, I walked downstairs to the tack room where Rocky had a freshly brewed pot of coffee and two dozen doughnuts. Rocky smiled and said, "Eat a couple of these doorknobs and wash 'em down with a cuppa joe." Looking me straight in the eye, Rocky broke into a silly song…"Good morning to you, good morning to you, we're all in our places with sunshiny faces. Oh, this is the way to start a new day." He slapped me on the back and said, "This is the only day you have to live, Red. Make the best of it!"

By now the tack room was full of coffee drinkers exchanging cheerful greetings. Rocky said, "OK, boys and girls, let's go to work. We have horses to track."

— 7 —

Grooms perform a number of important duties regularly as they care for the three or four horses in their charge. On arrival each morning, feed tubs are checked to determine if the horses "ate up." Unconsumed food could mean the animal is "off his feed," a possible warning sign of sickness or too much exercise. Knees and ankles are examined by the groom by placing the palm of his hand on each joint, feeling for heat. A feverish joint requires a detailed examination, as it can signal more serious problems such as internal damage. Fever is more easily detected before the horse has walked or been exercised. If no heat is found in the joints, the groom inserts a thermometer rectally as another check for temperature. All being normal, he begins to knock off, or brush, the horse. The water bucket is cleaned and filled with the first of some ten gallons the horse will consume throughout the day. Finally, the feet are inspected and picked out with a hoof pick.

As jockeys and exercise riders arrive, daily orders for each horse are reviewed. Depending on the current condition of the animal, some have orders to gallop, others to work out, and some simply to walk. Trainers make this determination of each animal every day, seven days a week.

Because I was new and green at my job, I was assigned to walk horses returning from the track. By ten o'clock, all horses had been tracked, bathed, groomed, and stalled with fresh bedding. Horses assigned only to walk were not bathed. We drank coffee intermittently all morning. By the time we policed the area and cleaned the tack and equipment, it was eleven A.M.

Rocky shouted, "Let's have a meeting."

The circle formed up in the tack room, the preamble was read, and Rocky introduced himself as a grateful recovering alcoholic. He reported to the group that I had answered the three questions satisfactorily. I received pats on the back, handshakes, and verbal affirmations such as "Awright," "That's cool," and "Welcome to the club."

Rocky had chosen love as the topic. "The ancient Greeks used three words to describe different love: Philos, Eros, and Agape. Philos was used for brotherly or familial love, Eros for physical or sexual love, and Agape for unconditional love." Rocky suggested that unconditional love was what we received from God, and He loved us regardless of our words or actions, even when we were unaware of Him. He said, "God loves the sinner but not the sin; He loves us even when we hate Him. God's love is constant and never-ending.

"You see," he continued, "It is some of our actions that God dislikes and not us. Romans 8:38 in the Bible's New Testament states, 'For I am certain that nothing can separate us from his love: neither death nor life, neither angels nor other Heavenly rulers or powers, neither the present nor the future, neither the world above nor the world below—there is nothing in all creation that will ever be able to separate us from the love of God.'"

He paused for effect, then said, "Fellows, that is about as plain as the nose on your face. I don't see how anyone can argue or dispute that not even sin, whatever that is, can come between God's love and us. Why would God withhold His love from us just because we made some mistakes? The wondrous beauty of all this is that God loves us in spite of our imperfection."

He leaned back in his chair, smiled and said, "If anybody here questions that, well, that's all right, too. Remember, God is of your understanding! If we practice what we truly believe, that God speaks to each of us, then it is wrong for me to try and change your understanding of God. If I decide I know better than you do, then what am I doing? Playing God. But I would like to relate this caveat, and that is, I believe there is but one God and today you are not Him, Her, or It."

We closed the meeting in the usual manner with the Lord's Prayer, and Rocky turned to me and said, "Red, go get some grub with Jack and Matt. They have horses in the fourth and the feature today, and you have to cool them out after the race."

− 8 −

I had been so absorbed in minding my own business and staying out of trouble I hadn't realized that this was opening day.

Over lunch, Jack, another groom in the barn, expressed a hunch that his gray filly had a shot at the feature and was worth a bet. He exclaimed, "She has the look of eagles about her head."

Matt, who was a student of the "pedigree," said that his horse was a maiden three-year-old colt running its first race, which was to be run around two turns. The race was at the distance of one mile and seventy yards. Matt said, "This sucker can run all day. If anyone asks you about my horse, be sure to cold water him."

I returned a blank stare.

Matt laughed and replied, "I forgot you're new at this. 'Cold water' means talk the horse down. Say he couldn't outrun a fat man, he's just as common as a stick, he's not ready yet, he needs a race...anything you can think of to steer them away from thinking he might be any good. Last week we worked this colt in the dark before any clockers could put a watch on him, and he galloped out three-quarters in fourteen. Man, that oughta put him in the hunt pretty good. I think he'll not only light the board, but probably win off by himself."

Jack and Matt each handed me a twenty-dollar bill and told me to put it on Matt's horse "on the nose, and then parlay it on the filly Jack had."

Jack added, "Everybody knows us and where we work, so if someone saw us at the windows placing a bet, the smart folks with a sharp eye might turn the colt into a steam horse."

I smiled and nodded enthusiastically. I got the message loud and clear. Post time was one P.M. for the first race. Matt said that he would bring his horse to the paddock right after the third race. He told me, "Don't forget to wait to go to the bet window until the last four or five minutes before the fourth. If you go up too early and somebody recognizes you're from our barn...well...you don't have to be a brain surgeon to figure that one out."

Immediately following the third race, entries for the fourth were walked up from the gap at the clubhouse turn along the track into the paddock. The paddock is the last stop before the race itself, where the horses are saddled. It's actually inside the grandstand area, at ground level, with galleries above where the bettors can view the entries.

Rocky had walked down into the paddock and had gone to stall four, where I waited. A minute later, Matt showed up and led his colt around the stalls in the center of the paddock. After two rounds, Matt led him into the gateless stall.

From the near side of the horse, Rocky removed the blanket and handed it to Matt. He placed a cut-to-fit sponge rubber pad between the saddle and its cloth at the rear of the withers, where the neck joins the backbone. The saddlecloth displays the race program number on both sides of the horse. Rocky completed the preparations and cinched the girth strap of the saddle.

Matt led the colt into the walking path and circled the paddock six times before returning him to the stall. By then the jockeys were waiting in the stalls, receiving riding instructions from the trainers. They stood at the horse's withers with the horse's head to their left, also known as the "near" side, and prepared to mount.

The paddock judge shouted, "Riders up." Holding the reins in his left hand on the front of the saddle, the jockey lifted his left leg and bent the knee to ninety degrees. Rocky clasped his right hand under the boot, and in one smooth lifting motion the rider jumped and swung his right leg over the back to the off side. They had executed a leg up.

Rocky led the colt toward the track. As the first horse and rider appeared from the paddock, a man dressed in riding pinks, boots, and derby raised his long thin brass horn and played "First Call." The horses were paraded in front of the grandstand and began warming up with a jog and a slow gallop. Most horses had a lead pony and outrider beside them. Their purpose was to keep the horses from getting too nervous and washing out. This calming effect sometimes prevents the horses from breaking out in a sweat that drips from the stomach like rainwater falling from a roof. Some can lather up as if they had soapsuds between their hind legs. This extra excitement and nervousness wastes energy and can lead to a losing race. The outriders hold the horse as it warms up. After galloping along the back stretch, each horse is placed in numerical order and led behind the starting gate located about eighty-five yards behind the finish line in front of the grandstand. Some races are longer or shorter, depending on the location of the starting gate.

One at a time, the horses are loaded in the gate and the starter waits for all heads forward. The doors spring open with a clash as the bell rings, and they thunder down the track to the finish line. Horses can run three-eighths of a mile at full tilt. Each horse has to be rated, or slowed, to about eighty-five percent of their speed. Otherwise, a horse cannot stay or last the distance of the race. Jockeys have to control the horse by knowing how much to hold back the reins. It is all timing, just like golf or basketball. We observers think it is so simple to make a basket or sink a putt.

I had made it to the betting windows moments before the race began and had placed two twenty-dollar win bets on number four. The odds board above the paddock showed number four as even money. The word had gotten out. A first-time starter going off at even money was a "hot" or "steam horse." Jack and Matt had thought they would get a price or a big return from their bet, but their horse was the solid favorite. It won the race under a "hand ride," which is in front of the pack, and the jockey didn't use the whip.

I walked onto the track where all the horses, except the winner, were being unsaddled. Rocky, Matt, and the owner, a cold knockout auburn-haired lady who appeared to be about thirty years old, were standing with the horse, posing for the winner's picture.

Rocky unbuckled the girth and pulled the saddle from the horse's back and handed it to the jockey. The jock held it while standing on the weigh-in scales. This would assure that the horse had carried its assigned weight. Rocky put a halter on the horse, attached a shank, and threw a blanket across his back. He handed the shank to me and said, "Lead this colt to the spit box."

Matt grinned and said, "Follow me, Red."

The "spit box" is a test barn run by the State Racing Commission to collect urine and saliva samples. These are analyzed at a laboratory for drugs. Some drugs can slow or disable a good horse, while others can improve a bad one. Testing is for the protection of the betting public. If drugs are found in the sample a week later, that horse's portion of the purse is forfeited. The bettors have long departed, and no recourse on their winning or losing is possible. Drugs found in a horse jeopardize the career of the trainer and everyone else involved.

In the spit box, a hot walker employed by the state racing commission took the horse from me and cooled him out in the shed row. After a couple of rounds, the horse was led to a stall where an official stood with a long-handled cup. Matt and Jack watched from outside the stall as the official softly whistled a tune beginning in an "A" half note followed by "F" quarter notes eight or nine times in succession. After four or five repetitions, the horse spread his hind legs in a semi-squat position and urinated. A cupful was collected and the sample harvester placed a cotton swab in the animal's mouth for a saliva sample. The spit box had performed its function.

When the colt was returned, I led him back to the barn for a bath. I walked him for an hour before returning him to the stall. Matt tied him to the back of the stall, rubbed him down, and packed wet clay at the bottom of his feet, level with his shoes. Brown butcher paper covered the clay to keep it from falling out. This helped soothe the sting of the hooves from hitting the track and also absorbed heat. Matt showered compliments and words of praise on the colt as if it were his own flesh and blood.

I gave the winning ticket to Matt. It was now worth forty dollars. In the next stall, Jack prepared the gray filly for the paddock. I gave the other ticket to Jack. Together, they led Bosheba, the gray filly, to the paddock "over there," or to the racetrack. Bosheba ran her race like a thief in the night and won by almost as far as you can throw a baseball. Matt and Jack whooped and hollered. They had won both their bets. The ritual after winning the race was repeated for her.

Darkness had fallen. The horses were fed and bedded down. I went to the kitchen alone, ordered a hamburger deluxe and a cup of hot chocolate to take back to the barn. It had been a long day and

I was bone tired. The barn was two for two and that brought many smiles and back slaps all around.

A faint smile crossed my face as I placed my head on the pillow that night. I was thinking of Matt's thwarted attempt to pull the wool over the eyes of the other horsemen.

God was in His Heaven and all was right with the world!

~9~

In the morning, I awoke from a deep sleep refreshed and with a clearer mind than I had had in a long time. The cobwebs that cluttered my mind were being swept away by sobriety. My attitude lifted immediately. It was a good day. It was a wonderful day to be alive.

I pulled on my comfortable work clothes and the down jacket Rocky had brought me from town and went downstairs to the shed row. I looked up at the heavens and took in a very long and deep breath. The mixed smell of the hay and early morning cold air rushed through my lungs and into my blood stream. It gave me the feeling of being accepted, at one with the world. It was such an invigorating feeling it surpassed the high of drinking. It was definitely a great day to be alive…and sober.

Only the night man, Jake, greeted me. Everyone else was still asleep. The night watchman keeps everyone and everything away from the horses and watches for fires. And he helps the cast horses, who have turned over and pinned their feet against a wall. With no leverage, they can only kick and damage themselves. The watchman helps horses roll over and regain their feet.

It was five-thirty A.M., and the night man was in the tack room. I walked down the row of stalls looking in on each horse, checking water buckets and feed tubs. They are the most magnificent of animals, these horses. I overheard Rocky say the other day that he believed the term "Sport of Kings" referred to the royalty of the horses rather than to their owners.

Pablo, the groom, whose nickname around the barn had become Blowy, had told me how a horse's height is measured. With a barely discernible smile, Blowy had muttered to himself, "Loco gringos," and explained to me the intricacies of equestrian standards and measurements. He said that the English had devised the measurement of a foot as twelve inches. Likewise, they used the human hand to measure horses. A "hand" is four inches wide, from top to bottom, and the horse is measured from the top of the withers to the ground. Most thoroughbreds are from fifteen to seventeen hands high, or sixty to sixty-eight inches.

The night man's shift stretched from ten in the evening through six the next morning, during which time he fed the stock their first meal of the day at four A.M. Most of the horses eat one to two quarts of cleaned oats in the morning and nibble at hay bales. As I made my rounds, some had their noses in the bales pulling out mouthfuls of the mixed fescue, alfalfa, timothy, and other sweet, fresh, pale green grasses. The bales were in thin rope bags with about eight-inch square openings through which the horses could stick their noses and smell the sweet hay and chew from it. The fresh sweet smell assured both man and animal that the hay was without mold, caused by baling it wet, which could prove sickening or even fatal to the horses. The hay served as roughage, a digestive aid, and although its food value was minimal, it contained bone-building calcium. Munching hay has a tranquilizing effect on horses and is probably their favorite pastime.

As I completed my rounds, observing the condition of horses, equipment, and surroundings, Rocky arrived and entered the tack room with two boxes of mixed doughnuts. He prepared and started a fresh pot of coffee. The workday had officially begun.

When the morning routine and chores were completed, the meeting hour arrived. Rocky opened it in the usual manner. His subject was the pride that comes with accomplishment. Winning two races the previous day had made him very happy, but he carefully had to guard against pride seeping into his program.

"Pride," he said, "is the psychological catalyst that ignites our selfishness and self-centeredness, which we think is the root of all our troubles. The only thing that can overcome these two archenemies is humility. But true humility can't be simply conjured up."

As an example, he related the story of the great racehorse Count Fleet. The very barn we worked in and met in was named Count Fleet, which was painted in large letters at both ends. The track tradition named new barns after famous horses that had stabled there.

"The Count Fleet story is known as 'Still Number One,'" continued Rocky. "The Count was one of the greatest thoroughbreds ever, and he slipped his earthly tether at the age of thirty-three, ascending into equine Heaven. Unlike his owner, John D. Hertz, whose car rental enterprise claimed it, Count Fleet had earned the title as Number One. Horses take five years to reach maturity and full skeletal development. In human terms, Count Fleet lived one hundred and sixty-five years, twice the average horse's life expectancy. His last and losing race with life had been as majestic as his sweep of the Triple Crown in 1943. His heart, bursting with age, was as big as all outdoors, for he would not give up in this race of life. He would not lose until his crown was passed to another Triple Crown Champion.

"Exactly thirty years after the Count's glorious undefeated accomplishment as a three-year-old, Secretariat, a flashy red colt, earned the right of coronation. Now the Count's long awaited rest and retirement were at hand, and he could lay down the awesome responsibility of being Number One. And so, he passed on with satisfaction.

"At the Pearly Gates, Count Fleet was mildly surprised to find a sign announcing the coming arrival of Number One, with his story of the greatest race in history. Humble pie and humility had never been found in the Count's feed bag; and the look of eagles had always been around his head. Pride now puffed an arch in his neck, and he bounced like a rubber ball as he entered the eternal pasture that anticipated his arrival.

"He was greeted by General Lee's famous mount, Traveler, who shared with him that here in the pasture, tender clover and sweet alfalfa were knee-deep to a Clydesdale and never-ending in any direction. Traveler related his admiration for the Count and his spectacular winning of the Triple Crown. But now he had to leave, and he would see the Count again at the Hill when Number One told the story of the most famous race in history.

"He spent a long time trying to determine who this Number One was and what race he had run. He asked War Admiral, another Triple Crown winner, and Seabiscuit, Gallant Fox, the undefeated Ribot, Nasrullah, Lexington, Whiskbroom and even Alexander the Great's famous war horse, Bucephalus. They all answered him the same way…you will know soon enough.

"Finally, the day arrived and they all gathered at the Hill. Count Fleet stood next to Man O'War in the throng of horses gazing upward. Quietly, a small brown ass appeared at the top and began to speak. He said this was the anniversary of his race against time, to get his rider, who was heavy with Child, to the Inn and an appointment with destiny at Bethlehem, Judea, about two thousand years ago."

⁓ 10 ⁓

Evening had fallen, and as I finished hanging the feed tubs in the stalls, Rocky said, "Red, we're going out to an AA meeting tonight. It's in that old church building down the street from the back gate. Starts at eight, as usual. It's a speaker meeting tonight, and I think you might be interested in what you hear."

At seven-thirty, Rocky returned to the barn for me, and we ambled through the back gate and down the street to the meeting place. It was a small, old building with a partially exposed basement that Rocky said was rented in perpetuity for a dollar a year from the Presbyterian Church that owned it and was once the occupant. The building was solid white, as if it had been whitewashed. As we entered the old church, Rocky said, "Red, the coffee is hot and there's a big box of oatmeal cookies next to the pot over there. Help yourself, and I'll join you on the front row in a minute."

Rocky turned and hugged a big, broad-shouldered, surly-looking man standing by the door. They exchanged greetings, spoke in low tones to each other, and laughed heartily together. With hot coffee and cookie in hand, I slipped into the very end seat of the unoccupied front row, as instructed. I looked over the crowd in the room and recognized the steward from the track office who had issued my hot walker's license. Our eyes met and the steward gave me a warm smile and signaled a thumbs up.

Suddenly, I noticed the handsome woman with the auburn hair behind the podium. It was the same one who had posed in the winner's circle with our stable's colt and filly on opening day. She appeared to be in charge.

In a loud voice she said, "Let's have a meeting." A hush fell over the crowd, and they hurriedly took their seats. "My name's Maggie, and I'm an alcoholic!"

The crowd in unison said, "Hi, Maggie!"

She read the AA preamble, and all joined her in reciting the Serenity Prayer.

After the announcements, Maggie said, "Tonight, it's my distinct privilege to introduce the one person most responsible for saving my sorry, irresponsible ass. He arrested me and hauled me in for DWI."

The group hooted and roared with a gut-wrenching and infectious laughter. I could not keep from laughing with them. It was almost embarrassing, finding humor in this woman's personal calamity, but I was acutely aware that everyone was laughing with her and not at her. As the laughter waned, Maggie said, "Please give a warm welcome to our Irish cousin, Sergeant Jerry Flanagan of the local constabulary."

There stood the big, surly man Rocky had hugged at the door. As he approached the speaker's stand, the crowd gave an accepting and affirming applause that brought a warm rush to me, and my eyes welled up with tears. This kind of personal emotion in public was a new experience for me. I realized for the first time that I was surrounded by people who might not know each other but were kindred spirits nonetheless, thrown together through the common bond of suffering. Together, their mutual refuge was an infinite sea of love, mercy, and forgiveness. Crossing this sea hand in hand, their common journey was to aid those "graced" with the disease of alcoholism. Oh, joyous fault!

The big man took the podium and said, "My name is Jerry Flanagan, and I'm an alcoholic."

The crowd joined together and shouted, "Hi, Jerry."

Rocky nudged me and whispered, "Jerry is the policeman who brought you to me."

My senses flooded into overload. "Gratitude" was too feeble a word to express what my mind was experiencing. My eyes filled again, and I felt an inner trembling of joy that made my chin quiver. I knew I was experiencing true humility, not feigned humbling experienced in the presence of superiors or at funerals. My mind stiffened to attention, reaching to hear and absorb the expectant message from one that had been so instrumental in my current sobriety.

Leaning forward into the podium Jerry said, "Most people are running around looking for God or for a real miracle. Well, let me share this with you. The Big Book, actually titled *Alcoholics Anonymous,* is a sure-fire miracle. I know this for a fact for me, because it saved my life. And if you stop and think about it, any book that has saved as many lives as the Big Book is bound to be an inspired writing. Remember, it took four years to write and get the first one hundred sober. But since then, maybe two million have made it to these rooms and had the benefit of this program of Good Orderly Direction. To me, that stands for G-O-D. In my opinion, this program has a better track record than organized religion.

"My favorite part of the Big Book is chapter four. The meat of the nut is found here. For instance, just the name of the chapter, 'We Agnostics,' describes all of us as we walked through that door the first time. The first paragraph portrays an alcoholic perfectly. It says 'If, when you honestly want to, you find you cannot quit entirely, or if, when drinking, you have little control over the amount you take, you are probably an alcoholic.'"

He said, "That's our problem! Then it gives us the solution. 'If that be the case, you may be suffering from an illness which only a spiritual experience will conquer.' A little further on it says, 'If a mere code of morals or a better philosophy of life were sufficient to overcome alcoholism, many of us would have recovered long ago.' Then it hits you over the head and knocks you to your knees with this wonderful wisdom, 'Lack of power, that was our dilemma. We had to find a power by which we could live, and it had to be a Power greater than ourselves. Obviously. But where and how were we to find this power?'"

He said, "Then the author sets the hook with the next few sentences: 'Well, that's exactly what this book is about. Its main object is to enable you to find a Power greater than yourself which will solve your problem. That means we have written a book which we believe to be spiritual as well as moral. And it means, of course, that we are going to talk about God.'"

He straightened and pointed at the gathering. "Now, ladies and gentlemen, that's something you can sink your teeth into. For those of us who have been atheist and agnostic, the last sentence in the chapter shows us exactly how to have an encounter with God."

He paused slightly longer than necessary for emphasis and said, "When we drew near to Him, He disclosed Himself to us.

"You see," Jerry continued, "God was not lost! He was right there all the while. We just were not aware of Him. We were too self-centered to be aware of anything past our noses. And, unless we took a trip to the soul-deep part of our hearts, we were never going to become aware of Him. If it weren't so sad, it would almost be humorous…how we tried to have God act like a small, trained dog that you can make jump through hoops. How for years, we tried to horse-trade with him, saying, 'God, You do this and I will do that!'"

Jerry paused again and turned almost stern as he said, "God don't need our horses!"

He continued, "On page sixty-two, the Big Book tells us the how and why of it. 'First of all, we had to quit playing God.' It doesn't say, 'Quit drinking, quit cheating, quit this, and quit that!' It's very, very, very specific. It says, 'First of all, we had to quit playing God.' That's simple advice for complicated people. And we must be convinced that any life run on self-will can hardly be a success."

"That's it!" I thought. "I've been in control all these years, not God. The barrier of intellectual self-sufficiency has always blocked me from Him. And all those special moments in my life were emotional experiences—not spiritual experiences. Until two nights ago, I had never had a spiritual experience. It's like an enigma. All my past life the negative or dark side has held me, but the light side finally pulled me into the warm brightness of understanding. St. Augustine knew it when he was asked if his love of God had brought him to holiness. He said he wasn't seeking holiness so much as he was backing away from the hell in which he was living!"

Jerry told his story—what he used to be like, what happened, and what he was like now. I hung on every word. But the message I received was what Jerry had read from the first paragraph of chapter four. It brought a new enlightenment into the darkness of my existence.

Now I was so emotionally drained that I excused myself from the fellowship after the meeting. As I returned to the barn, I was amazed at the starry, bright Heaven's closeness. It seemed to touch me, to surround me. I now knew I was no longer a leaf being blown aimlessly by the winds of selfishness to the empty and bottomless achievements of self-obsession. I imagined my new self as becoming star dust, the particles of light that gently settle from a shooting star as it returns to its beginning in Heaven. Stardust would help light the path of understanding to those living in the abyss of darkness.

I don't remember climbing the stairs or even getting in bed, but I would forever remember this signal night in my life that was planted firmly in the heart of my mind.

—11—

The next morning I awoke about four-thirty. I had never seemed so relaxed and felt so good. I immediately gave thanks to God for revealing Himself to me. After several minutes of quiet meditation, I dressed and went to the track kitchen, which opened at five every morning. There I got a small orange juice, one biscuit covered in cream gravy, and a cup of coffee. When I entered the next room where all the chairs and tables were, I saw Rocky and went over and sat down.

We exchanged greetings, and Rocky asked me how I liked last night's meeting. I let down and shared my feelings and what I thought had happened to me. I related to Rocky my spiritual experience. He smiled as he listened intently to my recent experience. After hearing me out, he studied my eyes for a few minutes before saying, "God bless and be with you, Red. It sure sounds to me that you let God come into your life."

Rocky then asked, "Red, do you admit that you are powerless over alcohol—and that your life had become unmanageable?"

I emphatically replied, "Yes! Yes! Yes! And thank God I finally came to understand my problem."

He congratulated me and then asked, "Have you come to believe that a Power greater than yourself can restore you to sanity?"

I stated further, "Before coming here I never in a million years would admit that, but today, I can honestly and without reservation say yes!"

Then Rocky asked, "Red, have you made a decision to turn your will and your life over to the care of God, as you understand Him?"

I said, "Without qualification, yes!"

Rocky reached across the table, clasped my hand in his, and reverently asked God to again bless my decision, and recited the Lord's Prayer.

I joined Rocky with an "Amen" at its conclusion.

Rocky said, "What a wonderful day this is already!"

He arose from his chair and told me that he would go ahead to the barn, and after I finished my biscuit and coffee I should come on over. I completed my breakfast and found Rocky in the stall of one of the horses. I leaned on the webbing and asked Rocky if I could help with anything.

He said, "Red, you better not stand so close! This old horse has a very nasty disposition and might reach out and bite a chunk out of your face."

I was surprised. "Are you kidding?"

"Hell no, this is one nasty bastard!" he exclaimed. "I'm just checking his left hind foot. Last week, he pitched a fit and bruised his foot when he tried to kick the wall down. This sucker should have been cut when he was a yearling. If he had been castrated like all the nickel-bred horses are, he would keep his mind on grass and not ass. That's a big problem with an entire horse this time of year when mares start coming into estrus. A stud horse has a nose like a hound dog and can smell a mare coming into season before she rounds the corner. But that's just one of his many character defects. Just remember, Red, when you walk by his stall, keep one eye on him. He can be a bad one. Common son-of-a-bitch!

"Red, remember this about horses: they are just like people. Some of them not worth killin' and some that will give you all the heart they have. Know something, Red? It's quite emotionally uplifting, almost spiritual, when a horse gives you everything it has and then some. It justifies the hope, sacrifice, care, concern, and many heartbreaking disappointments that come with loving horses. Even this sorry-assed horse! By the way, Red, he has the same name you have—Red. Red Stinger!" He laughed and slid under the webbing and we returned to the tack room for a cup of coffee.

The rest of the morning passed quickly for me. My mind had been occupied with the mysterious and strange new sensation of strength I felt flow into me. I eagerly anticipated our eleven o'clock meeting in the tack room.

After the standard opening, Rocky announced that he had had a talk with me during breakfast that morning and thought I was ready for Step Three. I grinned and nodded approvingly.

He continued, "Red, the way we take the third step in this group is on our knees."

I dropped to my knees and Rocky opened the Big Book to page sixty-three, handed it to me, and said, "Red, read the prayer in the second paragraph."

Out of habit, I crossed myself and began: "God, I offer myself to Thee—to build with me and to do with me as Thou wilt. Relieve me of the bondage of self, that I may better do Thy will. Take away my difficulties, that victory over them may bear witness to those I would help of Thy Power, Thy Love, and Thy Way of Life. May I do Thy will always!"

I arose and everyone took turns firmly hugging and congratulating me. Rocky said, "OK, let's all take our seats and get this meeting under way. Today, Lucas is going to share a story of a sure-nuff alcoholic."

Lucas said, "A man had two sons. The younger said to his father, 'Look here, Dad, I don't want to have to wait 'til you die to get my inheritance. Why don't you give it to me now?' Without hesitation the father gave his younger son all that he had coming to him. The boy hit the road for the next town, where he wasted all he had on booze and fast women. He wound up living and eating with pigs. Now this doesn't sound too bad until you realize this boy is an Orthodox Jew. For him to have any traffic at all with pork was sinful in the Jewish tradition."

Lucas paused here and said, "To me, what the scripture says at this point in the story is one of the most important events that can take place in any person's life. It says, 'He came to his senses.'

"Now to me, this means that he had been in denial and suddenly understood this new awareness. Personally, I think denial is a form of serious mental illness. One is in the state of denying the existence of reality. The Latin word that gave us sanity is 'sanitas!' It means whole, complete, sober. If one is insane—not whole, complete, or sober—then he has a slice of his pie missing. In some, it may be just a sliver, but in others, it might be half the pie. Regardless of the size of the piece, they are not complete and consequently are not in their right senses."

Lucas then asked, "Do you think God holds someone responsible for their actions if they are insane and not whole?"

After a long look at me that ended with a friendly and affirming smile, Lucas said, "The boy returned to his father, who didn't wait for the boy to come to him as he should have, according to Jewish tradition and authority, but ran out and hugged him and welcomed him back. He then dressed him in a robe and placed a ring on his finger. The ring had the family symbol on it and was used to seal business transactions and the guarantee of the family. So it was quite evident the father had complete trust in him. This surely is a supreme act of confidence and love by the father. Could it be possible that this is the way God treats us after we have transgressed, too? All the boy did was return."

After reflecting on Lucas's statement for awhile, Jack raised his hand to speak and after being recognized said, "The prodigal son is one of my favorite stories. But the version I like best is where an angel asked God if he could receive his inheritance immediately. He wanted to become human and have the freedom of choice that goes with being a man. God acceded to the angel's wish and let him become human and live on Earth and have the freedom of choice he so desired. The angel, now a man, became so absorbed in life's frailties and complications that he ignored God. After years of struggling to be something he wasn't by fighting misery and making wrong decisions, he finally came to his senses and surrendered. He pleaded that God receive him back in Heaven. He realized that being human wasn't a piece of cake, and he longed to be an angel again. God again granted his request and reached out and rescued the angel from the swamp of selfishness and self-centeredness in which he had become bogged down. The angel had experientially learned that acceptance is the key to humility that is needed to stay in God's protective light."

After another period of reflection among the seven, Rocky spoke. He said, "I really enjoyed the prodigal son's story and wish to share my interpretation of that scripture. To me, the story is not about two brothers, but one person who has two personalities, one dark and the other light. All of us live or have lived in the dark side. And only when we have had enough suffering, we begin to seek God to let us surrender to the light. He pulls us out of the muck and mire we have created in our lives and gently places us against His bosom. And there is not one word of retribution by Him. Not a word or action. Only celebration, because we have returned from an existence of death and now live in the Love and Light of His Mercy and Forgiveness."

He then brought out an important fact that is pointed out in the character of the older brother. "He had been living in the light, but because of his father's gracious reception of his brother, resentment overcame him and he could not forgive his brother's previous unworthy life of misdeeds."

Rocky wryly smiled and said, "Here's the world's first Alanon! The great importance this points out to me is, you have to forgive your brother as well as yourself. Why? Because both God and the Prodigal have forgiven the brother. And God forgives the Prodigal as well. But if you withhold self-forgiveness, then you have acted as if you're more important than God is! You're playing God! If God and you can forgive others but you can't forgive yourself, then you're denying the dark side of life that all of us have. Only God is Pure Light! Fellows, if God can forgive us, then we must do the same. In the fellowship, this is part of Step Five. 'God, ourselves and another human being.'"

I was thunderstruck by the inspired interpretation and spiritual wisdom displayed by these men. Generally, this level of theological thought is relegated to the innermost circles of the church. My God! I felt ashamed. I was experiencing God's wisdom coming from the mouths of ordinary men. I was coming to my senses!

I came...I came to...I came to believe. Thanks be to God!

The meeting then concluded in the usual manner.

~12~

I was preoccupied with the fearless and thorough inventory Rocky told me to write in the form of my life's story. This made the next few days pass unnoticed, lasting until a hard freeze kept the horses from going to the track for three days. The mornings were extremely busy walking all the horses that were jumping out of their skins with pent-up energy. With no races in the afternoon, I was able to almost fill a legal tablet with my story. Rocky told me an inventory included the good as well as the bad. "When a business takes an inventory, they count everything. That way, they know what to keep and what to throw away."

I took a break from writing my inventory and went to the kitchen. There I ran into Rocky sitting at a table with Maggie, the woman who had chaired the meeting Rocky and I had gone to. Rocky introduced me to Maggie and invited me to join in and help them pass the time. I sat down. Maggie was relating a story about a former horse owner who built a very nice barn next to the racetrack. She had obtained credit from the merchants in town to build this nice barn next to the gap at the three-quarter chute. She charged everything. Not one business ever sent her a bill and nobody filed a lien on the property to secure payment of her debt. As it turned out, she was the little sister of a Mafia godfather who was notorious for beating and whacking people who were not in his favor. Maggie smiled and said, "Can you beat that?" Then she looked at me and asked, "Red, where do you hail from?"

Having recently been imbued with spirituality never before experienced, I couldn't be untruthful. So I said, "I'm living just one day at a time, and today I hail from a bunk room in the Count Fleet Barn."

Maggie then turned back to Rocky and the two of them became absorbed in a conversation I did not hear, because my interest had been drawn to Maggie's bright and sincere smile, fair skin, and sky-blue eyes. A chemistry was surfacing that made me feel uncomfortable because I was still a priest. This was the same feeling I had experienced before many times: the perception of being incomplete, alone, and yearning to be wanted or needed. The sensation that I resisted all my life as a clergyman. I remembered how some women threw themselves at me. It could have been my collar. I had wondered at the time if this was something that all men of the cloth experienced. There were mental mazes where I found women attractive and pleasing to my eye and mind. I felt myself being drawn by an urge to touch...to feel...to draw closer...Those were the moments in life when two-fisted, white-knuckled prayers had to be summoned to wrestle the monumental tempting frailties of the flesh.

I excused myself and returned to the barn to take a cold shower.

~13~

The track thawed and opened the next day. It lifted everyone's spirits. Even the horses seemed to comprehend. There were many smiles and sighs of relief at the eleven o'clock meeting. We had a visitor—Jake, the night man. He called himself an "irregular" at the zyx club because he generally was fast asleep this time of day. After the traditional opening, Rocky said, "Jacob, whom we all know, has been kind enough to come and share with us today."

Jake was a light-chocolate-colored black man in his late sixties who was medium height, on the thin side, square shouldered and pridefully erect. He took off his California Angels baseball cap, exposing a shaved head, and said, "Now, don't get me wrong, fellows. I'm not trying to change your thinking, religious belief, or spirituality. All I want is to share some of mine. I wish to talk about the parables of Jesus and what my understanding is of them. The first thing I think about is what's the meaning of a parable. To me, Jesus is sharing His understanding that parables are not a way or rule to live by—but an explanation of God's nature. Also, they seem to always contradict all our expectations."

Jake then said, "My favorite is the Workers in the Vineyard. The kingdom of Heaven is like this. Once there was a man who went out early in the morning to hire some men to work in his vineyard. He agreed to pay them the regular wage and sent them out to work in his vineyard. He went out again to the marketplace at nine o'clock and saw some men standing there doing nothing, so he told them, 'You also go and work in the vineyard, and I will pay you a fair wage.' So they went. Then at twelve o'clock and again at three o'clock he did the same thing. It was nearly five o'clock when he went to the marketplace and saw some other men still standing there. 'Why are you wasting the whole day here doing nothing?' he asked them. 'No one hired us,' they answered. 'Well then, you go and work in the vineyard,' he told them.

"When evening came, the owner told his foreman, 'Call the workers and pay them their wages, starting with those who were hired last and ending with those who were hired first.' The men who had begun work at five o'clock were paid the same amount as those who were hired first were supposed to receive. So when the men who were the first to be hired came to be paid, they thought they would get more, but they too were given the same pay as the ones who started at five. They started grumbling against the employer. 'These men who were hired last worked only one hour.

We worked the whole day in the hot sun—yet you paid them the same as you paid us.' 'Listen, friend, I have not cheated you. After all, you agreed to do a day's work for an agreed-on wage. Now take your pay and go home. I want to give this man who was hired last as much as I gave you. Don't I have the right to do as I wish with my own money? Or are you jealous because I am generous?'

"And Jesus concluded, 'So those who are last will be first, and those who are first will be last.' Now folks, it's pretty easy to see and feel the resentment those earlier workers had. The last paragraph on page sixty-four of the Big Book tells us that resentment is the number one offender. It destroys more alcoholics than anything else does. From it stem all forms of spiritual disease, for we have been not only mentally and physically ill, we have been spiritually ill. When the spiritual malady is overcome, we straighten out mentally and physically."

He went on, "Page sixty-six of the Big Book says, 'It is plain that a life which includes deep resentment leads only to futility and unhappiness. To the precise extent we permit these, do we squander the hours that might have been worthwhile. But with the recovered alcoholic, whose hope is the maintenance and growth of a spiritual experience, this business of resentment is infinitely grave. We found it is fatal. For when harboring such feelings, we shut ourselves off from the sunlight of the Spirit. The insanity of alcohol returns and we drink again. And with us, to drink is to die. If we were to live, we had to be free of anger. The grouch and the brainstorm were not for us. They may be the dubious luxury of normal men, but for alcoholics, these things are poison.'"

Jake continued, "But the central and most wonderful thought I receive from the Vineyard Workers Parable is regardless of how much or how little we work, pray, or love God, His pay is the same for everyone. Constant, infinite, and overwhelming love for each of us! Nothing more…nothing less…and nothing else…"

Jake lowered his eyes slowly and said, "Thank You, Lord, for loving me that much!…Amen."

Again, I was shamefully embarrassed and struck dumb by the wisdom of a person that on first appearance seemed as plain as an old shoe. It seemed my unhealthy ego was beginning to recover.

After the meeting adjourned, I cornered Rocky and, as I handed him the yellow legal tablet I had filled with my story, said, "Here's my Fourth Step! When will it be convenient to get together to do my Fifth Step?"

Rocky glanced at the tablet, smiled, and said, "Looks like I might be reading for awhile. I'll let you know when I'm finished!"

‒14‒

Three days later, Rocky called me aside and said he would take me to lunch in town after the eleven o'clock session and to meet him at his Jeep Cherokee.

I was sitting in the front seat of his car nervously awaiting the ordeal of taking the Fourth and Fifth Steps. I wondered if it would take all afternoon. I had heard of some of them taking all day long. Rocky opened the door, got in, and handed me a brown sack that contained sandwiches, chips, cold drinks, and my yellow legal tablet. He drove through the back gate and told me we were going to one of his favorite spots where we would eat our lunches and then do the inventory.

Soon we were on the highway that led out of town. After about five miles, he turned into a cemetery. When I asked if the cemetery was one of his favorite places, he nodded but still didn't utter a sound. He drove to the top of a hill that overlooked the entire field of tombstones and stopped. Turning off the key, he asked me to hand him a sandwich and a cold drink. Then he said, "The reason I like this place so much is because it brings to mind the reality of my mortality. Please take notice that everyone buried here was once alive, just like us. Let's eat our lunch."

After finishing his lunch he said, "It appears to me that you've made a good attempt with your Fourth Step and now we'll proceed to your Fifth Step."

I couldn't believe my ears. All the time and work I had spent writing my story, confessing everything—including being a priest—and all he was going to say was I made a good attempt at it. My God!

Rocky noticed my consternation and said, "What good do you think it might do if we talked about how your life has been so screwed up? You've already covered that very well. Now, how would you like to share with God, yourself, and me the exact nature of your wrongs?"

I was still perturbed and was puzzled by his question, so I asked him, "I thought you wanted to go over all my wrongdoings. What exactly do you mean by 'the exact nature of my wrongs'?"

Rocky smiled and replied, "Let's imagine a large tree with many limbs and leaves represents all of your wrongs. If you begin to trim away at the leaves and limbs, you may be able to trim away a lot of the wrongs. And that's good. But many times, the pruning you have sought to accomplish backfires and the leaves and limbs grow back twice as thick. That could be very disheartening, Red! At this stage of your life, when your program is not real strong, failure can lure you back to the bottle."

I could feel the piercing look in Rocky's eyes travel straight into my soul. Then he said, "Let's take an axe to the taproot of this tree. When you kill the taproot, the tree will die! The taproot of this tree is your selfishness and self-centeredness. That is the exact nature of your wrongs!"

A soft smile that could look innocence straight in the eye crossed his face and he uttered, "Chop away, Red!"

At that moment, a spike of clarity cut through my murky mind, and tears flooded my eyes as I prayed that God forgive my life of selfishness and self-centeredness. That I completely understood and admitted these things to myself and to my friend and sponsor, Rocky. I thanked God for His Grace and for placing Rocky in my life.

As I was about to say "Our Father," the thought of Jesus calling God *Abba*—Dad—Gave me a warm feeling of belonging. For the very first time in my life, I had the sense of being a part of…not apart from.

After a period of reflection, Rocky said, "Red, I thank God for your coming into my life. It's like the manger scene at Bethlehem. The Wise Men were following a star that would lead them to their Higher Power. Remember the song the angels were singing that night? 'Peace on Earth to men of goodwill!' Red, that's our theme song in the program. Like the men on the camels following the star, when we begin the journey into our hearts, seeking a Higher Power, we too have to be wise. It doesn't take much of a person, but it takes all of a person to surrender and accept God into our lives.

"After the Wise Men presented their gifts, they were advised to take a different route home or they would have been killed. Red, that's one of the messages that we have to remember. If we go back the same way we got here, then we're doomed, too. After we arrive at the manger of Alcoholics Anonymous, we have to take a different path or we will die!"

Rocky's face was peaceful as he said, "I have had many wonderful experiences in life, but the finest and very best was when I have been allowed to be the star that led someone to the manger of Alcoholics Anonymous."

As we drove back, we didn't exchange another word until we reached the barn. Then Rocky said, "Go in peace to love and serve the Lord."

Humbly, I replied, "Thanks be to God."

~15~

Springtime has always seemed so feminine to me. The harshness of winter begins to die and becomes soft like the gentle touch of a woman. The pear and plum trees, which are always the first to issue forth with their bloom, are beginning to sprout their white buds.

One early spring morning, as I inhaled the misty, early morning fog, I felt as if the spirit of my mind was being freshened by the many fragrances released by the bondage of the buds. The new hay in the stalls and the occasional pile of steaming horse manure had an almost sharp yet halfway subtle aroma that was neither sweet nor rancid. It is one of the many wonderful fragrances that are abundant at the track's backside.

Also, there were many flowers that were about to burst into bloom from a kiss of the sun's warmth. If I closed my eyes I could feel a gentle breeze as I inhaled with a long and steady breath that filled my lungs like a fully stretched balloon with a lightly-scented, sweet aroma.

This womanly scent of spring reminds me of the special women in scripture that had such a great influence on Jesus: Mary his mother, the woman at the well, Mary Magdalene, and many more. But I remember as one of the most important the story in Matthew about the Canaanite woman who asked Jesus to cure her daughter who was tormented by a devil. She had Jesus change his mission and ministry by persevering and not taking no for an answer. He had told her that His ministry was only to the lost sheep of Israel. He said it was not fair to take the children's food away and throw it to the little dogs.

She retorted, "Ah yes, Lord; but even little dogs eat the scraps that fall from their masters' table."

Then Jesus answered her, "Woman, you have great faith. Let your desire be granted."

I meditated on the realization that this seemingly insignificant woman became one of the most significant women in Christian history. Jesus hadn't known his mission was to all peoples and not just to the Jews, and this woman changed his mind.

One of the most important things I think we can do as alcoholics—drunk, dry, or sober—is change our minds. In the Serenity Prayer it says we are to "change the things we can." We alcoholics hate change, especially in our minds and attitudes. So why can't we change our minds to bigger and better things just like Jesus did?

Then, as my last horse came down from the track and was groomed for the day, it was time for the meeting. After the usual opening by Rocky, he said that Spot had asked to have the meeting this morning.

Spot nodded acceptance from Rocky and remained seated on a bale of hay. He started by stating, "I have come up with a simile that Jesus was just like a sponge. In its natural state, it lives in the ocean and is permeated with water. The sponge has lots of holes through-out it and is very soft and pliable. The sponge material represents the historical human Jesus. The water throughout represents his Divinity.

"Jesus had to be one hundred percent human just like the sponge has to be one hundred percent sponge. And the water is one hun-dred percent Divine like God. Because of the human defect of imperfection, it is unlikely for Him to understand or know that he is God. For instance, how could you kill God? Or, how could you tempt God like Satan did in the desert? Would any of his suffering count if He realized He was God? How can you hang God on a cross to crucify him? Remember, in the Garden of Gethsemane, His prayer was for this cup to be taken away from Him. The indi-cation is that if Jesus knew he was God before He was crucified, God had played a celestial prank on us.

"I am just as sure, though, that he knew he had the Divine Spark in his soul."

Spot slowly and deliberately looked each one of us in the eye before he answered his own question.

"Remember, in the Garden of Gethsemane, His prayer was for this cup to be taken away from Him. This statement implies fear and anxiety. Certainly not characteristics attributed to God."

At this point in Spot's sharing, he began speaking of the woman at the well. He said, "Jesus told the woman at the well if she would drink from the well of His water, she would be refreshed and never be thirsty again. After that statement, Jesus said she had been married five times and she didn't even know the one she was currently living with. Whereupon, she ran through the streets shouting she had met the Messiah."

Spot said, "Guys, I really had a hard time trying to understand this parable. Then it came to me. I realized that Jesus was telling her that she was married to her five senses. The one she was living with and didn't know was actually herself. She didn't think of herself as a selfish and self-centered person that lived only for good feelings from her five senses. But having no spirituality at all, she had only the destructiveness of being self-obsessed." Spot concluded his discussion by comparing the woman at the well and her shortcomings, which were exactly like his.

−16−

All was well with the stock in the barn. Rocky called the morning meeting as usual. After the opening, Rocky said "The lesson today is about a great flood. It was raining for days and the National Guard came in a truck to rescue a man before his house flooded. When told to get in the vehicle, the man said, 'No thanks, I'm just going to depend on God to rescue me.' The floodwaters deepened to the roof of the man's house. A neighbor brought a motorboat to the house and said, 'You better come on now and get in the boat.' The man refused again, stating, 'No thanks, God will rescue me.' The next day the water was within one foot of being completely over the man's house. A helicopter came by, and the pilot told the man to grab a rope ladder, which would save him from drowning. The man said, 'I told you guys that I am going to wait on God to rescue me. Thanks, but no thanks.' Whereupon, the floodwater went over his roof and he drowned. When arriving at the Pearly Gates, he was really pissed. He asked God, 'Why didn't You save me? I just knew you would and I'm mad as hell You didn't.' Then

God said, 'First I sent the National Guard truck to rescue you. Then I sent your neighbor in a motorboat. As a last resort, I sent a helicopter to get you for one last saving try. But you were going to make me act like God. Do you think I'll jump through a hoop for you? You should have taken advantage of those three attempts at your rescue. Remember, don't get 'should' on."

Rocky explained, "This is really a no-brainer. It's essential that we look for God in everyone. Sometimes He's hard to recognize, but I believe He's in all of us, and all of us are in Him. I believe that it is a basic instinct that everyone wants to be with God. And He wants to be with all of us. He may even be known by different names.

"All of us are climbing the same mountain, but we take different paths to the top where God dwells and we all come together. Much has been said about religion versus spirituality. Religion has rules and spirituality doesn't. Many people profess their way is the truth and others do not. They may be correct and they may not. At the end of my life when I shed my coat of faith, with rigorous honesty I cannot state that I actually knew the reality of truth. Consequently, I try to abide in hope, faith, and love.

"One of the mysteries in religion is the Trinity. It really is not that difficult if you can find some medium that has the same molecular structure but different personalities. Take, for instance, water," he said. "Imagine God is water. Then Jesus is steam. And the Holy Spirit is ice.

"The molecules are exactly the same in water, steam, and ice. All are water. Only the molecules move faster as heat is applied reach two hundred and twelve degrees or slower when they are exposed to thirty-two degrees or less. So it becomes very simple that you have three personalities—water, steam, and ice. The very same thing, yet different personalities with a common medium.

"God, Jesus, Holy Spirit."

The group meditated for a time and the meeting adjourned when we stood and repeated the Lord's Prayer.

~17~

The following day I ran into Maggie. She invited me to the kitchen after the races were through for the day. There was a table in the corner that was away from the others. The food was good and generous. While we were eating, Maggie began to ask questions. Questions like "Where are you from? What have you done in life before coming to the track? Are you married? Divorced? Do you have children? A girlfriend?" and a litany of others.

I was scared to death of the questions. She was very intelligent, and her eyes and facial expression seemed to penetrate into the deep recesses of my being. I then began to tell my story. My personal history of a self-obsessed, self-serving ego. I felt that I had to come clean. I related to Maggie everything about me from A to Z.

The part of my life as a priest became strained. I found myself wanting to be rid of the many lies I had told. I had been told by Rocky that the absence of conflict in my life was the gateway to serenity. I decided this was the moment to begin my battle with discord in life. Noticeably, this strange feeling of being able to tell only the truth seemed to pierce my mind like a lance. It gave me the courage to go on with my tale of agony. It took an hour to flush my sick ego down the commode and replace it with a footing built on rock.

When I was finished she reached across the table and grasped my hands. The gentle squeeze made me feel warm and affirmed.

When we got outside the kitchen she carefully clasped my hand and entwined our fingers together as we walked toward the barn. Not a word was uttered, but I now realized the source of anticipation—projection. When we reached the barn she gave me a close embrace and then thanked me for an amazing evening. Then she got in her car and drove off, leaving me staring into infinity.

I was tempted to the core of my being. I realized that I had to be cautious because I was still a priest. After climbing the stairs and getting into bed I tossed and turned for a short period, then I began a

Centering Prayer. My mantra was the Serenity Prayer. I would inhale as deeply as possible, then exhale until my lungs were depleted of air. During this deep-breathing exercise I could focus on listening to my breathing. During the completion of each cycle I would meditate on one syllable at a time. The repetition became rhythmic and produced peace in the inner reaches of my mind. I don't know when I fell asleep but I was completely refreshed on awaking.

As I went about my chores, my thoughts reminded me of Jesus in the desert after His baptism by John the Baptist. Analyzing the temptations by Satan seemed to reveal the key of translating the message into contemporary thought and times. Remember that Jesus had been in the desert for a long time and afterward was hungry. The tempter approached and said to Him, "If you are the Son of God, command these stones to turn into bread."

Jesus replied, "Scripture has it: 'Not on bread alone is man to live but on every utterance that comes from the mouth of God.'"

Next Satan took Him to the holy city, set Him on the parapet of the temple, and said, "If you are the Son of God, throw yourself down. Scripture has it: 'He will bid his angels take care of you; with their hands they will support you that you may never stumble on a stone.'"

Jesus answered him, "Scripture also has it: 'You shall not put the Lord your God to the test.'"

Satan then took him up a very high mountain and displayed before him all the kingdoms of the world in their magnificence, promising, "All these will I bestow on you if you prostrate yourself in homage before me."

At this, Jesus said to him, "Away with you, Satan! Scripture has it: 'You shall do homage to the Lord your God; him alone shall you adore.'"

At that Satan left him, and angels came and waited on him.

The first temptation was with food because Jesus was very hungry. I thought, "This means that the devil was tempting Jesus with possessions."

The parapet being the highest place in or on the temple makes the statement that Jesus' holiness was above everyone else and not the humanness attributed to Him. Also, He would be commanding God to play God by rescuing Him. The second temptation related to prestige.

The third temptation is power.

The temptations Christ was faced with are just the same today as they were then. Possessions! Prestige! Power!

The morning passed quickly because I was preoccupied with the desert setting. It was now meeting time. When I arrived at the door of the tack room, Maggie was there with her beautiful eyes and bright smile.

"Hello, Red," she said. She then asked me to have lunch with her after the meeting.

I replied, "You bet."

Rocky opened the meeting in the usual manner. He then stated, "The Wizard of Oz story is an allegory that was written around the turn of the twentieth century. According to the story, Dorothy and the three main characters were in an imaginary world searching for someone to fix them." He said, "All of them were journeying to find this Wonderful Wizard of Oz. The tale goes on to say that Dorothy's sidekicks were in need of a brain, a heart, and courage.

"The Scarecrow needed a brain because he represented the agricultural community. The country's farmers just weren't very smart. The Tin Man needed a heart because he represented industry. The robber barons had their feet on the necks of the industrial workers who were poorly paid and worked like slaves. The Lion needed courage because he was a politician who voted for the people who donated the most money to him and against the people that needed the most help."

Rocky said, "The yellow brick road represented the gold standard the U.S. was using at the time for their monetary system. There are other interpretations, but the theme of the story is that Dorothy and her three friends are looking for help from the Wizard who had them spellbound with his booming voice."

He laughed and said, "Toto, the little Cairn terrier, grabbed the curtain in his teeth and pulled the curtain down. Lo and behold, the Wizard, without the microphone booming his words, explained in a small whiny voice that he was just a human being like everyone."

Still grinning, Rocky said, "The meaning of the story is that nobody can fix you. Only you can make yourself whole. And only with God's help."

"I have one more short story to share," Rocky said. He began by describing a small group of men walking down a road when they came upon a drunk lying in the gutter. All but one started laughing and making fun of the man who was lying in his vomit alongside a jug of wine turned on its side and apparently empty.

The one who had been silent said to the others, "There, but for the grace of God, go I." This statement was like a bolt of lightning that made the others aware of their shame and failure that only God's grace could alleviate. After that, Francis and the small band of followers continued on the road to Assisi.

Rocky said, "There, but for the grace of God, go I!"

The meeting closed in the usual manner, and I joined Maggie in her car.

— 18 —

Maggie parked her car at a drive-in restaurant. I could slice the silence with a knife. We ordered hamburgers with fries and ice tea. When we finished eating, Maggie said, "Now it is my turn to talk.

"Up to the age of eighteen, other than being very aloof, I led a normal life, which included being raised in a good Christian environment. My life seemed incident free. Then I joined a religious order named the Daughters of Charity. On the annual anniversary of my vows I was required to sign an agreement that I would follow all the rules of the Order, including Chastity, Obedience, and

Poverty, for a one-year period. If I didn't sign my pledge on that anniversary again, it would mean that I wasn't renewing my vows.

"After five years of wearing my habit, I made up my mind that the church was headed in the wrong direction. Most of my problems were in the province of feminism and dominant male power. The pyramid of power in the church was turning me off, and my drinking to lessen my constant inner battle with being lonely and alone became a struggle. I think it is fair to say that I had a pretty good problem with booze.

"I remember the first time Mother Superior called and ordered me to go to an AA meeting. Naturally I didn't think I had a drinking problem. After trying some unsuccessful controlled drinking, two sisters from a nearby community contacted me. They told me their stories about how they had quit drinking. They then asked me three questions. 'Do you believe in God? Would you go to any lengths to get sober? Would you let us guide your life during this period One Day at a Time for twenty-eight days?'

"I answered the first question with a yes and the second 'maybe.' They said, 'That's OK. Honesty is what we are looking for.' Then, reluctantly, I agreed to let them manage my life for the time required. Then after the three of us said the Serenity Prayer in unison one of them responded like a memorized slogan, 'I alone can do it, but I cannot do it alone.'

"My start was not good. I picked up a 'desire chip' to quit drinking at practically every Friday or Saturday night meeting. I lived with two other sisters and worked for the diocese in the Religious Education Office. Having been furnished a car for my work, I could visit other parishes throughout the diocese. This gave me the opportunity to purchase my vodka throughout the state. It also made it possible for me to avoid getting caught frequenting the same liquor store. And I bought only half-pints so I'd be able to hide them easily. My favorite hiding place was in the water tank attached to the commode. Who would think to lift the lid and look in there?

"It seems like I would drink a whole bottle every Friday night after evening prayers. In the AA program I am known as a periodic drunk because my drinking was occasional. If I didn't watch closely, my occasions became Friday night, Saturday afternoon and night, and Sunday afternoon and night. I had a ceaseless struggle with the poor me's. You know, the eternal conflicts that come with the territory—depression, personality problems, and anything negative that I could latch onto. We have a revealing adage in AA. It is simply: 'Poor me, poor me, pour me a drink.'"

A very gentle smile, like the Mona Lisa's, came to her lips as she pondered refuge from her frailties. "Although I thought I was in complete control, after leaving the Daughters the fabric of my life began to unravel faster even when I wasn't drinking. My life was becoming unbearable and my thinking untenable. It is called 'Stinking Thinking.' I went on a leave of absence from my order and came here hoping I could quit. But it just didn't happen.

"Since this town is a mecca for tourists, you can find a party somewhere every Saturday night. And I found lots of them until Jerry Flanagan found me swerving back and forth in my car and pulled me over."

I asked, "Maggie, what was the name you chose as a Sister?"

She replied, "Sister Mary Joseph."

She continued in almost an apologetic voice, "Red, I could easily become intimately involved with you because I am a passionate human being, and you are the first man I have met that excites me. I believe that we may have some chemistry going on. But my spirit is restless and I yearn for God's love, mercy and forgiveness. My soul is searching for completeness. I need to be at peace. Therein lies my struggle. You see, Red, I feel better physically, mentally, and spiritually than ever before. And I have mostly continued to grow in those areas, but there seems to be a longing, a thirst that cannot be satisfied or quenched. I feel God is calling me back to a religious life. Back to the Sisterhood."

Then I perceived her sensitive nature as tears began to seep onto her soft cheeks. I drew her near and gently kissed the tears from them. With both arms she softly and closely embraced me for my gesture of caring.

~19~

Rocky opened the eleven o'clock meeting with the usual introduction. Then he said, "This morning, I wish to expose you guys to some powerful Jewish scripture that is a favorite of mine.

"In the Old Testament, Song of Songs, Chapter Two, Verse Eight, called the Second Poem in The New Jerusalem Bible, these few verses give me a strong belief that God beckons me home as I take my final breath, discard my cloak of faith, and enter into a new experience in my knowledge of existence, surrounded only by love. In the following verses, think of the lover as God.

"I hear my love.
See how he comes
leaping on the mountains,
bounding over the hills.
My love is like a gazelle,
like a young stag.

"See where he stands
behind our wall.
He looks in at the window,
he peers through the opening.

"My love lifts up his voice,
he says to me,
'Come then, my beloved,
my lovely one, come.
For see, winter is passed,
the rains are over and gone.

"'Flowers are appearing on the earth.
The season of glad songs has come,
the cooing of the turtledove is heard in our land.
The fig tree is forming its first figs
and the blossoming vines give out their fragrance.
Come then, my beloved,
my lovely one, come.

"'My dove, hiding in the clefts of the rock,
in the coverts of the cliff,
show me your face,
let me hear your voice;
for your voice is sweet
and your face is lovely.'
Catch the foxes for us,
the little foxes
that make havoc of the vineyards,
for our vineyards are in fruit.

"My love is mine and I am his.
He pastures his flock among the lilies.

"Before the day-breeze rises,
before the shadows flee,
return! Be, my love,
like a gazelle, like a young stag,
on the mountains of Bether.

"Now think on and about these verses after we dismiss with our prayer," Rocky said.

— 20 —

While eating lunch at the track kitchen, I kept hoping that Maggie would show up. But she didn't, and I was beginning to miss her company and companionship. When she dropped me off at the barn the night before I had told her that I was going to kiss her. As I pursed my lips together for just a peck on her mouth, I thought it would be an innocent touching of our lips and nothing more. The next moment thrilled and filled the essence of my mind's heart. She pressed close to me in a smooth deliberate move and opened her mouth slightly to accept my tongue onto hers, which was warm and tasteful. She then turned her head slightly as she disengaged our lips and said in a soft voice, "Thank you for being a wonderful listener, but I have to be careful because I am still thinking of returning to the Sisterhood." I thanked her for everything and got out of the car and went to bed.

I could not get her out of the desires of my mind that night when I went to bed. My eyelids seemed pried open. My mind was spinning with thoughts that were anything but innocent. Momentarily I realized how selfish my thinking was, but I couldn't quit wanting her. The desire in my heart seemed as big as all outdoors. While turning over and over in my bed, I knew I had to meditate strongly through centering prayer, in order to get her off my fantasy-filled mind. I imagined sleep might be a stranger tonight.

After some time elapsed, however, I dropped off into what became a peaceful sleep.

— 21 —

The following was a splendid day. The temperature was in the mid-sixties. The plum and the dogwood trees were in full bloom with the beautiful white blossoms that only God could make. I could feel the warmth of the noonday sun soaking through my long-sleeved shirt, giving me a feeling of belonging, acceptance, and surrender of the selfish motives I had harbored all my adult life. This was a huge change from my former feelings of loneliness and insecurity. I knew God was in his heaven and all was right with the world.

After I had put the feed tubs in the stalls for the night, Maggie drove up and asked me if I would like to go for a drive. My heart leapt like a gazelle bouncing across the plain as I entered her car. As we drove along the town's main thoroughfare, she asked whether I would enjoy parking the car and aimlessly strolling around the streets.

I happily replied, "Why not?"

We got out of her car and began slowly and pointlessly walking along under a canopy of large magnolias that stretched for several blocks. She then put her arm gently around my waist and patted me with that hand. Then she squeezed me and laid her head on my shoulder. The inclination of her sensitive nature thrilled me.

The previous night, my mind had ached like a clenched fist that was being squeezed as hard as it could be. Suddenly, my nostrils widened as the rich smell of her recent shampoo burst the grasp off my mind. Simultaneously, a passion pierced my mind like an arrow being released from a full-drawn bow.

She asked, "How do you like the smell of my perfume? It's Shalimar."

To smell it, I put my face near her ear and lightly sniffed. It was more than wonderful. I felt like a jet engine's afterburner had turned on my longing passion. The fragrance filled my lungs and made me weak in the knees as if intoxicated. I had never realized there were physical and mental sensations like this.

As we walked with our arms around each other's waists my passion subsided slowly. By now, we had walked to the end of Bathhouse Row. At that point, she sat on a two-foot high concrete and rock wall about a foot wide. It separated the sidewalk from a pond created by hot springs coming from the fissures on the side of a hill. The springs were about fifty feet in front of us.

I sat down on the wall and stuck my hand in to test the water. It felt warm and interesting. I told Maggie, "I remember reading that this hot water, which circulated up from the bowels of the earth and into this catch-pond, is rain that fell about four thousand years ago. Just think, this could be some of the water that showered Moses."

She took off her shoes and socks and placed them at her side. She then swung her legs over the wall and immersed them in the tepid water halfway up her calf. In a strong voice, she moaned, "Ummmm!" and said, "Take off your socks and shoes and come on in." With a guttural sound she added, "The water's grrrreeeaaattt!" My mind filled with only the thought of her slightly opened, puckering lips coming at my mouth.

It was about nine o'clock and we passed insignificant conversation for about fifteen minutes. After a long pause, she asked, "Why don't we get a room at the hotel across the street?"

I was unbelievably stunned. The only thought that entered my mind was, "Should I pinch myself to see if this is real?"

We put our shoes and socks back on and walked across the street and up the steps of a landmark hotel. I registered for the room in the name of Mr. and Mrs. James Clay. Neither of us uttered a word while we went up the elevator and down the hall. Stopping at room 733, I placed the key into the keyhole and gently pushed it in flush to the hilt and the back of the tumbler. It was a good firm fit and went in easily, making me think how it was very Freudian.

As I opened the door and we entered the room, Maggie asked that I turn out the light as she walked into the bathroom and closed the door behind her. While she was in the bathroom, I quickly undressed, turned down the bedspread, and crawled between the sheets and under a blanket. After a few minutes Maggie appeared in the bathroom doorway. She was completely nude, silhouetted by the light behind her. She then pulled the door to and it became pitch black. Then she opened the door slightly ajar. The soft light banished the darkness. A vision of splendor filled my eyes.

For an instant I remembered I was still a priest. My mind flooded with doubt and confusion. Quickly she entered the bed and snuggled up to me. She strongly embraced me. She ran her fingers through the hair on the back of my head then placed her hand on the nape of my neck. She kissed me all over my face and lips. Next she began to hold and hug me. She bit me with a slight tug on my earlobe, then, with her gentle warm breath and tongue, fluttering like the wings of a butterfly, kissed the orifice of my ear and I was covered with goose bumps. This sparked a sensation that raced through my entire body, my entire being—even to the tips of my toes and the center of my cerebellum. I was grossly unfamiliar with a passion that was this exotic.

I remembered a line from a movie where an actor said, "If this is foreplay, then I'm a dead man."

The mixed emotions occupying my thoughts an instant before were completely melted away by the super-charged thought steaming in my mind. I could no longer be passive. I had a supreme sense of urgency for her love.

After we completed the act of love, I told her that she was the potter and I was the clay: she could fashion or mold me anyway she wanted. I was hers forever. She turned on her side with her back at my chest and pulled my arm across her body. Then she gently placed my hand on the lower part of her soft, smooth, and warm-to-the-touch abdomen. She bent her knees forward and, like a magnet, mine fitted the backs of hers. I scooted the insteps of my feet on the bottoms of hers. For the first time in my life, I had realized the experience of oneness between two people. My thoughts reached back to the times I had counseled couples who had posted their Bans of Marriage about uniting two people into one. Now I had had the supreme experience of the oneness with another human. It was almost the same feeling of fulfillment and wholeness I felt about my encounter with God, and I would always treasure its memory.

Realizing that I had to be at the track at six, I phoned the desk and put in a wake up call for five A.M.

When the phone rang, we dressed, drove to the track, and had breakfast in the kitchen. As we finished eating, she walked me to the barn, hand in hand. We took turns occasionally squeezing each other's hand. We maintained practically continuous eye contact. When we reached the barn, we hugged, and then she gave me a slight kiss. She said, "Thanks, and *Dominos Vobiscum.*" Then she left and drove out of sight.

I immediately began to miss her. Yet my flooding thoughts of her seemed to overflow the brim of my mind. I silently spoke the words of Shakespeare's twenty-ninth sonnet:

> When, in disgrace with fortune and men's eyes,
> I all alone beweep my outcast state,
> And trouble deaf heaven with my bootless cries,
> And look upon myself, and curse my fate:
> Wishing me like to one more rich in hope,
> Featured like him, like him with friends possessed,
> Desiring this man's art and that man's scope,
> With what I most enjoy contented least:
> Yet in these thoughts myself almost despising,
> Haply I think on thee, and then my state,
> Like to the lark at break of day arising
> From sullen earth, sings hymns at heaven's gate;
>> For thy sweet love remembered such wealth brings
>> That then I scorn to change my state with kings.

The last two lines were imprisoned in my heart. I had never, ever been filled with this kind of passion and love. Then I remembered lecturing couples that were to be married that God should become a partner in their marriage. I could feel the Holy Spirit moving in our new love.

~ 22 ~

Blowy did not show up that morning, and my chores almost doubled. I didn't have much time to rejoice in last night's magnificent moment. The eleven o'clock meeting came quickly.

Before he opened the meeting, Rocky said he'd seen Blowy swigging on a Carta Blanca with one hand and eating a taco with the other. He went on to say that he would only allow a person that he was sponsoring to have one slip. "If he does it again, then he's outta here. Poor Blowy probably thought that just one beer wouldn't hurt. He could handle just one cerveza. Ha!"

Rocky explained that he always told the pigeons he sponsored that if they slipped more than once while he worked with them, they would have fired themselves from his sharing with them and he would not be their sponsor any longer.

"The reason is very simple," Rocky said. "What I've been doing is apparently not working with the slipper's search for sobriety. And it's not my fault. I think one of the biggest mistakes we make in the program is to get a person and keep sponsoring him even after a number of slips. I hope and pray that they obtain sobriety, but as I see it, my job is not to baby-sit drunks, but to be available for the many out there who want to get sober."

Jerry Flanagan called the barn and wanted to know whether or not this was Blowy's first slip. He was told yes and arrangements were made to bail Blowy out of jail. Then Rocky smiled and said, "But I think I'll let him cool out in there 'til tomorrow."

Rocky requested we all pray the Serenity Prayer together for Blowy. He charged us to remember that prayer gives us the wisdom to see that each of us needs change in our attitudes.

My attitude was the only thing I could change. Not to change Blowy, but me. I had to accept Blowy the way he was. To love him as he was, not as I would have him be. And it didn't take a rocket scientist to the see the wisdom of that.

After we prayed in unison, Rocky dismissed us for an early lunch.

— 23 —

One of the tidbits of learning how to stay sober is not making any big decisions for one year. Generally, by the time that anniversary came around, you would innately know if it was the right thing to do.

In the early stage of sobriety many of us get bitten by the "love bug." A new job with a new start in a new town appeals to us too. Changing locations is called a "geographical." We go where nobody knows us. Good health and a short memory are referred to as "the newcomer's disease."

These are the danger signals of stinking thinking.

Most of us have a change of heart or mind before the year is over. Then, if we have made commitments too early, it takes a toll on our emotional well-being.

Remember that we have to be selfish only in our own sobriety. With the rest of life we are beckoned to be selfless.

If we aren't sober, forget it.

Also, the Big Book says if we don't clean house, we cannot carry the message. For me, the message is love and acceptance of others as well as ourselves.

The message of God's will for me is very simple: Just show up! Stay sober so He can work with me. When it seems that God is showing me the path, if I don't take every step the journey requires, the road gets bumpy and I have to just hang on or start forcing my will. When I force things, it usually follows a disastrous pattern that can burst the balloon of sobriety.

With only ninety days into the program, I am gonna have to practice "Easy Does It" for at least another nine months. This will become a big leg of my journey. Will it become triumph or tragedy?

—24—

In a short period of time, my life had taken a new tangent that was leading me on the path of an ecstatic existence. My cup overflowed. I could feel the presence of God. I could see the presence of God in the blooming trees, in the AA room, in my friends, in Maggie. I had become what William James calls "twice born" in his famous book, *A Variety of Religious Experiences.* I had experienced a new meaning in life.

Maggie and I talked about getting married on my one-year sobriety anniversary. The feeling of hope occupied my thoughts night and day. I was able to live in the now, not projecting as I used to do all the time.

Looking back, it is easy to see that I never liked myself. Now, if someone came up and asked me if I liked myself, I would have replied, "Hell yes." I had thought before that I was the neatest dude you would ever meet, but still, I always wanted to be someone else, such as the priest Bing Crosby portrayed in *The Bells of St. Mary's,* or John Henry Newman, the converted Cardinal whose thinking had a great influence on Vatican II; or the great modern theologian Karl Rahner; or Jesuit Pierre Teilhard de Chardin, scientist and metaphysicist; or the famous writer of many religious books, Thomas Merton. But never me. Never Clay James.

Upon realizing this, it became pretty clear that my always wanting to be someone or something that I wasn't reflected a person who didn't like himself.

And not only that, I always wanted to be in another time frame. Last Friday night; next Saturday; never liking the right now. I was living in the future and the past. The two biggest thieves in the world are not in the penitentiary; they are in my mind. They are called "Yesterday" and "Tomorrow."

Slowly, I was becoming more aware of me. My real self. By going through the Twelve Steps, I had honestly begun to enjoy my own company. To be me. In the here and now.

It may be hard to comprehend, but for the first time in my life I could actually stop and smell the roses.

Halleluiah!

-25-

The days in my new life seemed to zip by. Only through Maggie's maturity and serenity was I able to keep myself from childish actions. I wanted to leap and jump, to shout and skip, to swing on a gate—the fun things that an eight-year-old would enjoy. The simple pleasures of life excited me to no end. I honestly felt that I was the happiest and the luckiest man on the face of the earth.

Then, one night, nine months into my sobriety, a dark cloud of doom and gloom shattered my life. A drunk driver had gone to sleep at the wheel, crossed the median, and run head-on into my Maggie. She was dead on arrival at the hospital.

I went into a deep state of shock. I was unable to fathom the reality of what had happened. One minute she was like the flame of a candle dancing in a gentle breeze. The next instant the flame was snuffed out. My whole being yearned for her presence, her smile, her gentleness—her everything. I needed her in my life.

The thought of joining her in death preyed heavily on my mind. I so much wanted to be with her that my spirit was broken. My soul suffered.

I had never had the opportunity to meet her family until after the Rosary at the funeral home. Her mother came over to me while I was still sitting in the pew and said, "Maggie talked about you a great deal. She told me she thought you were so wonderful because you had helped her develop an 'attitude of gratitude.'"

She continued in a soft and almost angelic voice, "It will be a long while before my tears will dry, but I can see a smile on her face because she was able to overcome the adversity in her life with the gratitude you helped her to develop."

With tears streaming down my face, I rose and with a trembling voice said, "Thank you, and God be with you at this tragic time."

She then clasped my hand between both of hers with a kind grip and asked me to sit with the family at the funeral mass.

─26─

In the next weeks after Maggie's funeral my steps were slow, heavy, and lacked deliberation. As hard as I tried, I still couldn't get my head together. My thoughts were aimlessly spinning and colliding into one another like a ping pong ball ricocheting back across the table after a slam with a paddle.

Rocky came by the barn during the races and asked me if I would be his guest at dinner that evening. Still mopping around with my hangdog expression, I said, "I don't feel up to it, but thanks anyway."

He looked sternly at me and said, "We're goin' to get your act together. I'm coming by for you, so be out front at six."

─27─

When Rocky arrived, I got into the car without speaking. After settling in my seat, I looked at him and noticed his entire demeanor wore a firm look. I then asked, "What's wrong?"

With a strong voice he said, "You!" After a slight pause he said, "I cannot abide someone who's supposed to be sober swimming in their own pool of misery. Some people in the program enjoy living in a pile of manure, because it is warm and feels familiar." He followed that line with, "You're going to have to get a hold of yourself and try to get back to that sense of ease and comfort that comes with lack of conflict in your thoughts and life."

Within a few blocks, he drove into a drive-in restaurant and parked. After rolling the window down, he turned the key off and ordered a cheeseburger basket and a diet coke through the speaker/receiver box attached to the stand between cars. Then he turned to me and asked, "What would you like?"

I replied, "The same please."

Not a word was spoken as we received the food from the waitress. Still without further talk we ate our food. When finished he said, "Red, life is not like basketball. You cannot call time out when things aren't going your way. And it's not a dress rehearsal, either."

Then he asked, "What do you intend to do about this? You've been living in the problem and it's time that you start living in the solution. That's the way we are supposed to act."

I mentally moaned and wanted to tell him to kiss my ass and mind his own business, but before I could, he said, "Red, I too was a priest and lost my way in the eternal abyss of drinking. I wallowed in my own self-pity while walking through the Valley of Death. The fear and loneliness instilled the many negative thoughts that drove me from the church. I didn't think I could face the world another day. My thoughts were of ending it all."

I was again stunned beyond belief at what he had told me. In his next breath he said that he had walked in my shoes and lived as I had lived, and he was not going to let me piss my life away.

With words that sounded like the clang of the bell to begin the round of a boxing match, his next phrase was like an uppercut that sent me to the mat for the ten count. He said, "You are just before taking a drink. That drink would not only drive you deeper into the crater of alcoholism, it would kill you."

The things he said jolted me into a numbness of mind. All I could think to say was, "Please take me back to the barn."

I didn't even feel like undressing as I crawled onto the bed. All I could think of was the third step prayer. I repeated it until I drifted into a deep sleep.

– 28 –

On awakening, I heard Rocky's booming voice from the tack room announcing that coffee was hot and there were two dozen doorknobs.

After washing my face and combing my hair, I walked down the stairs to the tack room where the aroma of the fresh coffee invigorated me. My mind was clear as a bell, and Rocky noticed a changed expression on my face as I sipped my hot coffee.

With a smile he said, "Whatever you did last night certainly agreed with you, Red."

– 29 –

The hours became days and the days turned into months as we went to Kentucky, New York, and then back again in December to Spa City.

On Christmas Eve after we finished with the horses, we met at eleven o'clock A.M. in the tack room. Rocky greeted each of us with a big hug as we sat down.

After the meeting started, Rocky said, "Fellows, I want to tell you the story of my first sober Christmas." He lowered his head almost like he was in prayer with his eyes closed and began to relate how he was alone and lonely, lying in his bunk at the Serenity House. He had just started his twenty-eight day program and didn't think he would be able to go through with it when one of his instructors came over and asked if he would like to have supper with him in his room.

"I nodded yes," said Rocky, "and followed him out back of the house where his room was. He politely asked me to sit down at the card table that was bare except for two paper napkins and a white candle. He then placed a pair of cheeseburgers on paper plates and two cans of cokes alongside.

"He lighted the candle, sat down, and extended his half-bent arms in front of him. The palms of his hands turned in toward his face with their fingers separated and straight.

"While crossing himself, he said, 'In the name of the Father, Son and the Holy Spirit.' Then he began thanking God for this wonderful meal and the one day of sobriety that was given to him today. He finished with the Lord's Prayer."

Rocky's eyes welled with tears as he said, "My friends, this was truly one of the best meals I ever had, and it saved my life." Then he lifted a cardboard box and passed out cheeseburgers and cans of cokes to each of us. Silence drifted over the tack room as we meditated about what he had just told us.

– 30 –

The days, weeks, and months seemed as if they had been compressed over the next two years. I had written the Abbot at St. George a letter of apology and related my journey to the present day. Then I asked if he would allow me to re-visit the Abbey since I had been sober for three years.

It was with some uneasiness and two-fisted prayers that I awaited the answer to my letter.

Within a week, a letter returned and I anxiously tore it open. It began with the Abbot telling me how sorry he was that the previous abbot had died over a year ago and that he had been elected abbot.

He continued that he had been known as the "Drunk Monk" for about twenty years. Then he joined Alcoholics Anonymous and sobered up.

Then he wrote, "And for the past ten years of sobriety, I have still been known as the Drunk Monk. Come on up, I need some AA fellowship."

My heart lept. I gave Rocky notice that I was leaving as soon as he could replace me.

It wasn't long before I was going back to the place where I had needed to be since my bishop had sent me.

Thanks be to God. I'm going to be in the priesthood again.

~31~

About a year after I returned to St. George, Rocky had a bad stroke. He was alive, but just barely. He had to be placed in a nursing home and was there for the next three years. Then he expired. There was nobody left in his family, so I got permission to go and give the funeral mass. Rocky had requested his funeral be held at the Serenity House where he sobered up.

About twenty people who were living in the house working on the twenty-eight day program were seated in the steel fold up chairs. The casket was not open. A small organ, played by one of the men going through the twenty-eight day program, sounded very much like a bagpipe.

I was thinking about how many lives this man had touched as I struggled through the service. I was so emotional that when I opened my mouth to begin the eulogy, nothing came out and I was only able to finish by reciting the Lord's Prayer.

After the service, I sat on the first row of chairs in front of the casket silently thinking my mantra, "Come Lord." Then I overheard someone behind me say, "Who was this guy, anyway?"

Another answered, "There were no mourners, even family, so I guess he was just some good-for-nothing who never amounted to anything. Good God! He's probably better off dead. After all, what's a man like that ever get out of life?"